ONE LAST DANCE

BOOK FIVE

THE CLEARWATER SERIES

JULIE MAYERSON BROWN

Edited by Virginia McCullough

Cover by Sapphire Midnight Design

For Myrna Brown
my incredible mother-in-law

and

Jen, Sara, Marina
you know why

Note to my Readers

"The best friendships are fierce lady friendships,
where you aggressively believe in each other, defend each other, and
think the other deserves the world."

Sarah Michelle Gellar

∾

Thank you for welcoming my stories into your life! I've loved creating this town and all of its fun, lovable, quirky characters. Cece, Patty, Tessa, Rebecca, and now Natalie have come full circle. I hope you've enjoyed their journeys as much as I have.

PROLOGUE

*T*he suitcase lay open on her bed, clothing arranged in neat stacks. The outside was a colorful collage of postcards from around the world. A clear message—*travel, seek adventure, spread your wings.*

Natalie stared into it, clutching a pair of jeans to her chest.

The oversized case had been a graduation gift from her father. Perfect for a young woman about to embark on a new life. That was only a few months ago, when anything was still possible.

She swallowed hard.

It was as if her father's gift had opened a locked door and given her a glimpse of the world outside. And just as she was about to walk through that door, it slammed shut. The cruelty of a gift snatched away.

Natalie dropped the jeans on the floor, dumped out the contents of her suitcase, and zipped up the empty container. She snapped the tiny lock into place and pushed the case into a dark corner of her closet where she wouldn't see it. A brand new suitcase never used would be a constant reminder of the hardest decision she ever made—and perhaps the biggest mistake of her life.

∼

HER MOTHER, Ilana Lurensky, put up a fight.

"Vat is zis gap year you speak of?"

"It's only a break, Mamma, one year off of school. I called the admissions office at NYU and told them what happened. They were very understanding."

Her mother narrowed her sharp green eyes. The former ballerina from Russia struck her angry pose, hands on hips and chin high and extended. "Your fawzer would not approve. He wanted you to go to college, to spread your wings, to see zee world."

"And I will, in one year's time. I—I don't want to leave you so soon after losing him."

"You stay for me? Or for yourself?"

Natalie considered the question. "Both of us," she said honestly.

Her father's death had been swift, a cough that turned into pneumonia. For a sixty-year-old man who had smoked for decades, ill health was not unexpected. Yet his death was still a shock.

A flicker of anger caught Natalie off guard. How could she be angry with someone for dying? But what-if questions made her aware of her own dark side. What if he'd died sooner? Maybe then her dream of going to college and escaping her small town wouldn't have been derailed. What if his sudden death had occurred after she'd left, after she'd settled into the dorm and started classes? Sure, she'd have come home for a while, but she would have gone back. It seemed her father had died in the narrow window of time that guaranteed she'd stay right where she was.

Natalie hated herself for having the thought. Petrov Lurensky had been a good father who wanted to see his only child soar.

"Vell," Ilana said, regarding her daughter with a mix of suspicion and sympathy. "Vat vill you do for one year?"

Natalie had the ready answer to that question. "Work at the studio, Mamma, with you. I might not have been the best ballerina, but I know how to dance. And I know how to teach others to dance."

"But ballet teacher? It is not vat you vant."

"It's one year, probably less than a year." Natalie grew impatient. "Besides, you'll pay me to be an instructor now that I'm out of high school."

"Pay you?" Ilana was notoriously frugal. Did her mother presume that room and board was sufficient compensation? But then Ilana grinned. "Yes, I vill pay you. You earn money, you save money, you have money for school next year. A good enough plan, I suppose."

Natalie hugged her mother. It was a good enough plan. It gave Natalie one year, time to heal her heart and to help her mother carry on. Soon enough she would pull her dream out of the closet and let it soar.

CHAPTER 1

*N**ineteen and a half years later*

FEBRUARY

The restaurant screamed of money, society, privilege. Certainly not Natalie's favorite environment, but she was accustomed to fine dining, especially at this particular place in downtown San Francisco. Her boyfriend loved old time steak houses. Leather seats, dim lighting, baked potatoes, fine whiskeys.

The waiter set a vodka martini in front of her. "Here you are, Ms. Lurensky."

Natalie smiled up at him. "Thank you, Walter."

"Icy cold, three olives." Walter lingered. "Are you sure you wouldn't like an appetizer? The crab cakes are very popular tonight."

"Thanks, but I'll wait for Brian. I'm sure he'll be here any minute."

"Very well, Ms. Lurensky."

"How many times do I need to tell you to call me Natalie? I call you Walter, don't I?"

"I suppose you do." The waiter, with his pomaded gray hair and tidy mustache, could have come from another era. As it was, he reminded Natalie of her father, which made her not mind the fact that Brian was late. She enjoyed Walter's soft-spoken care.

"I will say, if I were meeting a lady as lovely as you, I would not leave her waiting for a single moment." He spoke with a wistful air, a reminder that gentlemen were no longer what they used to be.

"Thank you for that, Walter." If only she could find a man like him—or snap her fingers and make Walter thirty years younger. And unmarried. "Maybe I will try the crab cakes."

"Excellent choice, Miss Lur—Natalie."

Alone at the table and enjoying the quiet, Natalie sipped her drink, savoring the cool, clean taste. When Brian bustled in through the front door and handed his coat to the maître d', she watched him wind through the crowded tables toward her, stopping to say hello to an attractive couple along the way. Brian was always the most dashing and charming man in the room, but his ego diminished his appeal.

They'd been together for over a year, somewhat off and on, but mostly on. It had been the kind of relationship Natalie preferred—flexible, low maintenance, undemanding.

She swept her dark hair over her left shoulder and raised her face.

"Sorry I'm late." Brian pressed a cold kiss against her lips. "The traffic was awful, my day sucked, and two of the partners are on vacation so everything's landing on my desk."

"Sounds stressful," she said with as much sincerity as she could muster. "You must be tired."

"Not that tired." Brian Steel, at forty-six, was nine years older than Natalie, practically her age considering her history of dating men older than that. Not as old as Walter who was nearing seventy, but definitely mature. Brian was handsome in the way that old-time movie stars used to be. Clean shaven with short brown hair beginning to gray around the edges.

"So, how was your day, Nat?" He reached for her hand, but she drew it back and repositioned her silverware.

"So-so, not great."

A bemused smile appeared. "Did a little ballerina twist her ankle?"

"No ballerina mishaps, thankfully. Other stuff, you know?"

His wry smile reversed itself. "Oh, right. Sorry. I didn't forget. I know it's been a hard time for you."

An understatement for sure. Natalie had spent years caring for her mother, who slipped away from her bit by bit. Dementia had stolen every piece of Ilana, turning her into an empty shell that recognized nobody. Natalie couldn't erase from her mind her mother's desperation to hold onto her memories, to avoid turning into the person she was destined to become. Her death a month ago had been devastating but at the same time, a relief.

Walter appeared and set a highball glass next to Brian's plate. "The usual, sir." His drink was always the same, whiskey sour with orange slice garnish.

"Thanks Walter. Give us few minutes, would you?"

"Of course." The solicitous waiter took his leave.

Brian sipped his signature drink, glancing around the room as if looking for someone he might know. It was his style. Natalie often thought he'd make a good politician.

He set the highball glass on the table. "So, other than that, you good?"

"Sure." Natalie swallowed the rest of her martini and ate the olives. "I'm perfectly fine."

He shook out his napkin and spread it over his lap then flipped it over a few times. Most people were uncomfortable with death, so Natalie understood his avoidance of the subject.

He'd accompanied her to Ilana's memorial service a few weeks prior, but they'd hardly seen each other since.

"It's been almost a month, Nat. And I think your mom's in a better place. Don't you?"

If Natalie hadn't already finished her martini, she'd have flung it in his face. "Did you know that what you just said tops the list of things you never say to someone who has lost a loved one?" She had no idea if that were true or not, but it sounded about right. People never know what to say to a grieving person, so they resort to clichés and platitudes.

"I don't think it's such a bad thing to say. It means, well, I'm not sure what it means. But if it's not what you wanted to hear, I'm sorry. Again."

"Forget it." Natalie forced herself to cheer up, or pretend to. "And sorry I snapped at you."

There, at least they'd gotten over that hump. The *I'm sorry, I'm sorry too* routine always smoothed things over.

After dinner, a second round of drinks, and mundane conversation about work and weather, Brian loosened his tie and pulled it out from under his collar. He rolled it around one hand and slipped it into his suitcoat pocket. "So, well, what's next?"

"What do you mean?"

"Now that, um, you don't have to take care of your mom anymore?"

Natalie put her napkin on the table. His question was reasonable. Her worries and inability to control any aspect of her mother's health, including the slow, excruciating process of watching her die, had ended. It was like being released from prison, a thought that brought a rush of guilt. But there was no denying the countless times she wished for her mother's suffering, as well as her own, to end.

"I'm going to do what I've always done," Natalie said. "Get back to work. God knows I've got a lot of catching up to do."

"I know that." Brian leaned in and lowered his voice. "But I, well, I only meant that now you might be able to spend more time in the city. More time with me. I'm going to New York on business next week, staying at the Carlyle. Why don't you come with me?"

New York? The thought made her dizzy. The city where she was headed, once upon a time.

Her dream of leaving Clearwater was long gone. Her plan had been a college degree, perhaps even a masters, in whatever subjects she found most thrilling—biology or history or English. Now it was little more than a passing thought, a dalliance she'd imagined.

Dreams don't have an expiration date. But they can be forgotten. Somebody had said that to her once, but she couldn't remember who it was.

"I can't go with you, Brian. But I appreciate the invitation."

"You don't sound like you appreciate it," Brian said.

"I do, but there's no way I can leave right now. I've neglected the dance studio for months."

Brian leaned back and crossed his arms. "I figured you'd say that."

Natalie bristled. His request to spend more time together should've delighted her, but instead it felt like another thing to put on her to-do list. In that moment, she realized how shallow their relationship was. Wide and stunning on the outside, no depth underneath.

"Brian," she said, her voice apologetic. "My mom's been gone barely a month. You might think that's enough time to grieve, but it's not for me. I'm still reeling. Plus, my house looks like an out of control nursing home, and my business, well, I hardly even know what's going on there. The last thing I have time for is a needy boyfriend."

Brian drew his shoulders back. "Needy? I'm needy because I want to take my girlfriend to New York?"

"I'm sorry. That wasn't what I meant." Natalie lifted her hair and fanned the back of her neck.

"What did you mean, then?" Brian asked. "I think I've been pretty patient the last six months, and very understanding when you cancelled plans or forgot to show up, even on New Year's Eve when I had to go to my partner's black tie affair without my girlfriend."

Natalie almost rolled her eyes. Poor guy, showing up at some over the top New Year's party without her. How humiliating to have to explain that his girlfriend was by her dying mother's bedside.

"I get it that you had your hands full, Natalie, but that's over now. It's time to move on."

Move on? How does someone move on when she's lost the most important person in her life—when she's engulfed in sorrow for the way it ended and for all the words she left unsaid?

The dark paneled walls seemed to be closing in on her. She'd do anything to be able to move on, to get her life in order, to feel relieved and unburdened. To taste the freedom she'd once dreamed of. But too many years had gone by since the day she gave up on her dream. She settled into adulthood, gradually taking over the family business. She'd never intended to be a ballet teacher, yet here she was. A good ballet teacher and a competent, serious business owner. That was her priority.

"I am moving on, but perhaps not the way you want me to."

"Great," Brian said. "Where does that leave me?"

The bitter taste of his selfishness caught her by surprise. The walls moved in even closer, as if she were being squeezed into the back of an elevator. "I need some air." Natalie shoved her chair back, grabbed her purse and jacket, and dashed toward the front of the restaurant. A large party had just entered, creating a bottleneck at the door.

"Miss Lurensky." Walter grasped her elbow. "Are you unwell?"

The crowd pushed Natalie against him. "I need to get outside."

"Stay close, my dear." Walter forced his way upstream and led her to the exit.

The cold mist touched her skin, sharpening her senses. She took some deep breaths.

"Better?" Walter asked.

"I think so. Thank you, Walter. I—I don't know what came over me."

"It was warm and crowded in the restaurant. That's all."

"Natalie!" Brian's voice rose above the noise on the street—cars speeding past, horns honking, valets whistling.

Walter pulled Natalie a few steps away. "That man is not good enough for you. You deserve better."

His warning caught her attention. "Why do you say that?"

"I have four daughters. And a father of girls knows how to protect them. It might sound old-fashioned, but it is the truth." Walter's concern made her eyes burn. And deep down she trusted him more than she trusted Brian. Way more.

"Natalie!" Brian shouted again.

She turned to Walter. "Thanks for looking out for me." She gave him a hug, which unbalanced him for a moment.

He steadied himself and enfolded her in his arms. "Good night, my dear."

Walter vanished just as Brian appeared by her side.

"Are you okay? You looked like you were about to pass out."

"Sorry, I didn't feel well. I'm okay now, just exhausted."

"Right, well, let's go then." Brian gave the valet his card. "You can leave your car here overnight."

"No Brian, I need to get home." Her home, the place she'd lived her entire life, was an hour's drive north of San Francisco in the heart of wine country.

"You can't go, not yet. At least come over for a nightcap. I'll bring you back here after, well, you know."

Natalie considered the proposition. It sounded like a cheap booty call. Her body was dead tired, and the idea of a sexy, romantic encounter made her want to collapse in a heap. On the other hand, a hot bubble bath in Brian's jacuzzi tub would be heavenly. But that would be unfair and dishonest when she knew what she had to do.

"Brian, are you seeing other women?" The question popped out of her before she thought twice. Whether Walter knew or only suspected it, she had no idea. But it made perfect sense. Men like Brian attracted women like flowers attracted bees.

"What?" He drew back. "Why would you ask me that?"

"It's okay. I mean, I know I've been distant... and neglectful." Her words unfurled like a piece of fabric caught by a gentle wind. "So I don't fault you for it."

Brian shifted from foot to foot. The valet motioned that his car was ready. "Come home with me, please. I'll explain everything, and we'll figure this out. I didn't cheat on you, I swear it. Not in the—"

"I said it's okay." Natalie rested a hand on his shoulder. "But I do think we've run our course."

"Wait a minute. Are you breaking up with me? Seriously?"

"I'm sorry. I just can't find the energy to be there for you in the way you want."

"Can't or won't?" Brian said through gritted teeth. "It is a choice, you know."

"Does it matter? I'm sure you'll have no trouble filling the void. And if you already have, well, as I said, I don't blame you."

Brian refused to give in or give up. "Come on, Nat, please, we can work this out. I'm so sorry."

"I told you, it's fine," she said, already relieved of the burden Brian had become.

The valet called his name, but he ignored it.

"You're not even upset? You don't care that I *might* have been seeing someone else? You don't care that we've spent over a year together and now you're ending it as if it were nothing? You don't care that I'm standing out here in the cold begging you to stay with me. I don't get it. You're devoid of emotion, indifferent, cold-hearted. It's like you've turned to stone."

A stone, indeed. Natalie hadn't shed a tear in ages.

"I'm afraid I have." She handed the valet her card, then turned back to her now ex-boyfriend. "Goodbye, Brian."

His jaw slackened. He looked at her as if she'd lost her mind. But it wasn't her mind she'd lost. It was her heart.

CHAPTER 2

*T*he days and weeks blurred as Natalie struggled to acclimate. On the surface, in front of her students and the ever-demanding dance parents, she was back to her old self. The hand-squeezes and quiet whispers of "I'm sorry for your loss," and "if there's anything I can do," finally dwindled. Natalie was sick to death of thanking people for kind thoughts —then angry with herself for not being more appreciative.

The only way out of her funk was to stay the course and bury the heartache. Put on a brave face. Strength could hide a multitude of emotions.

Valentine's Day popped up like an unwelcome houseguest. Natalie tried to avoid walking past Betsey's Blooms on Main Street, where roses and lilies and pink daisies spilled onto the sidewalk in giant buckets and glorious displays. But there was no avoiding it on her way to Nutmegs Bakery. She scooted past with only a quick wave at Betsey inside.

Nutmegs, one of Clearwater's original businesses, was as dependable as the sunrise. Although it had been remodeled and updated a few times over the years, the bakery never failed to bring comfort. In the last few months of Ilana's housebound existence, Natalie still took her to Nutmegs. It was the only place other than the studio where she seemed to know where she was. The aroma of bread baking, the taste of her favorite butter cookie, the smooth surface of the wooden tables—all had remained a familiar experience in the far reaches of Ilana's brain. It was odd what one could still remember when everything else had been forgotten.

As Natalie approached, the faint scent of cinnamon and freshly baked cookies beckoned. Her friend Tessa was seated at a round table on the patio under a heater.

"Oh good, you're here." Tessa Mariano, owner of the famed Mariano's Cheese and Wine, was like Natalie's big sister. She'd been her babysitter once upon a time and then, when Natalie's father died, Tessa stayed by her side as a constant companion and unending source of comfort.

Tessa handed Natalie a coffee. "Let's walk. I'm short on time."

"Same. My afternoon class starts at one."

With lattes to go and cookies in little white bags, the women crossed the street into Town Square Park. They made their way along the center path, passing the duck pond and community garden. The familiar smells and sounds took her back in time— flowers that bloomed sweet and pungent with the promise of spring, the hum of quiet conversation, birds chirping, children laughing. A duck plunged its head beneath the surface, exactly like the ducks had been doing for as long as Natalie could remember.

An entire lifetime spent in one place.

"Could you slow down a little?" Tessa said. "Your legs are much longer than mine."

Natalie shortened her steps. "Sorry, I always forget how tiny you are. Your presence is so large that you seem taller."

"I have to agree with you there." Tessa gave her a friendly nudge.

They sat on their usual bench under a giant oak tree near the children's playground.

"So, how are you doing?" Tessa asked with genuine interest.

"How am I doing with what?" Natalie had so much to deal with, her friend could be referring to any number of issues.

Tessa ticked them off. "Your mother's death, your break-up with Brian, your business woes, your expired driver's license. Should I go on?"

Natalie groaned. "I took care of my license. My business is hanging by a thread. I could not care less about the break-up. And as far as my mother goes, I'm completely numb. I still think she's going to be sitting on the sofa every time I walk in the house. It's like trying to turn on a broken lamp over and over because you keep forgetting it's broken."

"That's quite the analogy."

"It's the best I could do on short notice."

"Fair enough." Tessa sipped her coffee. "You know how I feel about therapy, don't you?"

Natalie raised an eyebrow. "Yeah, you hate it."

"Absolutely hate it," Tessa said, as if the sentiment needed confirmation. "And I hate meditation, too."

"I know."

"But, and I am loath to admit this, both do help."

"Forget it." Natalie bit into her dark chocolate chip cookie. "I know how to deal with my mother's death. I don't need a therapist."

"That's what I said when I had my episode four years ago."

"You literally had a mental break, Tessa. You fell apart." Natalie shuddered at the memory of her friend's crisis. "You almost lost your business."

"Now you're exaggerating," Tessa said. "But never mind that.

16

If you say you don't need therapy, I promise I won't bring it up again."

For the millionth time, Natalie thanked her lucky stars she had Tessa in her life, the kind of friend who knew when to push and when to let up.

"We'd better go." Natalie stood and extended a hand. Tessa took it and squeezed, allowing herself to be pulled to her feet.

They walked along the path until their routes diverged at the gazebo, Natalie's dance studio to the right and Tessa's shop directly across on the opposite side of the park. Earlier that morning, the women's club had hosted a Valentine's Day brunch, leaving the gazebo still awash in flowers, paper hearts, and streamers.

"I hope these decorations are gone by tomorrow." Natalie'd already had more than enough of the romantic holiday, and it wasn't even half over.

"Don't count on it. Just try not to look." Tessa faced Natalie with a gentle smile. "Remember when I used to babysit you? I always told you, *you're my girl*. Well, you are still. You're the little sister I never had."

Natalie hung on Tessa's words, gratitude swelling her heart.

"You probably don't remember this," Tessa said, "but when *my* mom died you were like three years old. And you and your mom came by with food or something. I was in my room in bed. You walked right in, crawled onto the bed with me, and with your little hands you wiped my tears. Then you snuggled against me and we fell asleep together."

"That's a really sweet memory."

A tear dropped onto Tessa's cheek. "It's one of my favorites. And consider this a rare moment. Very few people can crack my hard shell."

"I'm well aware," Natalie said.

"My point is this. I'm here to wipe your tears, if and when they fall."

The offer almost made Natalie cry then and there. Almost, but not quite. "Good to know," she said, surprised by the hitch in her voice. She pulled Tessa into a tight hug then released her. "Alrighty, you have a happy Valentine's Day."

"Blech." Tessa waved the idea away. "One of my least favorite days of the year. But very good for business."

CHAPTER 3

*a*t six pm, after her final dance class of the day, Natalie settled at the antique desk in her office where her mother had sat for over thirty years. Bills and paperwork covered the dark wood surface. She was trying to organize everything by date and subject when Cece Redmond, the Lurensky Academy's brilliant artistic director, flopped into a chair across from her.

"What are you doing tonight? Want to come for dinner?"

Natalie sat back. "Absolutely not. It's Valentine's Day. You should be having dinner with your husband."

"Brad's prepping for a case. I'll be lucky if he can sit at the table with me for ten minutes."

"That's too bad, but I still can't come. Tons of stuff to do at home."

"Like what, watch another episode of *Law and Order?*" Cece's lips tugged at the corners. "It's been weeks since your breakup with Brian. You never go anywhere except for work and home. It's not good."

Natalie unwound her tight ballerina bun and shook out her hair. She rubbed her scalp where it ached from being pulled taut all day. "For the record, I like being at the studio and at home." She paused, a swell of emotion flooding into her voice. "It's where I feel close to my mom, you know?"

"I do know." Cece's features folded in sympathy. As Natalie's childhood best friend and one of the most celebrated ballerinas ever to come from the Lurensky Academy, Cece fully understood Natalie's obligations and her commitment to her mother's legacy. Years ago, Cece had stepped up and taken over as Assistant Director when the competition circled like hungry sharks, spreading the rumor that the Lurensky reign had ended. But Natalie and Cece, with their tremendous artistic abilities and similar management styles, kept the dance school going strong.

"Never mind," Cece said. "Rain check?"

"Rain check."

The two former ballerinas strode down the quiet hallway lined with cubbies and hooks before exiting through the front studio. As Natalie locked the door, she dropped her massive key ring on her ballet slippered foot. "Youch."

Cece picked it up. "Do you really need this many keys? You look like a high school janitor carrying this around."

"I do. One for the front doors here, another for the back door, plus the closets, the bathrooms, the office, the PO Box. Then I've got keys to three neighbors' houses. And my own keys as well."

"That's ridiculous. They're really weighing you down."

"Tell me about it." Natalie sat on a bench on the wide veranda. She removed her ballet slippers and replaced them with sneakers.

"Are you sure you don't want to have dinner with me and Brad?" Cece asked.

"Yes, I'm sure. Enjoy yourself, and don't worry about me." She zipped up her dance bag and slung it over her shoulder.

"If you say so. But the door is open if you change your mind."

Cece tossed her things into the back seat of her car. "See you tomorrow."

Natalie waved as her friend drove around the park, past the gazebo, and up Main Street toward her home on the expensive side of town.

Natalie's house, the one her parents bought before she was born, was in the other direction. She drove the short distance and turned onto her street. Tidy ranch houses in various shades of yellow and cream lined the avenue in neat rows, each one with small patches of green grass and narrow planters across the front.

She pulled into her driveway, parked in front of the single car garage, and went inside. She turned on a lamp. In the corner, her mother's wheelchair remained, a thin throw pillow on the seat. Natalie occasionally sat there, trying to normalize its presence, even though it was no longer needed.

The fluorescent kitchen light flickered to life. She opened the freezer and stared at stacks of foil covered casserole dishes. She couldn't stomach one more serving of creamed chicken or soggy lasagna.

With a box of Triscuits in hand, Natalie sat on the couch with a blanket and turned on an old episode of *Law and Order*, Ilana's favorite show. They'd watched it together countless times over the years. There was something cathartic about the predictability of every episode and how justice, in the end, was always served.

Halfway through the show, right when the perp was being arrested, the doorbell rang. Natalie hit pause and went to find who had interrupted her quiet night.

Cece stood on the porch, arms weighted with plastic bags. "I brought Chinese."

Although the last thing Natalie wanted was pity, especially on Valentine's Day, she didn't mind her friend's surprise visit— or Chinese food.

"That's very sweet. Come in." Natalie took one of the bags. "What happened to your dinner with Brad?"

"I told you it'd be short. He went back to work, so I put Noah to bed and decided to come eat dinner with you. Besides, I've been craving Chinese for weeks."

"Thank you. Have to admit, I'm tired of casseroles." Natalie unpacked the bags and opened the containers. "You know there's enough for like ten people here, right?"

"Good, leftovers for lunch," Cece said just as the doorbell sounded.

Natalie's head shifted like a dog on alert. "What did you do?"

"It's Tessa. She was alone tonight, too."

The front door opened and slammed. "Hello, girls!"

The workaholic sommelier waltzed in with a bottle of wine in each hand. "I brought Sauvignon Blanc. It pairs well with Asian cuisine." She set the wine on the counter.

"This is crazy," Natalie said. "Where's your husband tonight?"

"At the hospital," Tessa said lightly. "He's on call."

Natalie hemmed. "You didn't mention that to me earlier."

Tessa brushed it off. "I guess I forgot."

The door opened again.

"What is going on here?" Natalie's annoyance, tempered by amusement, grew.

"It's me!" Rebecca, everyone's favorite and the youngest of the group, blew in like a gust of warm air. "With heart cookies from Nutmegs."

Patty trailed after her. "You didn't think you could have a party without us, did you?"

"I'm not having a party," Natalie said. While each of her friends brought their own unique brand of camaraderie and humor, she was in no mood to entertain.

"Patty," Cece said, "did you come empty handed again?"

Patty jutted her chin. "It's kind of my thing. Besides, what more do we need? Food, wine, and dessert. That should cover it, right?"

"Wait, I know," Rebecca said. "You can be the entertainment. You tell such fun stories."

"No stories tonight," Patty said, loading her plate. "Except to tell you that Adam cancelled our dinner reservation because of a problem with the cooling unit at the winery."

Patty's boyfriend, Adam Hawk, was one of the most famous and successful winemakers in the region.

"That could be a disaster," Tessa said. "Taking care of his cooling unit is way more important than taking you to dinner."

"Really, boss? Like I don't know that?" Patty had worked for Tessa since moving to Clearwater several years ago. As manager of the illustrious wine shop and girlfriend of the esteemed owner of Hawk and Winters winery, she'd become a wine expert herself. "Anyway, Adam will be making it up to me over the weekend, so don't worry."

"Nobody's worried about you," Rebecca said. "It's Natalie we're worried about."

All eyes shifted. Tessa gave Rebecca a warning look. Patty and Cece exchanged glances.

"Oh no," Natalie said. "Please tell me this isn't some kind of intervention."

"It's not," Cece said. "Come on. Let's take our food to the table and enjoy dinner."

Suspicious but hungry, Natalie acquiesced.

With plates piled high with chow mein, egg rolls, and assorted other dishes, they took their seats around the old dining room table. Tessa poured the wine. Nobody spoke, until Patty voiced yet another opinion.

"For God's sake, Nat, why is your mom's wheelchair still sitting in the middle of the living room?"

Natalie sat back. "This *is* an intervention, isn't it?"

"We're a little concerned, that's all," Cece said. "We think you need to get out more. Do something different."

"What do you suggest I do?" Natalie grew defensive. "Start online dating?"

"That's a great idea," Rebecca said, long noodles hanging from her chopsticks. "Or better yet, Chris has a few single friends. We can set you up with someone."

"Speaking of Chris," Natalie said, changing the subject, "why aren't you dining with your wonderful new husband tonight?"

"I will be. We have a late reservation."

"Then you can't eat all that chow mein." Patty pulled Rebecca's plate away.

"Yes, I can." Rebecca pulled the plate back. "I'm super tall, plus I walked twelve dogs today and got in over sixteen thousand steps. You think I can't eat two dinners? I could probably eat three."

Natalie laughed, her first real laugh in forever, and lively banter filled the room. That was until Tessa brought up online dating again.

"Look, it's a place to start. No harm in creating a profile. You never know who might come your way."

"I will say this one time and one time only." Natalie dipped an eggroll into hot mustard sauce then pointed it at each of her friends. "I will not be putting up a profile of any kind anywhere. If I'm meant to meet someone new, it'll happen organically."

"Not when you never leave Clearwater," Patty said. "What do you think is gonna happen? You'll walk into Nutmegs one day for a latte, and the man of your dreams is going to be there eating a sticky bun?"

"Hey, isn't that how Cece met Brad?" Rebecca held her chopsticks midair. "I love that story!"

"I was the one eating the sticky bun," Cece said. "But Patty does have a point. I don't think there's been a new man in Clearwater in years. And the current selection isn't vast."

Natalie sighed. "I'll figure it out. I just need more time." How much time she might need, Natalie couldn't say. "Truth is, I've been so preoccupied for so long, I've forgotten how dull this town is."

"It's not dull," Rebecca said. "It's perfect."

"Oh, to be Rebecca," Tessa said. "You really are our Mary Sunshine, aren't you?"

"I try to be. Anyway, I have to go." Rebecca shoveled the rest of her noodles into her mouth, opened the bakery box full of sprinkled sugar cookies, and wrapped two in a napkin. "I'll let Chris know you're open to a set-up."

"No, you won't," Natalie said. "Now take your sugar cookies and have a wonderful night."

Natalie walked her to the door. One down, three to go.

But the others made no move to leave. Tessa refilled the wine glasses. Patty kept eating. And Cece put cookies on a plate.

"What's next on the agenda?" Natalie asked. "You going to suggest I paint my house?"

"That's not a bad idea," Tessa said.

The house certainly could use a facelift. It hadn't been painted in years. The carpeting was threadbare. And the bathrooms still had pink tiles from the sixties.

"And maybe the painter will be a stud," Patty said. "Lot of women have affairs with their contractors, you know."

"Oh, a sleazy affair, just what Natalie needs," Cece said. "I should've made you stay home, Patty."

"I'm kidding, geez. I know Natalie's too classy for that."

"That's sweet, sort of." Natalie wondered briefly what a sleazy affair might feel like. She'd never had one. Relationships, whether satisfying or not, were more her speed. "Now, don't get excited, but I'm going to admit something."

Her three friends leaned in, as if she were about to espouse brilliance.

"Because I've spent the last seven years wrapped up in my

25

mother's health and consumed by the studio, I have ignored the fact that I pretty much have no life."

"Now you're making progress," Tessa said. "Recognition is the first step toward change. I learned that in therapy."

"But I'm almost thirty-eight," Natalie lamented. "I wouldn't even know where to start."

"You could start by getting rid of that wheelchair over there." Patty shook her hand toward it.

The evening devolved from there into laughter and gossip and more wine. Two hours later, the intervention/party ended.

"Thanks for coming over," Natalie said, ushering them to the door. She wrapped them in her arms for a big group hug. "My life might be a disaster, but I'm so lucky to have all of you."

After her friends left and everything was put away, Natalie took her cookies, sat on the couch, and watched the rest of *Law and Order*. It ended, so she watched another episode. And then another. If that wasn't the definition of *no life*, what was?

CHAPTER 4

$\mathcal{N}$atalie mulled over her friends' advice. A few days after the impromptu Valentine's Day intervention, she quit digging in her heels.

On Sunday morning, her only day off, she woke up with a six o'clock alarm, ate a hearty breakfast of eggs and toast, threw open every window, and set to work.

The bookshelves were covered in a thick layer of dust, cobwebs hung like curtains from the ceiling corners, and random stuff was everywhere. Natalie took stock of where to start. She moved the wheelchair to the 'to be donated' area in the garage, then tossed the flat throw pillow into the trash. That single act was cathartic. She dusted every surface in the living room, swatted away the webs with a broom, vacuumed the carpeting from top to bottom and side to side.

From there she tackled the kitchen. The casseroles in the freezer, offerings of comfort from friends and neighbors, were covered with frost. Natalie couldn't remember how long the food had been there, much of it delivered in the last weeks of Ilana's life. She filled two giant trash bags, washed down every inch of the refrigerator, then put in a fresh box of baking soda to absorb the old smells. Once the floor was mopped and counters sanitized, she moved on.

Wiping down walls, airing out beds, washing laundry. She worked until it turned dark and cold outside. Then, with her last burst of energy, she attacked the bathroom, tossing out her mother's pills, eyedrops, cosmetics, expired skin creams.

A tube of lotion dropped to the floor. Natalie picked it up and rubbed a small amount between her palms. The soothing scent, a mix of lavender and eucalyptus, evoked memories of her mother's fragility.

Natalie had never allowed the caregivers to bathe her mother. She did it herself almost every night. In her prime, Ilana had been proud and dignified. Natalie was grateful her mother never knew how vacant she'd become. If she had been aware of her inability to care for herself, she would've prayed for death. Ilana Lurensky, who had escaped fascism, endured weeks in steerage on a boat across the Atlantic, and rose to become one of the most accomplished ballerinas to dance in America, had been reduced to being bathed like a child.

Natalie cupped her hands over her nose and inhaled again.

"Here, Mamma, sit. Let me rub your legs." She guided her mother to the pink upholstered stool at the vanity and lifted her right foot into her lap. Mamma's legs, once so muscular with smooth, clear skin, were now blemished with bruises and age spots and swollen veins. The toes that had been tortured by years of dancing on pointe were twisted and misshapen. As Natalie tended to her mother, Ilana stroked her daughter's hair and murmured softly, her words a jumble of English and Russian.

The once refined and extraordinary woman had struggled to hide her condition, and she'd succeeded for a while. It was slow at first. The doctors called it mild cognitive impairment, intermittent episodes of confusion or forgetfulness, as if the lights had been dimmed. Then, as quickly as it came, it went. And the strong, decisive, brilliant dance instructor would return, giving

Natalie great relief and a reason to believe her mother was perfectly fine.

Ilana could remain stable for weeks, sometimes months. Then, without warning, the episodes would reappear. Natalie managed to keep it quiet for almost two years. The Lurensky Dance Academy had a reputation to uphold, and that reputation was built on the fame and glory of its founder. Eventually, however, the news leaked and spread. The rumor mill churned, alerting dance schools across Northern California that Ilana Lurensky could no longer run her business. And Natalie, the heir to the throne, would never be able to carry the torch.

But everything changed when Cece stepped up and took over as Assistant Director. With her friend's support, Natalie was able to move forward with direction and vision. If not for Cece, she'd have lost everything.

Natalie shook her head, forcing the memory aside. If she allowed herself to ponder long enough, she'd find herself in an endless spiral of doubt and regret.

Early on, it was obvious Natalie was not destined to become the ballerina her mother had been. She was good, very good, at times excellent. But by her mid-teens, Natalie knew she was set to take a different path.

And then, just when she was on the cusp of starting her own life, her father died and everything changed. Natalie stayed in her mother's world, by her side, year after year, doing everything in her power to take over the business she'd never wanted to begin with.

Life was funny that way. One choice, one seemingly small decision, and Natalie's future was altered in ways she never could have predicted. So be it, she often thought. What's done is done. She took great solace in the knowledge that if not for that choice, the Lurensky Dance Academy would have been shuttered years ago and her mother's legacy buried along with her.

Natalie scrubbed the bathroom with cleanser and a stiff brush until the tiles gleamed.

Exhausted, her hands red and raw, she filled the tub with hot water and bubble bath. She dipped her toe to test the temperature, then sank into the therapeutic scent of lavender. Steam rose and fogged the mirror. With her knees bent, Natalie could get her shoulders beneath the bubbles. She closed her eyes and listened to herself breathe. She dozed, lingering in the soothing space between sleep and wakefulness.

Her cell buzzed, breaking into the blessed calm. Natalie splashed as she straightened her legs and pushed herself upright to reach the phone.

It was a text from a Maura Keaton, the owner of another dance school, asking her to lunch. Natalie was far too busy to slip away for a lunch date. And knowing Maura, the request was not simply a friendly invitation. While they weren't exactly rivals, there was a sense of competition between their studios, stirred mostly by the dance moms. Maura was a good business person with a long roster of students. She'd bought her dance school some years ago and often had questions for Natalie, everything from how to manage demanding parents to where to have costumes mended. It was always something. But Natalie did her best to be generous and kind.

Right now, however, she was too tired to think about it. She dropped her phone on the mat beside the tub, ran more hot water, and submerged her shoulders back into the water.

CHAPTER 5

The Lurensky studio occupied the entire first floor of the Old Mayfair Hotel, a southern style inn with white siding, black shutters, and a wide veranda that extended across the front. The inn had been built in 1925 and boasted a carved plaque from the historic registry on a post near the steps.

Natalie entered through a side door and went straight to her office, the office that used to be Ilana's. Black and white photographs of ballerinas lined the walls. More than a few of Ilana's students had succeeded and performed with illustrious dance companies. In recent years, Natalie and Cece had turned out several professional ballerinas as well. One of their star students had gone on to dance in New York, another in London. It had been quite an achievement, and Natalie was proud of the reputation she and Cece had built together.

Natalie straightened her desk and plumped the pillows on the couch. She dusted the shelves and picture frames.

"What are you doing?" Cece asked, walking in and taking a seat.

"Cleaning." Natalie threw the rag into the trash. "Maura Keaton is coming."

Cece straightened like an arrow. "That's interesting."

"Yeah, she texted last night and asked me to go to lunch."

"And?"

"And I didn't respond. I was in the bathtub. Anyway, she called this morning. Said she had to be out this way, which makes no sense because why would she come to Clearwater? There's nothing to do here other than—"

"Natalie, how many cups of coffee have you had?"

"Two."

"Only two?"

"Well, two double espressos."

"That's a lot of caffeine." Cece dug through her purse and pulled out a baggie of little orange crackers. "Here, eat some Goldfish."

Natalie accepted. She needed something to absorb the acid in her stomach. "Thanks."

"Okay, so, Maura's coming by. What does she want?"

"No idea," Natalie said, nibbling the tasty snack that belonged to Cece's son. "But if it were something ordinary, she'd just text or email me."

"But she asked to see you person this time." Cece cocked her head. "That is curious, isn't it?"

"Curious, indeed."

NATALIE STOOD on the veranda as Maura parked her Prius in front of the inn.

Her visitor bounded up the steps and greeted her with a hug. "So good to see you." In black stretch pants, matching jacket, and wedge sandals, she looked both casual and professional. Maura was an indiscernible mix of nationalities with flawless dark skin and short brown hair. She'd grown up in Wisconsin and had traces of a Mid-western accent that put one at ease. Sort of.

"You too, Maura." Natalie relaxed as she escorted her inside.

Maura stopped in the center of what was once the grand ballroom of the hotel and lifted her nose like a dog sniffing steak. "God, I love this place. You can smell the history. And wow, those crystal chandeliers. Imagine the parties they must have had here back in the day. Sometimes I think I was born into the wrong era."

"I know the feeling," Natalie said. "But then we wouldn't have cell phones."

Maura laughed. "That's what I love about you—always looking at the practical side."

Natalie started toward the office, but Maura lingered in the cavernous hall, eyeing the ceiling, the walls, the floor.

"We have repairs starting soon," Natalie said, self-conscious about the state of disrepair her studio reflected. "Deferred maintenance and all that, but I've been waiting on the contractor." It wasn't like Natalie to spin a story, but Maura's keen eye set her on edge.

"Oh, don't I know it. Dance studios take a real beating. You should see the floor in my tap class room. Looks like someone's been hitting it with a hammer."

"Can I get you a cup of tea or something?" Natalie asked, anxious to move Maura to the office.

"No, thanks." Maura ran her hand over the worn wood ballet barre. "Where's Cece? She still works for you, doesn't she?"

Natalie tensed. Maura knew darn well Cece worked for her. There were online gossip groups dedicated to who worked where in the industry. If someone of Cece's reputation made a move, it would be headline news.

It was no secret that Maura had lured numerous dancers from the Lurensky academy and vice versa. Sometimes the needs of a dancer were better met by a different instructor.

And the best instructor of all was Cece. She had a waiting list of aspiring ballerinas, those who showed tremendous promise but needed to be molded. Cece could turn raw talent into a work of art.

"Cece's my Artistic Director." Natalie gave her doubtful look. "But of course you know that."

"You're right. I do. Just, you know, small talk."

Small talk, the last thing Natalie had time for. "You sure I can't get you something to drink?"

Maura glanced into one of the adjoining rooms. "No, thank you."

Natalie's patience was wearing thin. She unfolded two plastic chairs and sat in one. "Maura, what is this visit about? We're not exactly in a *drop in on each other* kind of relationship."

"That's true, so I'll get right to the point." Maura sat in the second chair and placed her purse on the floor. "I've lost a couple of my best dancers in recent months. One family moved away, supposedly, and another said they couldn't afford lessons after I raised my prices."

Natalie crossed her long legs and steepled her fingers. "They didn't come here, if that's what you're suggesting. But even if they had, you know that's how this business works. Dancers move around. And dance mothers move around, too."

"I agree completely. Which is why I'm here. What would you think of us, well, us working together?"

"How do you mean?"

"Merging." Maura moved her hands in a circular motion. "You know, like merging together."

"I know what merging means. And I have no interest in *merging*."

Maura's mouth twisted to one side. "Well, then, would you consider selling?"

A shocked laugh escaped Natalie's throat. "Selling my business? Are you kidding?"

"I'm not kidding."

"What on earth makes you think I'd ever sell the Lurensky Dance Academy? My mother devoted her life to this business."

Maura's blank expression seemed to ask, *So what?*

Natalie's dramatic reaction settled down as she puzzled over Maura's request. "Wait, I know what this about. You want Cece, the *great Cecilia Rose*, don't you?"

"And you, of course."

"You mean my name." Natalie spoke matter-of-factly. Everyone knew how much the name meant. It was one of the few things Natalie had that mattered anymore.

"The Lurensky name is big. I'm not going to pretend it isn't. And I like your location. While my studio's in a busy strip mall, yours has that small town charm. I mean, an historic hotel ballroom? Who wouldn't want to dance here?" She spread her arms in a grand gesture.

Maura's modern studio, an hour away, had the best of everything. Brand new, top of the line, state of the art. Six huge rooms, sound proof walls, and a menu of classes for all ages. Ballet, tap, jazz, hip-hop, cheer. A chunk of Maura's students joined the dance teams of major sports organizations. But what she had never done, could not do, was produce a prima ballerina.

That was Natalie Lurensky's ace in the hole. Ilana Lurensky had produced three of them.

"It's known that you've been struggling for a while, Natalie."

Natalie hated that the situation with her mother had had such an impact on her bottom line and made her vulnerable. Money from bake sales and fundraisers went straight into scholarships. Building maintenance was a boring line item in the budget nobody wanted to think about. And her studio was in dire need of updating.

Although the Mayfair hotel was listed on the historic registry, most of the upkeep and maintenance focused on the outside. Inside was a different story. There were cracks in the mirrors and breaks in the dance barres that looked like missing teeth. Parents occasionally mentioned that repairs were needed, and Natalie had responded with little white lies about the handyman being busy or new materials on back order.

Maura walked from one end of the room to the other, her shoes squeaking on the hardwood floor.

"I'm very sorry to hear about your mom, by the way. I really admired her."

Natalie paused before asking. "Did you ever even meet my mom?"

Maura halted her steps. "Don't you remember? I came to a production of The Nutcracker shortly after I bought my studio."

"Oh, that's right," Natalie said, although she had no memory of it.

"Ilana and I chatted for a few minutes. She was gracious and, well, dignified. Less intimidating than I thought she'd be."

Natalie was tiring of the conversation, but she couldn't be rude. "Yes, my mom was—"

One of the French doors opened, and Cece entered. "Oh, hi," she said. "Hope I'm not interrupting."

"Not in the least." Natalie was relieved to see her. Cece's presence always diffused tension. "You know Maura, don't you?"

Maura stepped forward, slightly star-struck. "Hello," she said with genuine admiration. "Of course we know each other."

Cece, probably the nicest person in the world, dove in for a hug. "Nice to see you again. How's Olivia doing?"

"Good. Great, actually."

Natalie pursed her lips. Olivia had danced with Cece for years, but a few months ago she'd switched over to train with Maura's cheer team instructor.

"She's very talented," said Maura. "But not as talented as her little sister. And you know how dicey that can be."

Sister rivalry, dance schools vying for the most talented dancers, business owners competing for every edge and angle— a day in the lives of all of them.

Cece set her bag in the corner. "I'm headed to Nutmegs. Anybody want to join me?"

"No." Natalie responded quickly. "Maura was just leaving."

"I'd love to join you," Maura said. "I haven't had one of those famous sticky buns in ages."

Cece threw a curious glance in Natalie's direction. "You sure, Nat?"

If there was one thing in her crazy life she never questioned, it was Cece's loyalty. If Maura wanted to make moves on her, she was welcome to try. Nothing would come of it.

"I'm sure. I have a ton of paperwork to do." Natalie turned to the interloper. It was laughable if she thought she could undermine Natalie by cozying up to Cece. "Nice to see you, Maura. Good luck with your expansion plans."

"Promise me you'll reach out if anything changes," Maura said.

"The only thing I can promise," Natalie said curtly, "is that nothing is going to change."

CHAPTER 6

*C*ece sat on the edge of Natalie's desk. "No, she did not offer me a job."

Natalie was skeptical. "Didn't even hint at it, huh?"

"Nope. We drank coffee and ate sticky buns and talked about how hard it is to find shoes for our big feet."

"Is that so?" Natalie lifted the lid off the decaf cappuccino her friend had brought from Nutmegs. "Did you braid each other's hair, too?"

"You funny girl. What do you think is gonna happen? Maura is going to steal me away and make me *her* best friend?"

"Well, you're my best friend, but Patty is your best friend," Natalie teased. "So I already have a chip on my shoulder about that."

"You have nothing to worry about. The truth is, I'm too busy to take on more friends, especially one like Maura. I sense she's a little high-maintenance." Cece dropped her coffee cup in the trash. "Oh, by the way, I have good news."

Natalie perked up. "I could use some of that. What?"

"We've got four candidates for the instructor position. I'll narrow it down to my top two. If we're lucky, we'll get both of them."

Natalie pushed her laptop toward Cece. "If you can find room in this budget for two new instructors, let me know. I'm not sure we can afford one at this point."

Cece studied the screen with focus and pressed her lips. "I didn't know things were so tight."

"To tell you the truth, I didn't either. I was so preoccupied with my mom, I stopped watching the numbers."

Cece scrolled the spread sheet. "I wish you'd have let me take this over months ago."

Natalie wished she had, too. "I couldn't ask you to do more than you were already doing. You picked up so many of my classes I probably owe you thousands in overtime. I hope you kept track."

"Natalie," Cece said, "we've known each other since we were little girls. You rescued me all those years ago when my life fell apart. I loved your mother. There's nothing in the world I wouldn't do for you. And that includes helping to—to shore up this budget."

"No." Natalie's chest rose. "I will not take money from you. This is my responsibility."

"A loan then. Come on, Nat, let me help you."

Natalie covered her eyes with both hands. The tears she couldn't cry for her mother now sprang to life, but they weren't about sadness. They were tears of shame that her studio was falling apart, her bills were past due, and now her best friend had just offered financial aid.

"I can't."

"You're being ridiculous. Think about your mom and how many people she helped over the years. Remember that family across town when we were kids? The dad walked out and the mom couldn't afford lessons anymore? Your mom gave all three of her daughters scholarships."

"I remember."

"And the costumes you donated to that school in the city, the hours you spent volunteering at the women's shelter. You always step up when there's someone in need! Why won't you accept help when it's offered?"

Cece's rant was out of character, enough so to make Natalie soften her stance.

"Let me think about it," she said. "In the meantime, if it's okay, I'll pay your overtime bit by bit. Let me know how many hours."

Cece threw her arms in the air. "You are the most stubborn woman. Forget the damn overtime."

"I can't forget it. It took you away from your family, and you must've spent a fortune in babysitting when Noah wasn't in school."

"Actually, no. And if you want to dive into who owes whom what, then I owe the studio money."

Natalie scoffed. "You do not."

"Yeah, I do. I put Noah in beginning dance classes with Serena."

"Oh my gosh, that's wonderful. Did he like it?"

"Not in the least. He completely disrupted the class, but clever Serena brought him a soccer ball to kick around. We made it work, so let's call it even. That said, Serena racked up a fair amount of overtime, so we do have to pay her. She's been asking."

"I get it. And I hear you." Natalie placed her hands on the edge of her desk and rose to her full five-foot-ten inch height. "Tell you what. This weekend, we'll dive into the finances. You're better at accounting than I am, so I'll accept help with that. Deal?"

Cece gave her a satisfied nod. "Deal."

That night, Natalie slept a solid nine hours, relieved to have her financial situation out in the open with her most trusted friend and colleague. Clearing problems off her plate one by one would surely bring about the calm she desired, a sense of peace. Perhaps Brian had been right—it was time to move on.

CHAPTER 7

$\mathcal{N}$atalie sat at the table in Cece's newly remodeled kitchen poring over numbers with her. She hoped to find money hiding in a forgotten account, but no such luck.

After hours of work, Cece rubbed her eyes and pushed her laptop aside. "Well, it's not as bad as we thought it would be."

Natalie studied the notes she'd scribbled on yellow legal paper. "No, but it's not good either."

Cece cleared away the empty coffee mugs. "It'll take time to pay everything off, but at least we have a plan now."

"Right." Natalie appreciated a good plan. "I guess as long as we stay on track and no unexpected situations or disasters crop up, the Lurensky Academy will become profitable again."

"Yes," Cece said with confidence. "Exactly."

THE NEXT MORNING, Natalie rose with the sun. She showered, secured her damp hair in a tight bun, and applied a little make-up to her pale skin. With a fresh face and improved outlook, she searched her closet for something different to wear. It had been nothing but black or navy for months, as if in mourning, but today Natalie slipped a hot pink tunic on over her leotard and tights.

"There," she said to her reflection, determined to stay positive and not let anything distract from the goals she'd set out to accomplish.

A short while later, as Natalie sat her desk catching up on paperwork, returning emails, and making sense of her many scribbled to-do lists, a light tap on the door interrupted her concentration.

"Come in," she said, expecting Cece. Although Cece didn't usually knock.

At first, she didn't recognize the face, but when the woman smiled, Natalie remembered the young mother of one of her former ballet students.

"Holly, wow, nice to see you." Natalie stood.

"You, too." Holly Robertson approached with tentative steps. She wore baggy jeans and an oversized gray parka. "I like your tunic. Hot pink suits you."

"Oh, thanks. Thought a little color would do me good." Natalie couldn't remember the last time she'd seen her student's mother. "How's Kaylee doing?"

Holly rested her hands on the back of a chair. "That's why I came by. I was wondering if you've heard from her."

Natalie recalled the sweet teenager who was awarded one of the Lurensky scholarships when she was twelve. For five years, she'd been a dedicated student, but then her interest waned and she quit coming to class. It was not an uncommon scenario, but with Kaylee it was disappointing. She'd shown great promise.

"Um, no," she said. "I haven't talked to her since—I don't even remember. Is she okay?"

Holly hesitated, as if she didn't know how to answer. Although about Natalie's age, she appeared much younger. Fair skinned with wispy light hair and pale blue eyes, the mother of five carried herself as if her thin frame were a heavy burden. "Oh, I'm sure she is. I just wondered if you knew anything because, well…" her timid voice faded to a whisper. "I've got to go. Sorry I bothered you."

Holly started to leave, but Natalie had questions. Kaylee was the big sister to a houseful of much younger siblings. That could be the cause of all kinds of turmoil.

"Hold on a sec." Natalie walked around her desk, took Holly's hands in hers, and guided her to the sofa against the wall. "Sit for a minute. Tell me what's going on. Is she in some kind of trouble?"

"Actually, I don't know." Holly lowered herself onto the sofa and folded her hands like an obedient child. "She moved out three months ago. Found an apartment with a friend somewhere near Oakland and got a job waiting tables. I wasn't happy about it, because she was set to start community college. But she's nineteen now. Allowed to make her own decisions."

Decisions and mistakes, Natalie thought. A situation she knew well.

Holly twisted her fingers together. "When I was her age, I was already a mother."

A mother at nineteen. Natalie couldn't even fathom how difficult that must have been.

"Do you know where she's living?" Natalie asked. "Maybe you could visit her, take her to lunch."

Holly blew out a breath of air. "She's not the kind of girl who likes surprises, especially from me. Besides, the last time we talked, we had a huge fight. I told her she'd made a foolish decision not going to school. I probably used more colorful language though." Regret spread across her face. "I should have kept my mouth shut."

"Yes, well, you only want what's best for her. Besides, Kaylee could always change her mind. Maybe she'll reapply in a year or two. It's not that big a deal." Natalie looked away as she minced her words.

It's a huge deal. A rash decision, a seemingly insignificant disruption to the plan, can change the trajectory of the rest of her life.

"That's kind of what I told her, but she accused me of trying to make her live the life I'd wanted for myself." Holly pulled on a loose thread poking out of her sweater. "She was right, although I denied it. Anyway, we haven't talked since. And now she's not answering my calls or texts."

"How long has it been?" Natalie asked, hopeful Holly was overreacting.

"Two weeks, maybe three. I'm so busy with the boys, I've lost track. It's not that we talk all that often, but..." Holly stood abruptly, as if a sudden thought occurred to her. "Natalie, I'm so sorry, I really shouldn't have bothered you, not with all you have going on." She glanced at a photograph of Ilana on the wall. "I should've sent you a condolence card or something. To be honest, I—I didn't know what to say."

"Don't worry about it, please." Natalie meant it. "And you're not bothering me at all. I just wish I knew something that might help."

"I know." Holly forced a smile, as if the motion hurt her cheeks. "Please, forget I was here. I'm sure she'll call me back soon. I left a message last night, and, yeah, so, never mind."

Natalie rose and gave Holly a brief and awkward hug. It was like squeezing a slender tree branch. "All right then, but let me know when you do hear back from her, okay?"

"I will." Holly brushed a few strands of hair behind her ear. "And on the off chance you hear anything, you'll let me know, too. Right?"

"Of course I will. Take care now."

Holly left the office, her footsteps barely making a sound.

NATALIE AND CECE sat side by side on the office sofa, both of their laptops on the coffee table. As Cece explained a new spreadsheet she'd created outlining income, expenses, and potential additional revenue streams, Natalie's mind drifted.

"Do you remember Kaylee Robertson?"

"Of course." Cece's eyes didn't leave the computer. "Why?"

"Her mom came by the other day."

Cece stayed focused. "If she needs a scholarship, the applications are due in a few weeks. I can send her a—"

"She thinks Kaylee is missing."

"What?" Cece's head snapped to the side.

"I know, it sounds crazy, doesn't it?"

"Like one of your crime shows."

"I doubt she actually is, but I'm a little concerned. And sad to hear she's gone off track. I mean, Kaylee was a shining star before she dropped out. All that potential wasted. But her family is complicated, and her mom is so—so needy."

"Five children and no husband," Cece said. "I have only one kid and a great husband, and sometimes I think I'm about to go off the rails. Is there something we can do to help?"

Natalie stared into space. "I don't know. I could ask around, see if any of Kaylee's old dance friends have talked to her."

"Can't hurt to ask," Cece said. "Have you looked at her social media? Maybe she's posted something recently."

"Good idea." Natalie reached for her phone and opened Instagram. She scrolled through Kaylee's photos while Cece peered over her shoulder. Nothing stood out among the random shots of food, cute dogs, and a beach that could have been anywhere. "None of these are recent. Her last post was over a month ago. Maybe she's not into social media."

"Most girls her age are addicted to it," Cece said. She closed her laptop and tucked it into her bag. "I gotta run, but if you find out anything, let me know. A bit of a mystery, that's for sure."

After Cece left, Natalie switched from Instagram to Facebook. Kaylee's page hardly existed—an old profile picture from high school and a notice that her page was private.

Natalie's cell buzzed. It was a text from one of her instructors that she wasn't feeling well and couldn't teach today. With that, Natalie switched gears and returned to her own challenges.

CHAPTER 8

*W*ith no word from Kaylee's mother, Natalie tried to set her concerns aside. It was easy during the day as she was so preoccupied with work, but every night during bouts of wakefulness, worries hopped through her brain like annoying bunnies trying to get her attention, most notably the missing teenager.

Although it had been more than a year since Natalie had seen her former student, her affection for her remained. Kaylee hadn't had many friends or much of a social life, so she hung around the studio most afternoons, often helping with the younger kids.

Occasionally, she'd talk to Natalie about school or family, but most of the time she was little more than a figure in the background. Except for when she danced. She was talented— not to the degree of some of the others—but enough to dance some of the more difficult roles. What stole Natalie's heart, however, was the way dancing brought Kaylee out of her shell. Ballet made her shine. It made her happy. When Kaylee quit, sometime during her senior year, the studio was a little less bright.

After another night of wondering, Natalie grew impatient for news of Kaylee. Maybe Holly had heard from her daughter and forgotten to let her know.

In between classes that afternoon, Natalie slipped into her office and made the call.

"Holly, hi. It's Natalie."

"Oh, hold on a sec."

The sound of children bickering echoed through the line.

"Sorry about that. Did you hear from Kaylee?" Holly's voice carried a hopeful note.

Natalie's heart sank. "I'm afraid I didn't. I was actually hoping you had."

Shared disappointment settled into silence, making Natalie squirm. She'd opened a door she had to walk through.

"But I—I wanted to tell you that I might be going to Oakland." The fib formulated as she plowed ahead, spinning some truth into the story. "There's a designer out that way who makes some of our costumes, and I need to check in on something." *Need* was pushing it. The designer did exist, but Natalie had never once needed to check on her. They managed everything through email and occasional video calls. But an in-person visit wouldn't be out of the realm of possibility.

"When are you going?"

"Sometime this week, I think, maybe," Natalie said. "Um, if—or when I go, I could drop by Kaylee's apartment. Do you have the address?"

"I do. That would be wonderful. I actually was thinking about doing that, but you know how girls can be about their mothers invading their lives."

"Of course." Natalie wondered if she herself would have been more proactive if in Holly's situation. She wasn't a mother, but she certainly knew plenty about teenagers, especially girls. "I'm not sure exactly when I'm going, but I'll call you afterwards."

"Please do. Even if there's nothing to report."

Kaylee's mother recited the address. Natalie jotted it on a sticky note and stuck it in her weekly planner.

For the next two days, the hot-pink sticky note poked at Natalie like a thorn in a sock, reminding her of the offer she'd made without thinking.

～

"You're usually more decisive. It's unlike you to fumble your way into a predicament." Cece sat across from her at an outdoor table at Nutmegs sipping a cappuccino. It was a cool afternoon, breezy with a hint of spring trying to edge its way in and push winter aside.

Natalie tightened her sweater against the chill. "I should try to find her. I mean, it won't take more than few hours of my time."

Cece took a bite of their sticky bun and pushed the plate toward her friend. "Exactly." She lifted her curly brown hair into a quick ponytail and stood. "I've got to run a couple of errands before classes start, so I'll see you in a bit."

Natalie remained at the table an extra moment, ruminating on her dilemma.

If Holly were that worried about Kaylee, why didn't she go see her herself? Natalie couldn't remember the dynamics of their relationship, only that Holly was constantly overwhelmed and frazzled. She scrolled through the contacts in her cell and texted the designer asking to meet at her shop in order to drop off costumes in need of repairs.

To her surprise, a response came within minutes. The costume designer suggested Friday morning.

"Hmm," Natalie murmured as she texted back confirmation. "Done."

≈

ON FRIDAY MORNING, after a quick visit with the designer that accomplished more than she'd expected, Natalie hopped into her car, an impractical white Mustang convertible. She'd bought the used car with every last penny of her savings several years back, the only extravagance she'd ever allowed herself.

Natalie followed the GPS directions as recited by the pleasant female voice that never admonished her for going the wrong way.

Make a U-turn at the next intersection and return to route.

"Will do," Natalie said to the voice, hoping she would track down Kaylee, solve the mystery, and make it back to Clearwater in time for her afternoon class.

The destination is on your right.

Natalie parked in front of a pink stucco two-story apartment building and leaned over the steering wheel to take a closer look. The sight of a tall rusted gate, dead flowers in cement planters, and pieces of stucco missing along the façade of the structure dampened her chipper mood.

She locked her car and stepped onto the sidewalk. Much of it was cracked and uneven with tree roots lifting large chunks of cement. As Natalie pushed open the gate, the hinges groaned like the entry to a haunted house. Once inside the courtyard, she was further dismayed to see the kidney shaped pool water was green with algae. At least it had a fence around it, although someone had propped open the gate to the pool area with an old lawn chair. A lot of good that would do if there were any small children around. Natalie took it upon herself to move the lawn chair and latch the gate closed. She looked around for access to the second floor and spotted a stairway on the other side of the pool. Without touching the handrail, Natalie made her way up the stairs.

She found apartment 249 at the end of the open air walkway, the number painted in black on a beige door. With her hand poised to knock, Natalie hesitated. She'd texted Kaylee to let her know she was coming but received no response. Her appearance might be a delightful surprise or an unwelcome intrusion, if Kaylee were even there. She could be at work or at the gym or having coffee with friends. Regardless, Natalie knocked.

No answer.

She knocked again, slightly harder.

The door swung open. "About time you got here."

Natalie jumped back. A man who looked to be in his mid-twenties stood in the doorway. He wore shorts and a tight white t-shirt exposing muscled arms covered with tattoos. His brown hair was coiled into a man bun on top of his head.

"Excuse me?" Natalie said.

"I placed my order an hour ago. Where's the bag?"

"Bag of what?" Natalie obviously had the wrong apartment.

The man laughed. "So you don't have my lunch, huh? I would've been impressed if they hired delivery girls as pretty as you. Please tell me one o' my buddies sent you over as a surprise for my birthday."

The encounter threw Natalie off her game. Now self-conscious, she wished she'd worn something other than a flowery skirt with white sneakers and denim jacket. "I'm looking for Kaylee Robertson," she said, hoping she sounded more authoritative than she looked.

The guy shook his head. "Don't know no Kaylee Robertson."

Natalie resisted correcting his grammar. "I was told she lives here. Apartment number 249."

"Nope. She don't."

Footsteps on the walkway distracted them. Natalie spun to her right to see a delivery kid holding a plastic bag.

"What the hell took so long?" the tattooed guy shouted.

"Sorry," the kid said. "I don't cook the food. I just deliver it." He handed the bag over and jogged away.

The smell of chili and garlic made Natalie's stomach roll over.

"It's Thai. Care to join me?" The guy's slick, suggestive smirk sent Natalie three steps back.

"No, thank you." Natalie stood as tall as she could, making herself close to his height. "Perhaps I have the apartment number wrong. Anyway, maybe you've seen Kaylee around here. She's blonde, slender, quite, um—" Natalie stopped before saying she's petite and shy. Everything about this guy told her she'd better leave.

"Never seen a girl like that. Besides, not my type. I prefer tall brunettes." He grinned and stepped closer to her. "Come on in, have some food and a cold beer with me."

"Sorry I bothered you." Natalie walked away, her steps firm and purposeful to defy the lewd gaze pressing on her back.

CHAPTER 9

a s soon as she returned to the studio, Natalie called Holly and delivered the disappointing news.

"The wrong address?" Holly said. "I'm sure it's the one she gave me."

"Maybe the address is right but the wrong apartment number." Natalie lay her phone on the desk and put it on speaker so she could change her clothes. "Some guy lives there. Said he didn't know her, had never seen her around the building. I wish I had more information."

"Well, thanks anyway. It was sweet of you to try. I'll keep texting and hope she eventually answers me."

Natalie tied her ballet skirt around her waist. "It's only been a few weeks since you talked to her. Maybe she's out of town with her girlfriends. Or trying to keep her distance after your, you know, argument. She's always had a little rebelliousness in her."

A slight laugh from Holly. "I suppose."

A shriek from a child broke into their conversation.

"Dammit you two, quit fighting!" Holly's normally reserved voice ended there. "Gotta run, Natalie, take care."

The call disconnected before Natalie could say good-bye.

~

BY THE FOLLOWING WEEK, Natalie had moved on. One dance class rolled into another—beginner, intermediate, advanced— she could instruct in her sleep.

How long had she been so blasé? Months, maybe years? Ever since giving up her dream of going to college, she still had a purpose as her mother's partner in the dance academy. When Ilana started losing her memory and grasp of reality, Natalie's purpose shifted. Her fierce determination to protect her mother and be the steadfast custodian of her life's work occupied every piece of her.

But since her mother was gone, the truth could not be ignored. Natalie needed to be renewed by something—anything that would light a spark of interest.

"What's wrong with you today?" Cece asked as they left work that evening.

"Nothing." Natalie locked the door of the studio and dropped the heavy key ring into her bag. It landed with a thud next to her laptop. "I'm fine."

It was Tuesday, or maybe Wednesday. What difference did it make? Every day was just like the one before.

"No, you're not."

Natalie gave her friend a sidelong glance as they walked to their cars. "I'm in a funk. The last few years might have had me on edge all the time, but the stress kept me on my toes. Not necessarily in a good way, but at least I woke up every morning with a plan and a purpose."

"So you're saying your life has lost its purpose?"

"I think so."

"You know that's completely insane, don't you?"

"Maybe. But it's how I feel. Blah and purposeless."

Cece stopped her. "How do you not recognize the enormous value in what you do and the impact you have here?"

Value. Impact. Meaning. Purpose. "You're right, I know you are. It's just that nothing excites me anymore."

Admitting the truth, even to Cece, embarrassed her. She didn't divulge how she'd perked up when she was on the search for Kaylee. That mission, although fruitless, had pumped some adrenaline into her system.

"I think you need to start dating. I really do."

"Oh, no, not that idea again. I'm on a break. Besides, have you noticed I always seem to end up with same kind of man?"

"You mean divorced, too old for you, lives far away?"

"That's the type," Natalie said.

"By your own design, Nat. You told me years ago that you liked low maintenance—someone you could keep at arm's length. I remember, because at the time it sounded so sensible."

"Sensible or not, I have no desire to step into the dating minefield again. I can't even imagine it." Natalie recalled her last encounter with Brian. Maybe she had been too harsh, too hasty. He had always been a good distraction and usually not too demanding. Then again, he was a womanizer. He needed his ego stroked. He didn't love Natalie any more than she loved him. What he really loved was flaunting her, showing off his *hot-dancer-girlfriend*—his words, not hers. He'd used her, yes, but Natalie used him, too. Neither one of them had been interested in a deep connection or serious commitment. And it worked, until it didn't.

"Now what are you thinking about?" Cece popped open the back of her SUV.

"Brian. How, at the time, we were what we needed."

"What does that mean?" Cece asked.

"The relationship, how shallow it was. He needed a certain kind of woman to drag to parties and events, and I needed a man I could be with only when I wanted. Low expectations all the way around." Natalie cringed at how selfish and shallow she sounded.

"At least you realize that. But come on now." Cece pointed at her." You deserve better. Much better."

Do I? she thought. What was the point of pursuing better when she, herself, was lacking?

CHAPTER 10

$\mathcal{N}$atalie parked in front of the designer's storefront to pick up the costumes she'd left last week. Winding her way through stacks of fabric bolts and naked mannikins, she greeted the seamstress behind the counter.

"These look great," Natalie said, admiring the perfect seams. "Thanks for the quick turnaround."

She paid the bill, which was higher than expected. But costume repairs were practical and a good investment. They'd get at least another few seasons out of these. While many parents could afford new costumes for their children every year, some could not. Ilana had always provided options, and Natalie was determined to do the same.

She loaded them into the Mustang, carefully tucking the plastic covered garments into the small space.

Traffic on the freeway was stop and go. As she passed a familiar exit, a flurry of something stirred in her chest. It was the off-ramp to Kaylee's apartment complex. The slow traffic gave her time to mull over whether or not to make one last effort. Maybe she'd find someone other than the creepy guy who knew nothing. It was worth the quick detour.

The courtyard gate groaned the same spooky groan it had before. In the pool area, a couple of bikini clad girls lay on cheap folding lounges. Both appeared to be about Kaylee's age, perhaps a few years older.

Natalie approached casually. In black pants, white blouse, and low-heeled pumps, she probably looked like someone's mother or an office manager at an accounting firm.

"Excuse me."

One of the girls looked up from her phone but didn't say anything.

"Sorry to bother you, but I'm looking for someone, a young woman about your age."

"Okay," the girl said. Large, black framed sunglasses covered much of her face.

"Her name's Kaylee Robertson." Natalie waited for a response, her heart beating faster than normal. "I think she lives here, or maybe she used to."

The girl slapped her friend's leg. "Hey, wake up."

The second girl, wearing a blue and white polka-dot swimsuit, mumbled some unintelligible words and rolled onto her side.

The girl smacked her friend's leg again. "Do we know someone named Kaylee?"

"I don't think so," the second girl said, rolling back over. "Hey, what time is it? I gotta get ready for work."

"It's a little after eleven," Natalie said, wondering what kind of work she might do. "I really could use your help. Kaylee's a— a friend of mine, and I'd like to track her down."

"You got a picture?" the first girl asked.

"I do." Natalie pulled her phone from her purse and scrolled. "Here's one. It's a couple years old and from a show, so she's in a costume."

It was Kaylee's last performance—the Sugar Plum Fairy in The Nutcracker. The photo of her, shimmering in white chiffon and a jeweled tiara, gave Natalie a twinge of regret. If she'd kept in contact with her former student, maybe she wouldn't be missing.

"Cute girl, and a ballerina, too." Polka-dot girl grinned, as if being a ballerina were some kind of joke. "But she doesn't look familiar to me."

Natalie grew antsy. What a waste of time. She was about to tuck her phone away when the first girl leaned in closer.

"Hold on. This is crazy, but doesn't she look a little like Robin?"

"Robin?" her friend said. "No, she doesn't. Robin has dark hair."

"It's the face. It really could be Robin."

"Who's Robin?" Natalie asked.

The original girl hesitated. "Who wants to know?"

Natalie took stock of the situation. She was part intrigued and part annoyed. "I'm an old friend of Kaylee's family, and I...I have some news for her. Good news." Natalie didn't know where she was going with her latest story, but spinning the truth seemed her only option. And it wasn't a lie. The good news for Kaylee would be that her mother loves her and just wants to know she's okay. That would be very good news, she reasoned.

"Listen," Natalie said, softening her tone. "If there's any connection between Kaylee and the girl you call Robin, let's figure it out."

Natalie envisioned herself pulling a twenty, or a fifty, from her wallet and sweetening the deal for an exchange of information. She almost laughed at herself.

"I gotta get to the restaurant, Mel. You're on your own here." Polka-dot girl snatched her towel from the lounge and scooted out the pool gate, her flip-flops smacking the cement.

Natalie waited until she was out of sight before sitting on the empty lounge chair. "So, Mel, I'm Natalie."

Mel pushed her arms through the sleeves of lacey coverup. When her head popped out, her sunglasses fell off her face. She couldn't have been more than twenty-two.

"Honestly," Mel said, putting her glasses back in place, "I don't know what to tell you. I haven't seen Robin, *or Kaylee*, around lately."

"Well, before I give up," Natalie offered, "do you have a photo of Robin?"

"I might." Mel picked up an old model I-phone and scrolled with one finger. "I don't think, oh wait, this is her." She turned her phone around. Through the cracks in the screen, a dark photo of a group of girls in a bar appeared.

Natalie looked closely. "I don't see her."

Mel zoomed in on a girl with dark brown hair and heavy make-up. It was the smile, the tiny chip on one front tooth. Even with all the squiggly lines running through the screen, Natalie could see it was Kaylee's smile.

"That could be her. Was this at a party or something?"

"A friend's birthday." Mel said. "A bunch of us work at the same restaurant. At the time, Robin was hanging out around here, but like I said, I haven't seen her in a while."

"I understand." Natalie sensed that Mel had more to say. "You two don't text or anything?"

Mel shook her head. "To be honest, we're really not friends, just, you know, acquaintances. Besides, I work nights and week-ends. I only see the people I see."

A man wearing shorts and a sweatshirt entered the pool area. He seated himself at one of the round metal tables with a laptop and a Starbucks drink.

Mel rose and gathered her things. "I gotta go," she said. "And I wouldn't talk to that guy if I were you. He's a perv."

Natalie glanced over her shoulder. Another reminder that there was no end to the uncomfortable, potentially dangerous situations young women might land in. Working with girls of all ages for so many years, she felt protective toward that segment of the population. Most of her students stayed on track, went on to college or continued with dance or established themselves in careers and solid relationships. But the ones who veered off course often found themselves in deep trouble. And the farther off track they went, the harder it was for them to recover.

It worried her that Kaylee had fallen off track. Why would she color her hair, go by a different name, have no friends, and avoid her mother? At this point, all she knew was that Kaylee had been around this apartment building. There was no way to know if she had actually ever lived at this address.

"Thanks for your help, Mel." Natalie checked the time. Her to-do list was a mile long. She should've been on her way back to Clearwater already. "I don't suppose there's anyone else around here who might know something."

"Well," Mel's mouth twisted to the side. "The only person I can think of is Jimmy. He's really cute, and all the girls want to hang out with him. Maybe he knows something."

"Oh, okay." Natalie said, almost sorry she'd asked. "And where might I find Jimmy?

Mel pointed to the stairway. "Up those stairs and down the hall to your left. Apartment 249."

CHAPTER 11

*N*atalie rapped on the door, loud enough to indicate she meant business, but not so hard that she sounded aggressive.

The man who opened the door was not the one she expected.

He resembled the first man she'd run into but taller and broader, like a running back, and much neater. His hair was clipped close to his head, almost a military cut. He wore jeans, a spotless white polo shirt, and what appeared to be expensive leather sneakers.

"Who are you?" the man asked. He had none of the disgusting lewdness of his friend or roommate, or perhaps brother.

"Are you Jimmy?" Natalie asked, intimidated by his dark stare and towering presence.

"What do you want?" His non-answer left her wondering.

"I'm looking for someone, that's all." Natalie itched to go inside, have a look around, but to enter an apartment with a strange man would be a stupid move. Dangerous, even. Besides that, with his wide stance and broad shoulders filling the doorway, he sent the clear message that she was not a welcome visitor.

"You a cop?" the man who might be Jimmy asked.

"Me? A cop, oh, um, no." The fact that he thought she might be infused her with confidence. And a bold-faced lie came out of her. "I'm actually a private detective. A family hired me to find a young woman gone missing." Okay, three quarters lie, one quarter truth.

The man remained expressionless.

"Her name is Kaylee Robertson. Also goes by Robin. Blonde hair, but maybe dark brown. Tall and skinny." Natalie used clipped, short sentences hoping it made her sound authoritative like the cops on TV.

There was a slight shift in his expression, as if he recognized Kaylee's description.

"Does that sound like someone you might have seen around here?" Natalie proceeded cautiously, making sure not to reveal herself as an imposter.

"Sounds like a lot girls I might've seen around here."

If Natalie had actually been a private detective, she would've known what to say, the follow-up question that would chip away at the subject's brick wall. All she had was an abundance of common sense and years of experience watching cop shows on TV.

"Where's the other guy who lives here? Younger, long hair, lots of tattoos?" She was grasping at straws. A beginner's mistake. Everything was about to unravel.

"Well, now," Jimmy-maybe said. He leaned against the door jam. "You've been here before, haven't you? And if I had to guess, you're not really a private detective."

Now it was Natalie's turn to say nothing, neither confirm nor deny. But the confidence that had bolstered her was leaking out like air from a slashed tire.

"I can't help you. Don't come back." He closed the door in

her face, literally *in her face*. If she'd been an eighth-inch closer it would've hit her nose.

ACCORDING to the map on her phone's navigation, the police station was only a few blocks from the apartment building. She placed a quick call to Cece to let her know she'd be returning late.

"Is there a problem with the costumes?"

"Costumes are fine," Natalie said. "What's all that noise in the background?"

"We're at the park. Hold on a sec." Cece shouted to someone to watch Noah. "Okay, I'm back. What's going on?"

"I stopped at the apartment building where Kaylee lives. Or lived. And something's weird."

"Okay, so you're on the way back now?"

"I have one quick stop to make," Natalie said, sharing as little information as possible.

Cece hemmed. "Quick stop where? You're up to something, I can tell."

"I'm, I'm thinking I need to—to talk to the police."

"Are you kidding me?" Cece sounded like a disapproving parent. "What exactly are you going to tell them?"

Natalie pulled into a parking space. "I'm not sure yet. I'll see what they say when I tell them about Kaylee and take it from there." She got out of her car and stood a moment. Perhaps she should reconsider. But all she had to do was tell somebody the situation. After that she'd be done. She'd already gone above and beyond in her quest to help Holly.

"Nat? Are you still there?"

"I'm here. I'm going in now. I'm sure it won't take long. There aren't many cars in the parking lot, so they're probably not even busy. See you when I get back."

Evidently, the number of cars in the parking lot was no indication of a police station's activity.

At least twenty people scrambled around the entrance where everyone had to pass through security. Natalie stood wide-eyed until a young woman in uniform waved her over. She searched Natalie's purse then directed her through a metal detector.

People waited in line at the counter. A few kids sat on benches tapping their feet and chewing their nails, as if waiting for grim news. A uniformed officer escorted a handcuffed man in pajamas into a room.

Natalie's heart thumped. This was not the kind of place she belonged. She turned, but there was no exit, at least none that she could see.

The woman searching bags glanced at her. "You look lost, ma'am."

"Oh, um, yeah, I—I think I should, I mean, how do I get out of here?"

"Hold on a second, okay?" The officer called a colleague over to take her place.

Natalie lingered, self-conscious of how she stood out in the crowd, like a child's game of *what doesn't belong.*

"Before you leave, is there something I can help you with?"

"Maybe. I don't know." Natalie had never been so flustered in her life. "I can't exactly say I'm reporting a crime, but I have a problem I'm not sure how to handle."

The officer pressed her palm to Natalie's elbow. "Come with me." She guided Natalie to the other side of the counter into the back. It looked sort of like police precincts on TV with rows of cluttered desks topped with file folders, computers, and coffee mugs. The officer pointed to a desk by the window. "Take a seat over there. Someone will be with you shortly."

"Okay. Thanks." Natalie wound through the maze of desks, trying to come up with an explanation for why she was there. She sat in a hard metal chair, knees pressed together, and perched her purse on her legs as if she were sitting in church. Nobody paid any attention to her until a man approached with a stack of file folders.

"Hello, there." He fell into his desk chair, which wheeled backwards a couple of feet.

Natalie took in his appearance—a few wisps of hair on his bald head and a face full of gray whiskers. He wore Levi's and a plaid flannel shirt and a grin he seemed unable to hide.

"Don't see pretty gals like you around here much," he said.

Natalie would've been offended if he hadn't been such a grandfatherly figure—a grandfather with a gun in a holster strapped around his torso. "I'm Sergeant White, but you can call me Fred." His kind voice didn't match his scruffy appearance. "So, you have problem?"

"Yes." Natalie managed the one word. Her legs were bouncing so fast she could be generating electricity.

"Alright then, what's your name?"

"Natalie Lurensky, L-U-R-E-N-S-K-Y."

He wrote it down as she spelled it out. "May I call you Natalie?"

"Sure."

"What's the problem you're having?"

She steadied her nerves with a deep breath. "I went somewhere."

Fred pursed his lips. "Oh-kay. Where'd you go?"

Natalie recited the address by memory. "It's not far from here. An apartment complex, unit 249, upstairs and to the left."

"That's very specific." Fred continued taking notes, as if she were providing important information.

"And I've been there twice now. The first time I met a guy, a young guy, kind of inappropriate and creepy. Then today, there was a different guy. It all happened at their apartment, well, it might be their apartment. I'm not sure about that part. Anyway, I went there to find out if anyone had seen—"

"Were you assaulted?" Fred showed genuine concern.

"Assaulted? No! Why would you ask that?"

"It's an ordinary question."

"Okay." Natalie sorted her thoughts. She'd certainly put herself at risk going there. "I'm here about a friend. She's a former student of mine, a young woman."

Fred leaned toward her. "Was she assaulted?"

"She wasn't assaulted. Although, I can't say that for certain."

"What did your friend tell you then?"

Natalie could not believe how convoluted her story had become. Her head was a whirl of confusion. "She didn't tell me anything. I can't find her, which is how I ended up at—"

Fred put his hand up. "Hold on. You can't find your friend?"

Natalie shook her head. Answering yes/no questions was much easier than trying explain something she didn't understand herself.

"You think she's missing?"

"Missing. Well, yes, she's definitely missing."

"Alright, you need to talk to someone else." He spun his chair around and pointed. "See the guy wearing the baseball cap? He's the one."

"I have to start over again?" Natalie wanted to stay with Fred. He was growing on her.

"Yeah. Just start at the beginning. Try to be succinct. Danny doesn't like ramblers. And if he seems impatient, don't worry about it. His bark is worse than his bite."

Natalie rose from her chair, hesitating. "I'm very nervous," she whispered to the fatherly figure.

Fred stood and shook her hand with both of his. "It'll be fine. Off you go, now."

"Right. Off I go." Natalie moved slowly in the direction she'd been sent, chin high, shoulders set—like a dancer about to go on stage.

CHAPTER 12

A plastic name plate on his desk read Detective Garrett. Natalie halted a few steps before reaching him and observed his activity. He was hunched over a laptop reading something and eating pistachios with impressive speed—break open shell, pop nut in mouth, discard shell, repeat. A mountain of empty shells covered a large paper plate.

Natalie moved closer and cleared her throat.

No response.

"Excuse me, Detective Garrett? Sergeant White sent me. He said you're the one I need to talk to."

The detective glanced up from his laptop. He blinked, then emptied the plate of shells into an overflowing trashcan. He drank down the contents of a paper cup and grimaced, then swept pistachio dust off his desk with his hands. "Have a seat."

"Thank you." Natalie sat in the hard metal chair next to his desk. She used her best posture to appear confident. "I'm here to report a—a situation."

He wore black, all black—jeans, t-shirt, shoes. Light brown hair stuck out from beneath his black and orange Giants base-ball cap. The holster across his chest was empty, and Natalie wondered if his gun was in a drawer or behind his back or strapped to his leg like they do in movies.

The detective's expression was blank as he shuffled through the mess on his desk to uncover a pen and spiral notebook. "What's the situation?"

"Don't you want my name first?"

"Sure," he said without looking up. "What's your name?"

She recited and spelled it out for him the same way she'd done for Fred, but he didn't write it down. She was getting the feeling Detective Garrett did not take her seriously. It was hard to tell how old he was, around her age, but maybe younger.

"Okay, what is it you want to report?"

Natalie brushed off her annoyance. "I'm looking for someone."

"Can you be more specific?"

Before Natalie could respond, Fred meandered by with an empty mug that had *World's Best Grandpa* on it in big block letters. "All good here?"

Natalie's regard for him grew. She smiled up at him—he reminded her of Walter, her favorite waiter in San Francisco, although not quite as dapper.

"What do you want, Fred?" The detective asked.

"Making sure you're on your best behavior, Danny-boy. We have a celebrity in our midst."

Detective Garrett took a closer look at Natalie's face. "You're famous?"

"No, not at all. Sergeant White must have me confused with someone." Natalie glanced at a round clock on the far wall. If she didn't get out of there soon, she'd be late for her afternoon lessons.

"Nope, I don't," Fred looked star-struck. "Your name sounded familiar, so I looked you up. The Lurensky Dance Academy is one of the top ballet schools in California. I tried to take my granddaughter to a performance of the Nutcracker last Christmas but tickets were all sold out."

Natalie stood. She was at least two inches taller than her new friend. "Sergeant White, Fred, I'll tell you what. Tomorrow, you call my cell. That's the number I gave you. And I will put you and your granddaughter on my personal VIP list. Best seats in the house and backstage passes. How does that sound?"

"Wow, fabulous! Thank you. I'll do that. Can I bring my wife, too?"

"Of course."

"Thank you, thank you. And so nice to meet you. Good luck with everything." Fred stepped away, mug in hand, his face flushed with joy.

"That was nice of you." Detective Garrett clicked the clicker on his pen repeatedly.

"Fred seems like a lovely man, for a police officer that is."

"Touché." Finally, a smile.

Natalie warmed up to the detective, but only for a moment.

"Alright now, tell me the situation. And try to keep it short."

"Fine, I'll keep it very short." In a calm tone and with no extraneous details, she spelled out the whole story, ending with the strange encounter with the second man (who might be Jimmy) at the door of apartment number 249.

The detective took a few notes, but not many.

"Got it," he said. "When was the last time you saw or spoke with..." he checked his notes..."Kaylee Robertson?"

"It's been a while, a year or more."

Click, click, click on the pen. "You haven't seen a person in over a year and now you want to report her missing?"

"I'm not actually the one who thinks she's missing. Her mother does. Kind of."

"Then her mother needs to file the report."

"I don't think she'll do that," Natalie said.

"That's her choice. Ms. Lurensky, please don't take this the wrong way, but the situation here isn't much of a situation."

"I disagree." Natalie responded with respect but also in her firm ballet-instructor voice. "There's something going on in that apartment. And there is something untoward happening with Kaylee Robertson. I know I haven't provided you with any evidence of a crime, but I know a suspicious *situation* when I see one."

"It appears to be unusual, I'll grant you that. But there's nothing you've told me that would warrant an investigation. We can't show up there and start asking questions. That's not how it works." He paused. "Sorry I can't be more helpful."

"That's it then?" Natalie threw her hands out to the side.

"I'm afraid so. Your friend is over eighteen. So unless her mother wants to file a missing persons report, there's nothing I can do." He rose from his seat. "Now if you'll excuse me, I have to get back to work."

Natalie gathered her purse and faced him.

"Yes, you do appear to have a lot of work to do. If eating pistachios qualifies as work." She marched off, her face heating up with embarrassment.

Detective Garrett was right. She'd reported a whole bunch of nothing.

After using the restroom, Natalie hurried outside, anxious to leave the station and the awkward encounter behind.

She got into the Mustang and called Cece.

"I'm sorry I'm so late. I'm leaving the police station now."

"You're still there?"

"I should be back in forty-five minutes, an hour at most."

"Well, don't rush," Cece said. "I had to cancel afternoon classes."

"Why?"

"Lice."

"Lice?" Natalie smacked her forehead. "Seriously?"

"Yep. All our little ones attended a birthday party the other day, and now three of them have it. The moms are freaking out."

"What a disaster," Natalie said. "Nobody returns until they've been checked. The last thing we need is a lice outbreak."

"I'll let everyone know. Now you get to enjoy a little free time."

"Free time? What a concept." Natalie leaned her head against the head rest.

"Hey," Cece said. "Do you want to come for dinner tonight? Brad's throwing steaks on the barbeque."

"Now there's a nice offer." Natalie's stomach rumbled. "I'd love to."

"Great. See you about seven."

"See you then." Natalie ended the call. A shame to have lice disrupt the schedule, but she didn't mind having extra time to herself. She started her car and pushed the button to lower the convertible roof. As it folded into place behind her head, she scrolled through some messages, ruminating on whether or not to update Holly Robertson on her latest foray into Kaylee's life. There was nothing new to tell her, except the fact that Kaylee might have an ex-boyfriend of unknown identity. But that was such a vague piece of information, and its validity could not be—

"Nice wheels."

Natalie snapped to attention. Detective Garrett stood over her, still wearing his Giants cap. He'd added a scary looking gun to his outfit.

"Didn't mean to startle you. Sorry."

"It's okay." She was seeing him from a different angle and noticed a faded scar beneath his sparse beard along a strong jawline.

"Convertible, huh? You didn't strike me as a convertible kinda girl." He was looking at the car, not at her.

Was he trying to strike up a conversation?

"I'm not," she said. "I'm actually more sensible than that. This car is the only impulsive thing I've ever done."

"You don't do impulsive, huh?"

"Absolutely not," Natalie said. "Although I have to admit, coming here today was a somewhat impulsive move."

"Yeah, about that." The detective shifted his shoulders as if he had an itch he couldn't reach. "I'm sorry if I was short with you earlier. I didn't mean to make light of the situation."

"Don't worry," she said, meaning it sincerely. "I already feel foolish that I came to the police thinking I had something worthy to report. I'm sorry I wasted your time."

"It happens." His cell buzzed. "Excuse me a sec."

Natalie waited, wondering why he was lingering outside. Didn't he need to go back to work? Or eat more pistachios?

"Shit," he said.

Well, Natalie thought, that's a good conversation starter. "Something wrong?"

"Yeah, I need to get to my sister's. She has a plumbing emergency." His thumbs flew over his phone. "And my Uber just cancelled. Gimme a sec."

She waited, as instructed. What more could he have to say to her? He finished with his phone and slipped it into a pocket.

"Uber on the way?" Natalie asked.

"Twenty minutes. By the time I get there, my sister's kitchen will be flooded. Anyway, I wanted to tell you that if the mom believes her daughter is missing, she should file a report." He handed Natalie his card. "We take missing person cases very seriously."

"Thank you." She glanced at his name on the card. "Detective Daniel Garrett."

"You're welcome." He stepped back, but he didn't walk away.

And she didn't move either.

"Do you want me to drive you?" Had she really offered him a ride? Talk about impulsive, what was she thinking?

Detective Garrett stuffed his hands into his pockets. "Oh, no, that's okay."

"I don't mind, as long as it's nearby."

"Maybe ten minutes. But I, that, well, I don't know. It's not against any protocol that I know of, but—"

"What would Fred do?" Natalie asked.

The detective laughed. "He'd ask if he could drive your car."

"You want to drive my car?"

What had gotten into her? That sounded almost flirty. But the detective seemed to have a sweet side. And any guy who would leave work to go help out his sister couldn't be half bad. "I won't let you drive. But I will drop you off."

"Are you sure you don't mind?"

"I'm sure."

"Great. Thanks." He walked around the car to the passenger side.

This was almost like picking up a hitch-hiker who happened to be a cop. A cop with a gun and a baseball cap and an intriguing scar on his cheek.

CHAPTER 13

O n the awkwardness scale, the ride with Daniel Garrett ranked a ten out of ten. From what Natalie could tell, he was even more uncomfortable than she was.

He pulled on his seatbelt as if it were strangling him. "Sorry, I'm not used to being a passenger."

"Nothing to worry about," Natalie said. "I'm a good driver. Very cautious."

A slight smirk. "I can see that."

"Thank you," she said, wondering if he was teasing or not. She went with not. "I like driving. I find it relaxing. Plus, I'm usually the designated driver in my group."

Daniel faced her. "You don't drink?"

"Oh, I drink." Natalie responded too quickly. "What I mean is I can drink without being impaired. That didn't come out right—makes me sound like a lush who can hold her liquor. That's not what I meant."

"Relax." Daniel smiled, an actual real wide smile. "I'm quite certain you're not drinking and driving. Besides, I'm not on patrol."

"Good to know."

Silence filled the car. "Music?" she asked.

"Whatever. I mean, if you want. Go ahead. I have to listen to a voicemail, if you don't mind." He tapped the screen and held his phone to his ear.

Natalie suspected there was no message. He probably was using his phone as an excuse to avoid interaction. She wouldn't blame him if he were.

"Good news," he said.

"Your sister?"

"No, my mechanic. My truck's been in the shop."

"Car trouble. So annoying."

"It is."

"What's wrong with your truck?" she clutched the steering wheel. This had to be the most boring conversation in the world.

A chuckle, not quite a laugh, but a little more than grunt. "You really want to know?"

"I guess not," she said, returning the same amount of chuckle. "Cars are not my thing. Except for this one."

"Just as well, because we're almost there. At the stop sign, take a left."

She turned the corner onto a quiet street with cookie-cutter homes in a few different designs. Most had neat lawns, walnut trees, and curved paths leading from the sidewalk to the front porch.

"Right here," Daniel said, pointing to a square yellow house with white trim. "You can pull into the driveway."

"Nice house."

"What? Oh, yeah, it's, um, the house my—never mind." Daniel opened his door and swung one leg out. "Can you wait here a minute? Or, well, that doesn't make sense. My sister can probably drive me, unless her—"

"I'll wait," Natalie said, feeling more in control.

"Okay. I'll be right back."

She watched him jog up the steps. A little flutter of attraction made her squirm. "What's wrong with you?" she said aloud. If a person could be embarrassed by herself in front of only herself, that was Natalie. She shut off the car and leaned back, suddenly exhausted. So much to worry about—first Kaylee and now her youngest dancers all scratching their heads and having fine-toothed combs yanked through their hair. Those poor parents. And what if—

"Hi."

Natalie looked up. Inches from her face stood a little girl dressed in pink tights, tutu, and an orange Giants t-shirt. Her blonde ponytail hung down her back in one perfect ringlet.

"Who are you?" the young Giants fan asked.

"I'm Natalie." She adjusted her seat, charmed by the girl's adorableness. "Do you take ballet lessons?"

"Yes."

"That's wonderful. Do you enjoy it?"

"No."

"No?"

She shook her head, ponytail swinging. "I only take lessons because I have to. My mom says I need to try lots of different things and discover what sticks."

"That makes sense," Natalie said, her amusement growing. "What's your name?"

"Lola."

"That's a pretty name."

"I know." Lola's suspicious eyes widened, as if surprised by her own thoughts. "Hey, wait. Are you the lady who's going to mend my Uncle Danny's broken heart?"

Natalie choked. "Excuse me?"

"Yeah, my mom says he needs to find a—"

"Lola!" A woman in tie-died stretch pants, oversized sweatshirt, and bare feet ran down the steps and grabbed Lola's hand. "I've been looking for you!"

"I was right here, Mommy. Geez, you're so dramatic."

"And you are disrespectful. Go inside. Uncle Danny needs your help."

"But I'm busy talking to Natalie." Lola flung her arms like wings.

"You're done." Her mother pointed her toward the door. "Go."

"You're mean." She dragged her feet through the grass and up the steps.

"Sorry about that. My daughter's a bit of a drama queen."

"She's adorable." Natalie got out of the car and offered a hand. "I'm Natalie."

"Jennifer." The handshake was solid, her hand rough and discolored. "Sorry about the paint. I refinish furniture. "Are you a friend of my brother's?"

"No, I don't, um—what did he say?"

"He said, and I quote, '*Somebody drove me here. Go outside and tell her she can leave.*' I figured you were someone from work."

"Well, in a way, I suppose that is how we met."

"Doesn't matter." Jennifer waved both hands. "Thanks for getting him here. I had a plumbing problem under the kitchen sink, which ordinarily I could fix myself. But this one was tricky, even for me." A slight pause, then, "If you don't mind my asking, are you married?"

Whoa, Natalie could see where Lola got her cheekiness.

"No, why?"

Jennifer looked her up and down. "You're freakin' gorgeous, aren't you?"

Natalie wrapped her arms around her waist. "I'm not sure how to respond to that."

"Yeah, sorry, I tend to create awkward moments wherever I go. It's just that my brother needs a girlfriend in the worst way."

"Well, he didn't mention that," Natalie said, inching her way back into her car. "I'd better go."

"Right, and I gotta get back to Danny. Should I tell him you said goodbye, or see ya later, or maybe *hey, gimme a call?*"

"Goodbye is fine." Natalie smiled at the detective's wacky sister. "Nice to meet you, Jennifer."

She closed her door and backed out of the driveway, percolating on the plethora of new information regarding Detective Daniel Garrett.

CHAPTER 14

"*A*ll I'm saying is she's totally hot." Jennifer stood over her brother who was on his back with his upper torso under the sink. "You could have a cathartic fling before you leave town."

"Jesus, Jen!" He hit his head on the cabinet as he extricated himself from the small space. "Lola's standing right there."

"I know what a fling is." His niece made kissing noises at him. "But what's that other word mean?"

"Tell you later." Jennifer hoisted her daughter onto a stool at the counter and dumped a pile of Lucky Charms in front of her. "Here, have a snack."

Daniel groaned and got to his feet. He loved his sister, but she was a real piece of work. Ever since her divorce, he did whatever he could for her and Lola. It pained him to think of them on their own without him.

"You haven't had a girlfriend in two years. That's not normal for a guy like you."

"A guy like me? What does that mean?" Daniel separated out a few blue moon marshmallows and ate them, the taste reminding him of his childhood with Jennifer—a protective sister, five years older.

"Never mind, just tell me how you know her."

"Yeah, Danny, how do you know her?" Lola chimed in.

"That's Uncle Danny to you, Lola-granola." He tugged on her curly ponytail. His niece was seven going on seventeen, thanks to his hippy-dippy sister. "She came to the station today to, well, with information."

"Did she turn herself in?" Lola gasped. "Did she rob a bank? Steal a car? Sell drugs?"

"My God, Jen," he said. "What kind of shows do you let her watch?"

"Relax," his sister said, "it's only a video game."

"Even worse." Daniel plucked his niece off the stool and set her down. "Lola, can you go play with dolls or something?"

"I don't play with dolls anymore. That's baby stuff."

Jennifer ushered her into the den and gave her a cell phone. "Here, play a game or something. And no Tik-Tok."

Once again, Daniel questioned his decision to quit his job and take off. As much as he needed a fresh start, leaving Jennifer and Lola had bad idea written all over it. His sister was a great mom, but Lola needed balance, especially without a father in the picture.

"Quit thinking so hard," Jennifer said. "Lola and I will be fine. Probably."

Daniel marveled at how his big sister could read his mind. She could do it even when they were young. For some reason, it didn't go both ways. "You and I have never been apart," he said. "We've always looked out for each other, and I—I worry about you."

"I worry about you, too." His sister leaned over his shoulders and wrapped her arms around him. "But for entirely different reasons. Which brings us back to the gorgeous woman in the spiffy car who drove you here. What's the story?"

"There is no story. She's, I don't know, involved herself in something."

"That's mysterious, but not what I meant. Come on, she's totally your type."

Daniel laughed. "I don't have a type."

"Then she's my type for you—smart, stunning, nice, and Lola liked her."

"You figured all that out in what? Ten minutes?"

"Less." Jennifer was relentless.

Daniel unwound her arms. "I gotta go. Can you drive me home?"

"No. Stay for dinner."

"What are you having?" Daniel asked.

"Whatever you go pick up." Jennifer patted his shoulders. "Lola! Uncle Danny's gonna stay for dinner!"

His niece ran back into the kitchen. "Let's go get pizza, Danny." She wrapped her short arms around his waist and looked up at him with more devotion than a Labrador Retriever.

Those big blue eyes killed him every time.

DANIEL DROPPED his keys in the dish on the narrow table in the narrow hallway that led into his narrow, depressing apartment. He stepped around his second hand furniture—a sagging leather sofa and two hideous orange chairs—into the kitchen.

His refrigerator contained nothing but a brick of cheddar cheese, peanut butter, a few sorry apples, and a case of beer.

He popped a Budweiser open and downed half, thirsty from the pizza he'd eaten with Lola and Jennifer. Even though his departure was still months away, he already missed them. Maybe he should change his mind. He could keep his job, if he still wanted it, or get a new one at a different precinct. Good detectives were needed everywhere. No shortage of crime, that was for sure.

And that brought him back to his encounter with the beautiful dance teacher. He couldn't get her out of his mind. The way she stood her ground. Strong, but with a brush of vulnerability.

Where did she say she lived? Or did she say? Fred had mentioned it—some place he'd never heard of. And a well-known ballet teacher, last name something Russian. He should've paid closer attention to Fred gushing over her.

Daniel sat on the couch, opened his laptop, and googled *ballet schools near me.*

Dozens popped up. He scanned, looking for a name that rang a bell. Click, click, click.

"That's it," he said. *"Lurensky."* He searched further and landed on an obituary from back in January in the San Francisco Examiner:

ILANA LURENSKY, once considered one of the most accomplished prima ballerinas in the world, passed away after a lengthy illness. Lurensky defected to the United States in 1965 and performed with some of the most illustrious dance companies in the country, including the San Francisco Ballet. Upon her retirement, she and her husband established the Lurensky Dance Academy in the small Sonoma town of Lake Clearwater.

"My mother was a force of nature," says her daughter, Natalie Lurensky. "Her dedication to her art, devotion to her students, and love of the ballet will forever be unmatched."

Services will be held privately. In lieu of flowers, donations may be made to the Lurensky Scholarship Fund.

DANIEL STARED AT THE SCREEN. "WOW." He googled *Natalie Lurensky, Lake Clearwater.*

His screen lit up with photos of a pristine lake, a park with a duck pond and gazebo, a tree-lined Main Street, and an old inn called The Mayfair Hotel. It looked like a Disney movie set.

Then, Natalie herself. Most of the pictures appeared to be from her teen years, shows in which she performed. The costumes were elaborate, haunting, and (he nearly choked) sexy beyond belief.

He clicked some more and found a series of photos of her at the San Francisco Ballet. She wore a long red dress that flowed over her body as if it were a second layer of skin. "Holy shit."

In one of the photos, a man wearing a tuxedo stood beside her with his arm around her waist. The description read: *Owner of the Lurensky Dance Academy and former ballerina, Natalie Lurensky, with fiancé Brian Steel, a founding partner of CTS Investments.*

"What is wrong with you?" Daniel shut his laptop. What was he thinking? His sister was right. Two years with no girlfriend was not normal. Sure, he'd had the occasional fling, but unlike every one of his thirty-something friends, he hated hook-ups. As much as he didn't want to admit it, he was an old soul.

Daniel stood by the window that looked out over the street. A light spring drizzle shimmered on the pavement, reflecting the neon lights of the restaurant signs. He couldn't wait to get out of the city, away from his low-life neighborhood and the places that reminded him of all the years he'd wasted on a relationship he knew wasn't working but refused to give up.

He took a breath as Natalie Lurensky in a long red dress flashed before him. If only he could find himself a woman like that.

CHAPTER 15

"*B*rad," Natalie said to Cece's husband, "you have outdone yourself yet again. You should close your law practice and open a barbeque joint."

Brad Redmond, the Atticus Finch of Clearwater, finished off his wine. "That's my plan. Who wants to be a lawyer when being a chef is so much more fun?"

"You do," Cece said. "We can revisit the chef idea after Noah graduates from college."

"In that case, I'd better get back to work. I'll leave you two to it, whatever it is."

Cece lifted her face and received a quick kiss.

They had to be the cutest couple in town. Then again, Natalie was surrounded by perfect couples. Her four closest friends had found four wonderful men. And here she was, single, last woman standing.

As she rinsed the dishes and Cece loaded the dishwasher, they caught up on Natalie's failure to accomplish anything at the police station.

"So they didn't care about the guys at the apartment where Kaylee supposedly lives?"

"Nope. So I'm done with it," Natalie said with a pang of regret. "Hopefully, Holly will hear from her soon."

Cece opened a pink box from Nutmegs and set it on the marble topped island between their wine glasses.

"Oh yum." Natalie sat on a stool and searched for her favorite dark chocolate chip with pecans. "Found it!"

"Wow. It's good to hear you getting excited about something, even if it is only a cookie."

"Not just any cookie," Natalie said. "Best cookie in the world."

"You know," Cece said, "I was thinking about something earlier. Remember how, over the last year when your mom was so sick, you kept saying you just wanted to get your life back?"

Natalie dusted crumbs from her lips. "I know where you're headed. You're going to tell me that now I have it back."

"Kind of."

"I'm not even sure what I meant by it. *Get my life back,* such a cliché."

"Clichés are what we say when we don't know what to say."

Natalie agreed. "Reminds me of Brian's clichés. On our last date, he told me it was time to 'move on,' and that my mom 'was in a better place.'"

Cece broke an oatmeal cookie in half. "What a jerk. I'm glad you're rid of him."

"Not quite," Natalie said. "He actually called a week ago."

"You spoke to him?"

"No, he left a rambling voicemail asking if I'd accompany him to some gala. Even suggested we pretend we were still together."

"Did you call him back?"

"Absolutely not," Natalie said. "But I texted him my regrets."

"Can't blame him for trying. He sure looked good with you on his arm."

"I suppose he did." Natalie knew they'd made an attractive

pair even if the relationship was as hollow as a dead shell on the beach.

Her mind wandered back to Kaylee and how that lead her to the handsome detective with the adorable niece and presumptuous sister.

"Helloooo? Where'd you go?" Cece shook Natalie's shoulder.

"Oh, sorry, I was just thinking about work." Natalie redirected her thoughts. "With tonight's cancelled rehearsal, we have to juggle the schedule. The summer production will be our first since my mother died. It'll be in her honor. I want it to be perfect, different somehow."

Cece crossed her legs and eyed her with an expression Natalie couldn't quite discern.

"What?" Natalie asked. "Why are you looking at me like that?"

"I'm not looking at you like that."

"Yeah you are." Natalie knew her friend inside and out. She was hiding something. "You have something to tell me, don't you?"

"I do. It's only an idea. An opportunity I guess you'd call it."

Natalie leaned on her elbows. "Tell me."

"Okay." Cece flattened her hands on the table. "Promise you won't react until you hear me out."

Natalie's heart did a little uptick. "You're making me nervous. Just tell me what it is."

"It involves Maura. She came to me with—"

Natalie jumped up. "I knew it, dammit. She's trying to lure you away from me, isn't she?"

"Sit down," Cece said with authority. "I told you not to react. Or overreact."

Natalie returned to her seat. "How can I not overreact? There's no way I can run things without you." To her mortification, tears threatened.

Cece took Natalie's hands into her own. "I'm not going anywhere, I promise. How could you even think that?"

Natalie pulled her hands away and tucked them in her lap, fists tight. "I think that because this business, my dance school, is the only thing in my life I can control. And I'm struggling to control it."

"I understand," Cece said. "You know as well as I do that this wonderful life I have is because of you, the opportunity you gave me all those years ago. I wouldn't have Brad or Noah if not for you. I owe you everything, which is why you need to trust me on this."

Natalie closed her eyes. "Okay. Let's hear it."

Cece scooted closer. "Maura has a new student. Her name is Ashley, thirteen years old, and according to Maura she's got what it takes. Her mother brought her to the studio unaware of how talented her daughter is—said she loves music, loves dance, has taken ballet off and on for years."

Natalie's interest flickered. "Okay, continue."

"Before you ask, Maura brought this idea to me only a few days ago. And I wanted to think it over before telling you."

"Fair enough," Natalie said.

"Anyway, Maura believes that with the right coach, this student could be one of the ones who make it."

"Uh-huh." Natalie tapped a fingernail on the table. Referrals were not uncommon, but giving up a dancer who could build a studio's reputation? Not likely. "Obviously, you're the right coach, but I suspect Maura isn't going to just hand her over to us, is she?"

"No. She wants to partner."

Partner, a complicated and dicey proposition. It wasn't unusual for a dancer to have more than one coach, but a business arrangement with a competing studio didn't sit well with Natalie. Ilana would not approve.

"Do you even like Maura?" Natalie asked.

"What does that have to do with it?"

"Well, do you?"

"I hardly know her."

"Exactly, Cece. We don't really know her. She's a little cagey," Natalie turned her wine glass in circles. "And I'm not sure I trust her."

"That's why we'll have a contract. Let's take the meeting, okay? Go one step at a time."

Natalie hemmed. She didn't like the idea, but it was interesting. And her studio hadn't produced a prima ballerina in over ten years.

"You really want this, don't you?" Natalie said.

"I at least want to find out more."

The shimmer in Cece's eyes revealed her excitement. She'd given up her own chance at becoming a prima ballerina. Producing one would be the next best thing, not to mention a feather in all their caps. Thirteen was old to start, but if Ashley really had the talent and drive, an instructor like Cece could take her across the finish line.

"Okay," Natalie said. "I'm willing to meet with Maura. For you."

Cece shook her head. "No, not for me, for us. And for Ilana. Natalie, I knew your mom in a way you didn't—she loved me, but I wasn't her daughter. I was her student. And I was one of the Lurensky dancers who almost made it. To this day, I regret that I let your mother down."

Natalie's chest went heavy with emotion. Twenty years ago, at barely seventeen, Cece was about to become the ballerina to put Lurensky Dance Academy on the map. But then her parents divorced, her mother ran off, and her family fell apart. She quit dance, moved away, and forged a new path. It was Natalie who brought Cece back to her roots.

"If this young dancer is even close to as perfect as Maura

says, she could do what I didn't. I want to redeem myself, Nat, revive what was once *my* dream."

Natalie rubbed her forehead. Cece's words were like poetry, a plea for permission to write a new a story for herself. Cece couldn't do it without Natalie's agreement. And Natalie couldn't turn out a prima ballerina without Cece. They each held pieces of something that separately were good, even great. But put those pieces together, and they very well might be invincible.

ON SUNDAY AFTERNOON, Cece and Natalie went to Maura's studio to meet the young dancer. Ashley Clark was extraordinary. Smart, musical, committed, muscular. Her joints were flexible, movements fluid and unrestrained. Her facial expressions brought Natalie to tears. With Cece as her instructor and mentor, there was no doubt Ashley would soar.

Three days after Natalie met Ashley, the contract and schedule were hammered out over coffee at Nutmegs. Maura was so excited she tipped over her mug. "Oh, geez, sorry," she said, mopping up the spill with napkins.

Cece helped her. "No worries, I do that all the time."

Natalie smiled to herself. Cece never knocked over her coffee. She was an expert at putting people at ease, just one of her many skills. No wonder everybody loved her.

They were sitting at a square table in the corner by a window, Cece and Maura directly across from each other. Natalie observed closely. Although the decision to proceed was hers, the details belonged to Cece.

"That means," Cece said to both of them, "I'll work with Ashley twice a week. And she'll come to us for at least one of her lessons. That takes me out of Clearwater only one afternoon a week, if that."

"Right," Maura said, slicing off a thin piece of sticky bun and nibbling it like a bird. "My assistant director will be Ashley's private coach, and she'll be there for every session.

"Got it," Natalie said, one knee bobbing up and down. She channeled her inner *Ilana*, bringing up questions her mother would have asked. "Where does Ashley go to school?"

"Right now she's at the local middle school," Maura said. "But her mom is interviewing private tutors, so she'll be home schooled."

The conversation about logistics continued. As she absorbed the plan, Natalie acknowledged the arrangement was a good financial move for the studio. Maura had already found Ashley a sponsor—a wealthy patron of the arts who awarded grants to dancers who showed tremendous promise. Ilana would've liked that. Natalie stirred her coffee, as Cece dictated instructions for Ashley's schedule to Maura. And Maura, to her credit, took notes and nodded, her interest keen.

A win-win all the way around. Most of all, Natalie wanted this for Cece. Her best friend's enthusiasm was almost contagious.

Even so, one thing weighed on her. It was Natalie's responsibility to cement her mother's legacy. Not Cece's, and definitely not Maura's. Now that the arrangement was underway, Natalie had to see it through to the end.

CHAPTER 16

*E*arly morning sun threw shadows on the path as Natalie walked through the park, putting her in an almost meditative state. She loved being in the park by herself, complete quiet except for leaves rustling and birds calling. Her cell vibrated in her pocket. Natalie almost ignored it, but she changed her mind and checked the screen.

Natalie halted her steps. "Holly, good morning. How are you?"

"Hi, Natalie," Holly said, sounding overly chipper. "I wanted to let you know I finally heard from Kaylee."

"You did?" Natalie sat on a bench near the duck pond. "Is she okay?"

"Yeah, she's fine. She called last night," Holly said. "She'd lost her phone, so that's why I couldn't reach her."

Flimsy excuse, Natalie thought. Everyone on earth had a phone Kaylee could have used to let her mom know her cell had gone missing. But Natalie didn't see any point in bringing that up. "I'm so relieved."

"I'm sorry I dragged you into a situation that ended up being nothing."

"Oh, please, don't apologize." Natalie forced a lighthearted note into her voice. "Kaylee always was one of my favorites."

"That's nice." Holly could be so non-committal.

Natalie itched to ask more questions, especially about the address Holly had given her, but she didn't want to push. The stressed out, overburdened mother deserved a break now that she knew her daughter was alive and well. It would do no good to remind her that the apartment she thought her daughter lived in was occupied by others.

"Are you going to go see her?" Natalie asked.

"I didn't really get that far." Holly's chipper tone dropped a notch. "One step at a time, you know?"

"Of course."

"Gotta run, Natalie, have get the little ones ready for school. You take care now."

"You, too, Holly. And if there's any—"

As usual, Holly ended the call abruptly, leaving Natalie's last words hanging.

THAT NIGHT, Natalie went with Tessa to a quaint French restaurant in a neighboring town where it was unlikely they'd run into anyone they knew.

They sat at a quiet corner table, but before any conversation could begin, the restauranteur appeared. He went on and on with praise for the famous sommelier. Ever the professional, Tessa conversed with him politely and gave several wine recommendations.

He fell all over himself with gratitude.

Once they were alone, Tessa sipped her water then rested her chin on one hand. "Okay, I haven't seen you in days. What's going on?"

"Are you ready for me to dump it all out at once? Because it's a lot."

"Ready as ever."

Natalie unloaded everything from Brian's attempt to get back together to Cece's new protégé. And the most intriguing—her no-longer-missing former ballet student and the mystery Natalie still found troubling yet stimulating.

"Good Lord, that is a lot." Tessa studied the Chardonnay, lifting the long-stemmed glass toward the light, before diving into the first topic. "Let's talk about Brian."

"Nothing to talk about there. He and I are done."

"Good. I never liked him anyway. You need someone new." Tessa leaned in. "So it's perfect timing. You know we have our big fundraiser next week. It'll be crawling with eligible men. In fact, there's one guy in particular I'd love for you to meet."

Natalie shook her head. "Absolutely not. If you try to set me up, I'll walk out the door."

The server brought their entrees, herb roasted chicken for both of them. Natalie took a large bite. Hot and crispy, hits of lemon and thyme. Her eyes met Tessa's, and then she looked away.

"Uh-oh." Tessa frowned. "What are you not telling me?"

Natalie chewed and swallowed. Tessa would figure it out soon enough. "I know this fundraiser is a big event and that it raises money for my scholarships, but, and this really embarrasses me, I didn't buy a ticket."

"Oh for God's sake, is that what's bothering you? You don't need a ticket."

Natalie knew she'd say that. "I don't want to be that friend who needs special accommodations. I'll get my finances in order once I pay off my mom's medical bills and the health care workers." Natalie pictured the state of disrepair in her studio. It, too, needed an infusion of cash. "Until then, I'm going to be off the social circuit."

Tessa refilled their wine glasses. "Honey, why won't you let me help you? I think you're even more stubborn than your mother was. And she was damned stubborn."

"I'm not taking money from my friends. Not you, not Cece, not anyone. It's bad enough you're treating me to dinner tonight."

"As it turns out, I'm not. The owner's treating both of us. Evidently my expert advice is worth a bottle of wine and two entrees."

"If he pays you in dinners, we should come back." She took another bite of chicken. "This is delicious."

"The food at the event will be delicious as well."

"I'm sure it will be."

Tessa groused. "Stop tormenting me. You'll be there. People want to meet you."

"Ridiculous."

"It's not ridiculous at all. Some rich people are vapid and egotistical, but not all of us. We support causes that matter to our communities. And the Lurensky Scholarship Fund is one of them. You are an ambassador. Besides, you're already on the VIP list—Natalie Lurensky and a plus one, although there isn't a plus-one so, well, just you."

Natalie set down her fork and knife. "Fine. I'll be there. But you'd better not try to set me up. Promise?"

"I promise, but if this guy shows interest in—"

"No, no, no, don't you manipulate it," Natalie said, shutting down her friend's persistence. "If you want me to come, you have to promise."

"Fine, I promise. Now let's move on." Tessa sliced a round potato into quarters. "A budding prima ballerina—very exciting."

"It is, especially for Cece." Natalie poured herself more wine, happy to discuss something besides men. "She's over the moon."

"And what about you?" her friend asked. "You're not?"

"Sure I am, well, not over the moon, but definitely enthusiastic."

"Enthusiastic." Tessa repeated the word as if disappointed in it.

Natalie toyed with the cloth napkin on her lap, considering how to proceed. But Tessa was like a big sister. She could tell her anything. "I have a stupid confession to make."

Tessa's fork stopped in front her mouth. "Let's hear it."

"Well, you know how I've been kind of out of sorts and blah for months?"

"I noticed," Tessa said with an air of sarcasm.

Natalie struggled to explain her anguish. "I can't seem to get excited about anything. Even the new dancer we're bringing in doesn't thrill me like it should."

"I'm sure you're just being cautious in case it doesn't work out. Is that what's worrying you?"

"On the contrary, I think it will work out. I haven't seen a prospect like her in ages, maybe not ever. And I am—" Natalie rolled her hands in the air, "optimistic. Definitely pleased. But I should be exhilarated, gleeful, elated. My mom would've been."

"First of all, you are not your mom. And second, if that's your big confession, it's not much of one."

"It's not the big confession." Natalie steeled herself. Once she brought it up, put it out there in the world, there'd be no way to unsay or deny it. "It's this thing with Kaylee."

"I thought you said it's all settled."

"Maybe, probably. But here's the truth. When I went to that apartment and did my little investigation, I felt—different. Energized. I liked it." Natalie covered her face with both hands, ashamed by the admission.

Tessa pulled Natalie's hands down. "I should send you a bill for psychotherapy. Nat, I've known you your entire life. And in thirty-eight years, you have never veered off the path. You've stayed in one lane traveling at the same speed year after year. Did it ever occur to you that you're just bored?"

"I'm not bored. I hardly have time to do anything other than work."

"Being busy is not the same as being non-bored. Lots of people are crazy busy but bored at the same time. And let's be honest. Clearwater is not the most happening place. We have to import excitement. The fact that your foray into this Kaylee mystery made you *not bored* is not a bad thing."

Natalie mulled over Tessa's reasonable assessment. "Makes sense."

Now," Tessa continued, "who's the smartest person you know?"

"You, of course." Natalie smirked.

"After me," Tessa said, prodding the correct answer.

"Nonna. Nonna for sure."

Tessa's grandmother was a guru on life. Plus, she could put anyone in their place without offending.

"Exactly, Nonna. And my ninety-year-old grandmother says the only way to keep our zest for life is to do things we don't already know how to do."

"Are you saying I need a hobby?" Natalie covered her mouth to hide her amusement. As if she had time for a hobby. Ludicrous.

"Maybe." Tessa paused as if formulating how to proceed. "Everything you do, all the stuff you're so busy with, you know how to do. And you do it well, brilliantly even."

"Okay."

"The problem is, none of it excites you anymore. Your interest in Kaylee took you out of your lane. You ventured into something new that has nothing to do with what you already know how to do. So it sparked an interest, no shame in that. It was impulsive."

Impulsive. There was the word again. The detective's voice popped into her head. *You don't do impulsive?* he'd asked.

"And you don't do impulsive." Tessa had read her mind, and the fact she'd just used the same words as the detective meant something, although Natalie didn't know what.

"I've never seen you do anything without thinking it over every which way to the point of· making it painful. Except maybe that fabulous car you bought."

"Yes, that one was impulsive."

"And," Tessa said with raised eyebrows, "your choice to stay in Clearwater after your dad died. But I'm not sure that was an impulse at all."

"What do you mean?" Natalie could hardly believe her friend was bringing up an incident from so long ago. "I was on my way to New York, suitcase packed and everything." The suitcase, a gift from her father. She wondered if she still had it. "How could that decision not have been an impulsive move?"

"Maybe it was impulsive, but also, maybe, part of your plan. I have a feeling you were afraid."

"Afraid of what?"

"Afraid of change."

Change. She was swimming in a pool of nothing but change, upheaval, unrest. Every day she woke up worrying about what unknowns would fall in her lap or on top of her head.

"The thing is, Nat, change is scary. Trust me, I learned it first hand after my divorce. But it's also an opportunity. It's the one door closing and another one opening cliché."

"You hate clichés."

"I do, but sometimes they work." Tessa placed her napkin on the table and leaned forward. "All I'm saying is that if you're not willing to walk through that open door, all the pain and lessons learned will be for naught. Sometimes we have to stop protecting ourselves and take the leap."

Take a leap, another tired cliché. But true.

CHAPTER 17

"*A*re you crazy?" Daniel asked his sister. "I can't ask her out. For all I know she's married to that guy in the photo."

It had been almost two weeks since he met Natalie Lurensky. The image of her in the red dress on the arm of that millionaire financial guy was stuck in his head.

"She's not married." Jennifer accelerated and sped through an intersection, already late to Lola's soccer game.

"Slow down!" Daniel pushed his hand against the dashboard. "You almost ran that red light."

"Did not."

"Did too, Mommy." Lola chimed in with her opinion from the back seat. "And she never stops at the stop sign on our corner either, Uncle Danny. You maybe should arrest her."

"I'm not going to arrest her." Daniel glared in Jennifer's direction. "But I will give her a very stern warning."

"Thank you, officer," Jennifer mocked.

"You're welcome." He lowered his voice. "How do you know she's not married?"

Jennifer turned into the parking lot at the soccer field. "I asked her. She said she's not."

"That means you can marry her, Uncle Danny." Lola bounced her soccer ball against the back of his seat. "And then you'll be happy again."

Daniel turned to his niece. "You think I'm not happy?"

Lola hugged her soccer ball. "I know you're not."

FOR TWO DAYS, Daniel Garrett ruminated on how he could approach her. He needed a solid reason to call a woman who was so far out of his league it was laughable. He couldn't just present himself and declare it had been love at first sight. Every humiliating pick-up line he knew made him cringe. What had happened to his confidence?

He'd always assumed he would have a normal life. A good job, a wife he loved and who loved him back, a picket fence, a dog, a kid. But two years back, when the girl he thought was the love of his life walked away, everything changed. And he'd been floundering ever since.

IT WAS LATE AFTERNOON, and his desk was covered in paper and pistachio shells. Daniel had spent most of the day in various locations meeting with witnesses in a gas station robbery that ended up with a shooting and five people hospitalized, including the suspect. A typical day that started at four in the morning.

He guzzled what was probably his sixth coffee in the last twelve hours, finished typing up his report, stood and stretched. He went to the bathroom and splashed cold water on his face, then returned to his desk to straighten it before he headed home.

As he sorted notes and organized some file folders, his phone lit up with a text from Jennifer.

> Hey, we didn't mean to ambush you yesterday. Lola and I love you. We want you to be happy. Whatever you do, don't sell yourself short.

Daniel sighed. God, he loved his big sister. Despite her over-involvement in his lackluster love life, she knew what to say to bolster him.

He made sure nobody was nearby before opening his laptop to see what he could find out about Natalie Lurensky. Just because she told Jen she wasn't married didn't mean she wasn't still engaged to the guy in the photo. As damaging as social media was to society, it did serve a purpose. He began his search into the supposed fiancé, Brian Steel. The financier had an active presence on the gossip websites. It appeared he liked to hang out with celebrities, owners of sports teams, and race car drivers.

Daniel clicked through the photos, eating pistachios.

"Bingo."

A recent photo of Steel at some fundraiser popped up. He was with a woman who looked like a cheap version of Natalie. She had the height and the dark hair but no genuine beauty or warmth. Daniel continued searching, half-hoping to find proof that Natalie was involved with someone. Anyone. He needed an excuse to excise her from his mind.

"Danny!"

He slammed his laptop shut. "Jesus, Fred, what?"

"Didn't mean to scare you there. You remember the tall brunette who was here last week? The one who invited me to bring my granddaughter to a show?"

Daniel swallowed hard. "Uh, maybe? I'm not sure."

"Come on, you can't tell me you don't remember Natalie Lurensky. She was beautiful. And nice. A friend of hers had gone missing."

Daniel pushed his laptop aside, feigning indifference. "Oh, yeah. What about her?"

Fred sat backwards on the metal chair and leaned in. "Last night, a few guys were arrested after one of our patrols responded to a *10-80*."

Domestic disturbance call. Nothing remarkable about that. "So?"

"Victim was stabbed, a young male. Critical condition."

"Happens all the time," Daniel said, his interest waning. "What does it have to do with Ms. Lurensky?"

Fred's bushy eyebrows drew inward. "When she was here, she gave me the address of where that missing friend of hers supposedly lived. And that's where the disturbance was. The stabbing was right outside that apartment."

Daniel's interest took a sudden leap. He wondered if the young woman Natalie Lurensky was worried about had ever surfaced. He grabbed his spiral notebook, flipped the pages, and reviewed his notes. Apartment 249, couple of strange men, a suspicious situation she'd said. And he'd blown it off. Of course he'd had to—she'd reported nothing that would warrant police intervention.

But she'd suspected something was amiss. And she was right. Daniel added sharp intuition to his growing list of reasons Natalie Lurensky was stuck in his head.

CHAPTER 18

*N*atalie wished she could get out of going to Tessa's fundraiser. With back to back classes until six, she'd barely have time go home to shower and change. Not to mention, she would be exhausted. Why had she agreed to go?

"Natalie!" Cece flew into her office and slammed the door. "There's someone here to see you."

"Who?"

"I think he's a policeman." Cece's blue eyes, large to begin with, widened.

"You *think* he's a policeman?"

"Well, a detective actually. He's waiting out front."

"What's his name?" Natalie asked.

"I don't know. I don't think he told me, maybe he did." Cece yanked open the door. "You'd better go see what he wants. And by the way, he's really good looking."

Natalie closed her laptop. "He isn't wearing a Giants cap, is he?"

"No. Why?"

"Doesn't matter. Let's go." Natalie tightened her wraparound skirt over her leotard and followed Cece into the main studio.

The detective stood in the corner of the room, his thumbs flying over his smart phone. He wore khakis with a white dress shirt and loosened blue tie. Aviator sunglasses rested atop his head in a nest of wavy brown hair. His somewhat professional attire, sans baseball cap, matured his appearance, but the freshly shaved face countered that. The scar along his jaw line stood out. Natalie never imagined she'd cross paths with him again, yet here he was standing in her studio.

She approached, her slippered feet moving silently across the room. "Well, Detective Garrett." Natalie felt a flicker of—of something.

He looked up from his phone. "Ms. Lurensky." The detective shoved his phone into a pocket. "How are you?"

"Fine," Natalie said, fairly certain he hadn't come all the way out to Clearwater to say *hey how are ya.*

"I'm here with an update." He opened his jacket and showed a badge clipped to his belt.

"You don't need to show me your badge. I know you're a cop."

"Yeah, sorry. It's a habit." His boyish grin revealed straight white teeth.

"Natalie," Cece whispered. "Why don't you take this conversation into your office?"

"Oh, good idea." If the dance moms got wind that a cop was nosing around the studio, there'd be no end to the gossip. "Detective?" She motioned toward the hallway, and the detective followed, his shoes landing on the hardwood floor with purpose.

When they entered the office, he scanned the pictures on the walls, stopping at a black and white photograph of Ilana when she was twenty-one, resplendent in costume with one leg extended in an arabesque. "Is this your mother?"

"It is."

"She's quite beautiful."

"She was," Natalie said, taken aback by his interest. "She passed away in January."

"I'm sorry," he said with genuine sympathy. "She was an impressive woman."

Natalie cocked her head. "How would you know that?"

Detective Garrett turned a little red. "I, uh, well, to be honest, I stumbled across her obituary when I googled your name."

"You googled me?" Natalie asked, not sure if she was flattered or offended. "Why?"

"It was Fred." He sounded like a little kid blaming the broken cookie jar on somebody else. "He was so appreciative about your offer to get him tickets to a show for his granddaughter that he, well, you know how people are. Curious about other people. And Fred's very, uh, interested in—"

"It's fine. I get it." Natalie glanced at her watch. Too bad he hadn't come when she wasn't so busy. "Sorry to rush you, but did you say you have an update for me?"

"I do," he said. "Has Kaylee Robertson surfaced yet?"

"She did, thank God. Was I supposed to let you know that?"

The detective shook his head. "No, we didn't open a case, so nobody was waiting on information. But I'm glad to hear it. A few guys were arrested at that apartment complex where you said she was supposed to be living."

"Really?" She wondered if the guys were the two she had met. "I appreciate you letting me know."

"You can say you told me so—if you want to."

"Well, I'll admit the news is validating, but all I care about is Kaylee. Her mom said she's safe. And that's what matters, Detective Garrett."

"Call me Daniel." He blurted it, making it sound like an order. "I mean, if you're comfortable with that. I'm not going to be a detective much longer anyway."

Well, that opened an unexpected door. "Have you been let go?"

His grin relieved her. She meant it as a joke, but what if it had been the case?

"I wasn't fired, although I do push the proverbial envelope from time to time."

Natalie leaned against her desk and gripped the edge. He was becoming more interesting by the second. She tapped her cell phone beside her hip. Almost one o'clock, and she had a class to teach at two.

"Detective," she began. "I mean Daniel. Would you like to taste one of the best cups of coffee in the world?"

His eyes widened, and he took a half step back. "Uh, yeah. Sure. I'd love to."

"Great." Natalie slipped on her sneakers. "I have one hour. Let's go."

DANIEL EASILY KEPT up with Natalie's long stride as they crossed the park toward Nutmegs. Seeing Clearwater through the eyes of somebody who had never been in the town before was delightful. It made her notice the beauty and charm she often took for granted.

"Right over there is Mariano's Cheese and Wine. Have you heard of it?"

"Can't say I have."

"It's practically famous. My friend Tessa is the owner. She's one of the most sought after sommeliers in California." Natalie pointed out shops and small businesses like a tour guide.

"I feel like I'm walking through a movie set," Daniel said.

"A movie set, huh?" Natalie had never seen it that way. But the colors of the flowers were so vibrant they could be fake. The trees lining the sidewalk were pruned with precision and symmetry. "Spring in Clearwater is pretty magical. It's a nice place, I guess."

"More than nice. And I'll bet crime stats are low."

"There's no crime in Clearwater," Natalie said. "Evidently, it's in the town charter—*crimes are not allowed.* We tell all newcomers that if they want to break the law, go someplace else. I think we send most of them to Oakland."

Daniel's laughter echoed across the park. "And she's funny, too," he said as if speaking to himself.

They walked over the bridge to the other side of the pond.

"A duck pond? This place is out of a storybook. My niece would love it."

"Ah, yes, Lola," Natalie said. "She's adorable."

Daniel stopped. "You know Lola?"

They turned toward the community gardens and started up the path that led to Nutmegs.

"She and I had quite the conversation the day I dropped you off at your sister's house." Natalie didn't mention the extent of the information the little girl had revealed. "You should bring her here for a visit."

"Maybe I will someday."

At Nutmegs, Daniel pulled the door open and allowed Natalie to cross in front of him. Once inside, she motioned to the barista for her usual afternoon order—times two.

"Cute place," Daniel said.

"The cutest. And wait 'til you taste the sticky bun."

"Sticky bun, huh? I like the sound of that."

They seated themselves at a table on the front patio under a yellow umbrella. It was a quiet time of day, for which Natalie was grateful. Nobody stopping to say hello, no dance moms interrupting and insisting they only needed one minute of her time.

Daniel's gaze landed on her face and stayed there. "Thank you for bringing me here."

"Oh, sure. No big deal." But it was a big deal. She wanted to be in his presence, to ask him questions, to know why he would not be a detective much longer.

Their coffees arrived. Natalie added a bit of milk to hers and offered the tiny white pitcher to Daniel.

"No thanks. Station only has the powdered whitening agent, so I learned to drink mine black." He tasted it. "Mmm, you're right. This coffee's a thousand times better than the bitter sludge I get at work."

Just the opening she needed. "So, work, sounds like you're moving on?"

"I am. I have about a month left, and then I'm—I'm making a change."

Natalie sensed a wistful tone, as if he weren't sure. It made her want to comfort him. His niece had said something about a broken heart that needed mending. What kind of loss and disillusionment had he suffered?

"Wow!" he said when the decadent pastry smothered in warm caramel glaze and chopped pecans was placed before him. "What did you call this thing?"

"A pecan sticky bun, Nutmegs' signature treat. People come from all over Sonoma for them." She sliced it in half. "This will change your life."

Daniel accepted his half and bit into it. "Oh my God, I've never tasted anything this good."

"Told ya. Nobody ever forgets their first sticky bun. You'll remember this moment forever."

"I believe I will," he said.

Although Natalie had said it in jest, he seemed to take her seriously, as if she'd intended a double meaning. And maybe she had, because already this moment was cemented in her memory.

"Now I really do have to bring Lola here. Bakeries are her favorite."

Lola. He sure loved that little girl.

Natalie checked the time again. Only twenty minutes until her class started, but she had no desire to move. "You said you're making a change?"

"That's the plan."

Why did he keep looking at her with an expression she didn't know how to decipher?

"A career change?"

"I'm not sure yet. It's kind of hard to explain." He searched her face. "I've had some plans that haven't worked out so well. So, I'm at a crossroads, you know? Just need to figure it out."

Natalie's hands tightened around her mug. His intensity was unbalancing her, stirring unfamiliar but pleasant feelings. And she wanted to keep feeling them.

"Are you busy tonight?" she asked.

"Tonight? I don't think so."

"I'm going to a wine tasting at Mariano's. Would you like to go with me?"

He blinked a few times. "Excuse me?"

"A wine tasting," she repeated. "Would you like to go?"

His face reddened. "I'd love to."

CHAPTER 19

*N*atalie fluffed her hair with spray and applied her speedy make-up routine—tinted moisturizer, blush, eyeliner, mascara. A pile of random outfits covered her bed. If she wasn't wearing the uniform of a ballet teacher, she was at a loss.

Wine tasting fundraiser at Mariano's? Her cocktail dresses were too dressy. Black pants and silk blouse not dressy enough. It was the fashion version of Goldilocks.

She dialed Cece. "What are you wearing tonight?"

"The usual," Cece said. "Little black dress or maybe those vegan leather pants I got last year."

"I don't have a little black dress, at least not a cute one. And I definitely have no leather pants, vegan or otherwise."

"You could go in a sack and look great," Cece said. "Want to shop in my closet?"

"No time for that." Natalie rifled through more dresses, some of them from as far back as high school. "See you soon."

A closet clean-out was long overdue. She yanked a plain sleeveless black dress off its hanger and slipped it over her head.

"Oh, God," she said to her reflection. The last time she'd

worn the dress was at her mother's funeral. Granted she had topped it with a conservative cardigan for the occasion, but still.

She rummaged through some shoes and found a pair of red pumps with four inch heels. Painful, but they definitely elevated the funeral attire to night-on-the-town.

Natalie swiped on some red lipstick, dropped the tube into her purse, and drove to the studio to meet Daniel.

She yawned three times along the way, big yawns that made her want to sit at home in front of the TV. Then again, it was good to get out and about. For years, she'd planned her every move around her mother's doctor appointments and caregiver schedules. It had become second nature to say no to every invitation—one of the many reasons she and Brian didn't work out.

Daniel was in front of the studio when she pulled up, waiting on the sidewalk like an eager student ready for class. He'd changed his shirt and added a navy sport coat. Before she could open the car door, he was beside her with a hand extended.

Natalie placed her hand in his. Her red pumps touched the street, and she rose to her full height plus four inches. It put them almost eye to eye.

Guests filled the entire space of Mariano's Cheese and Wine. Natalie knew at least half the people there. Many, known and unknown, wanted to greet her and ask about the studio.

Daniel managed to hold his own, which Natalie found impressive. These events could be overwhelming. She kept reminding herself it was a not a date, not exactly. But he was her guest. Then again, did he think it was a date? Should she have made it clear in some way that this was just a—a what? Thankfully, Cece and Brad appeared seconds later.

Usually self-possessed, Natalie never stumbled over words, but now she found herself stumbling through introductions.

"You met Cece this afternoon, right? And this is Brad, her husband, and oh, he's a lawyer so you might—"

"Nice to meet you," Brad said, shaking Daniel's hand and cutting off Natalie's rambling.

"Honey," Cece said, "why don't you and Daniel go see what they're pouring tonight? I have to talk to Natalie about some work stuff."

Daniel gave Natalie a little nod and went off with Brad as Cece maneuvered her into a corner.

"What the hell?" Cece said with a laugh. "I can't believe you didn't tell me you invited him."

"It was last minute. I don't know what I was thinking. But if it looks like I'm here with someone—"

"That's what it looks like, all right! A tall, rugged, broad-shouldered detective who just stepped out of a movie. How old is he anyway?"

"I don't know. Our age, maybe younger." Natalie pulled her friend in closer. "This is crazy, but I kind of like him. I mean, I don't even know him, but I like being around him. He makes me feel—this sounds so juvenile—fluttery."

"Oh my God, Natalie Lurensky has a crush. How cute. And look how gorgeous you are tonight." Cece glanced toward the wine bar. "Do you want me to stay by your side or leave you alone? Maybe we should have a code word."

Before Natalie could respond, Patty, wearing an orange mini dress with black knee boots, was by her side. "Who is that hottie? I can't believe you have a date. This is so exciting!"

"Little missy," Cece said, "lower your voice. And where did those boots come from? They're so—"

"Perfect? I know, right? I've had them forever, but they never go out of style. And Adam loves them."

Adam Hawk, the famous vintner, swooped in and wrapped his arms around her like a bear trying to hug a puppy. "Ladies, how are you? Natalie, are you here with someone? A date, perchance?"

"No, he's not a date. He's my...my guest."

"A plus one, then?" Patty said.

"Yes." Natalie acknowledged that term. "Close enough."

"That's what we call a date," Patty argued.

"Well, whatever he is," Adam said, "I suggest you keep an eye on him. New man in Clearwater? That always gets attention."

"Would you all stop?" Natalie sidestepped her friends. "He's just someone I know, and he happened to be in Clearwater for a, um, a work thing."

"But how do you know him?" Patty demanded. "Where'd you meet? Where does he live? What does he do? Why have we never heard of him?"

"That's enough questions," Adam said. "Come with me, we have wine to pour."

"Oh, shit, I forgot. I'm working tonight." She pointed at both Cece and Natalie. "You two better catch me up on this tomorrow. I do not like being out of the loop."

As Adam pulled Patty away, Brad and Daniel returned and handed them each a glass of red. The four of them clinked glasses. Natalie swallowed, barely tasting it, self-conscious about showing up at an event with a man she hardly knew.

"Cece, you won't believe who's here." Brad took her hand. "One of my buddies from law school. You have to come meet him."

Cece gave Natalie a concerned look. "I'll be right back."

"No hurry. We'll be fine." Natalie pressed a hand against the fluttering in her abdomen. "Do you like the wine? It's a Syrah, I believe."

Daniel sipped. "I do. But I'm not much of a connoisseur. I can't tell the difference between this and a ten dollar bottle from Costco."

Natalie laughed. "Don't worry, most people can't. Even if they say they can."

A waiter came by with stuffed mushrooms, two left on the platter.

"One for each of us," Natalie said with a flirty wink. *Oh, why did I wink?*

They moved through the shop, tasting creamy cheeses, peppery salami, Greek olives, and spicy pickles. Small talk, that was all, but shared enjoyment. After perusing the impressive selection of silent auction items, they joined Adam and Patty at the back of the shop at a tall cocktail table for a small group tasting of Hawk and Winter's latest production.

They drank more wine.

Daniel and Adam found they had a common interest in baseball, both huge Giants fans. For a moment, Natalie's mind wandered to a place where a man like Daniel could fit into her world. Her imagination stirred up scenarios that would never happen for so many reasons. Exactly what did needing to 'figure things out' mean, anyway?

"Well now," Tessa said, slipping an arm around Natalie's waist. "You brought a decoy date so I wouldn't try to set you up? Clever."

"Shhh." Natalie turned and hugged her friend. "It's not that at all. Where's Owen?"

"Can you believe he's not here?" Tessa waved away her feigned annoyance. "On call tonight. Somebody had the nerve to fall and break a hip. My poor husband is missing out again."

"Shame." Natalie lifted her glass. "Well, here's to a successful event. Hope you sell a ton of wine."

"That's the plan." Tessa squeezed Natalie's hands. "And you look stunning tonight. A bit overdressed, but beautiful."

"Overdressed? I'm wearing a little black dress, same as you."

"I know, but I'm short and curvy, and you're tall and willowy." Tessa stepped back and pointed at Natalie's feet. "And those red stilettos. Wow. Anyway, I'm not breaking my promise, but one of my clients, a huge wine collector and totally your type, asked to be introduced to you."

"Good to know, but no." Natalie had no interest in a wine

collector, her type or otherwise. That said, based on her attraction to Daniel, it appeared her type might be morphing.

"He's over by the auction table, if you want to take a look."

"I do not. End of discussion. You can pester me all you want at our next girls night in."

"Count on it." Tessa melted into the crowd of admirers.

Natalie turned, but Daniel was no longer nearby. Adam had gone back to pouring wine and chatting with guests. She made her way toward the front. Had he left? He wouldn't do that, unless he'd overheard her conversation with Tessa, which would have been horribly awkward. She was about to go back to ask Adam if he knew Daniel's whereabouts when she spotted him at the far end of the shop. He was gazing up at the wall of wine that spanned the length of the room.

Flutters. Oy.

She walked over, heels clicking on the hardwood floor. "Hey, there."

He turned. Again, his eyes shone, as if delighted to see her all over again. "This is some wine collection. Massive.

"This shop is Clearwater's claim to fame."

"I thought the sticky buns were."

"Those too."

"You could be a claim to fame, as well. I've overheard people talking about you."

Natalie's modesty made her blush as she tried to come up with a clever response. But then the crowd thickened, and someone bumped into her, pushing her into Daniel. She put up a hand to steady herself as he caught her elbow.

"You okay?"

Her hand fell onto his chest. "Sure, yes, sorry. Didn't mean to bump you like that."

"I didn't mind," he said.

"It's getting so crowded." Between the lack of space and her

proximity to Daniel, Natalie overheated as if she'd just pirou-
etted across a stage.

"You look a little flushed. Are you sure you're okay?"

"Of course. I'm a little hot though." Oh, God, did she really
say she was hot? So much innuendo in that word.

"Do you want some cold water?" Daniel suggested. "Or we
could leave."

"You want to leave?" she asked, suddenly concerned he was
bored.

"Only if you want to."

Where would they go? What would they do? "We can," she
said. "Or not. Either way is fine with me. It's up to you, because
you have a long drive home and all." Ugh. She sounded like a
teenager at a sock hop asking the cute boy to dance.

"Why don't we go outside and get some fresh air?" Daniel said.

"Yes, let's do that. It's a beautiful night, and if we—"

"Natalie, hello."

She spun around and caught her breath. Brian? They hadn't
seen each other since their unceremonious breakup in front of
the restaurant two months ago.

"You look stunning, as usual." Brian's eyes flickered toward
Daniel as if he were annoying fly. "Is this your little brother?"

Natalie wanted to smack him, but all she managed was a
pathetic, "I don't have a brother."

"Oh that's right." Brian laughed.

"What are you doing here?" she asked, making no effort to
hide the fact she wasn't pleased to see him.

Daniel seemed to not know what to do with himself. Next to
Brian, who wore a black Armani suit and Gucci loafers, the
dashing detective looked like a college kid.

Brian held up his glass "Obviously, I'm tasting wine. My
cellar needs something new, and Tessa has never steered me
wrong. I'm thinking two cases of the Syrah."

How had Natalie put up with him for a whole year? He was beyond full of himself, bragging about his wealth.

"Are you going to introduce me to your friend?" Brian gestured toward Daniel.

"We're not friends," Daniel said, as if fending off an accusation. "More like acquaintances. We just met."

Brian gave him a condescending smile. "As in tonight?"

Natalie shouldered herself between them. "No, Brian, we didn't meet tonight, not that it's any of your business. Why don't you go taste your wine somewhere else?"

"Nat, please." He leaned toward her ear. "I was hoping we could talk."

"Hey," Daniel said, backing up. "I gotta take off. Listen, if there's any new information about the case, I'll let you know."

Natalie wanted to stop him from leaving, but that would be even more awkward. "Okay, thanks."

He wavered then shook her hand as if they were ending a business meeting. "G'bye." And like a flash, Daniel was gone, taking all the flutters with him.

"How dare you." Natalie smacked Brian's arm, almost knocking his wine out of his hand. "That was so rude and inappropriate."

"What? What did I say that was so bad?"

"Everything." Not only what he said, but the way he said it, too.

"Who was that guy anyway?"

"That is no concern of yours."

Brian scoffed, as if she'd made a joke. "Then what did he mean about some case? Is he a lawyer?"

"Again, none of your business." Natalie scowled at him. She turned to leave, but Brian was right on her heels.

"What are you doing with a guy like that anyway? He's practically a boy. And you don't do younger men."

Natalie contained herself. He was right about that. She

hadn't dated anyone even close to her own age since high school. And she'd never taken a second glance at someone younger. At least not until today.

"First of all, Brian, you don't have any idea what I do or don't do. And to be honest, since we broke up I'm finding younger men have certain—hmm, how do I put this delicately—strengths?"

His lip ticked up like a snarl. "I can't believe you said that. You and I had the best…" His expression changed. "Oh, I get it, you're playing me. Very funny. Now, can we just be friendly toward one another? Let's start over. You look beautiful."

"Don't even go there. Your compliments are meaningless."

"You're really making me work, aren't you?" He flashed his toothy smile. "It's still early. Let me take you to dinner."

Natalie glanced to her right. People were looking at them. Brian moved closer, shrinking her personal space. "Please?"

"No."

"Come on, Nat." He ran a finger down her bare arm. "We were so good together. And I, well, I've missed you."

Natalie shook her head, repelled by his ego and syrupy expression of longing. "We were good together for a short time, but it's over. Oh, so over. I want you to leave me alone."

He touched her again, this time with his whole hand. She swept her arm back in a circular move that almost knocked him on the chin. "Get out of here, Brian. Clearwater is my town, my territory. Go pay for your expensive wine, get in your fancy car, and move on with your life."

CHAPTER 20

*D*aniel merged his clunker of a truck onto the freeway, still burning with embarrassment. He laughed a pathetic, *I'm such a fool* kind of laugh. He'd scampered out of that party like a kid kicked by the bully.

Daniel pushed the accelerator, and his truck rattled in response. That jerk Steel probably drove a Maserati or a Lamborghini or at least a Porsche. Okay, a high end Mercedes for sure. What the hell difference did it make now?

Going to see Natalie in the first place had been foolish. Going to coffee with her had been a stupid mistake. But going to that over-the-top event (in a shop where he couldn't afford to buy a box of crackers, let alone a single bottle of wine) was a colossal, idiotic move.

An hour later, he was sitting at the counter in his sister's kitchen.

"You went to a wine tasting?" Jennifer dumped popcorn into a giant metal bowl and salted it. "In a place called Clearwater?"

Lola stuffed huge handfuls of popcorn into her mouth, eyes wide. "Where's that, Uncle Danny?"

Daniel copied his niece's method of eating popcorn, stuffing his mouth. He washed it down with beer. "Far away."

"I wanna see it. Will you take me?" Lola asked.

"No, sorry." He'd never set foot anywhere near that town again.

The three of them sat on stools at the counter like crows on a telephone line.

"I don't understand," Jennifer said. "Was it a date?"

"A date, Uncle Danny? You went on a date with that lady? She sure was pretty, and super nice, too."

"Lola," her mother said, "have you finished your homework?"

"Yes. Ages ago. Uncle Danny, do you know I go to math with the grade ahead of me and that I'm very gifted?"

Danny squeezed her skinny shoulder. "I sure do, Lola. You're a superstar. But there's more to a person than being smart." He imagined Brian Steel. That guy probably had a huge IQ in addition to his oversized ego—and wallet. "You need to be nice and helpful and caring, too."

Lola scooted from her stool into her uncle's lap. "Like you. You're all those things."

A lump in his throat? Is that what that was? "I love you, Lola-granola. Do me a favor though. Go watch TV. I need to talk to your mom alone."

"But I like grown up stuff. Let me stay, please. I won't talk, I promise."

"Let's go, silly." Jennifer pulled Lola off Daniel. "I'm going to put you in the tub, and after that you get extra screen time for good listening."

"You mean for staying out of your hair," Lola said, scuffing her way toward the bathroom.

"That, too." Her mother gave her a pat on the bottom. "Be right back, little brother."

Daniel picked at the popcorn, crunching the underdone kernels. "Ouch." A piece lodged between two teeth. He got it out with his pinky nail. How uncouth, he thought. But who cared? Wasn't like he was taking a beautiful woman with a mane of dark hair who was smart and kind and fascinating to dinner. Oh, and that coffee. Now he could never go back for coffee and sticky buns. How could he have blown it so royally? Then again, it wasn't his fault Steel had shown up. And it wasn't Natalie's fault either. She obviously hadn't expected him to be there. But what if she had? Maybe it was all an act, and she'd used Daniel to make her ex-boyfriend jealous. Nah. Daniel had enough experience with human behavior to know authenticity when he saw it.

"Okay, I'm back." Jennifer sat beside him on her perch.

"I wish I'd gotten Lola a sticky bun from this bakery called Nutmegs."

"Nutmegs, Clearwater? Sounds like something out of a storybook."

"It kind of is. She took me there for coffee." He sighed. "It was amazing."

"The coffee or the woman?"

"Both."

"Who are you, and what have done with my brother? Geez, Danny, you're pining after some woman like she's a goddess from a faraway land."

Goddess. The goddess ballerina. His stomach turned in on itself.

"Going to see her was a terrible idea." He finished off his beer and set the bottle down with a firm knock. "And it messed with my head. I gotta bring the old Danny Garrett back. I'm a cop, for chrissake."

Jennifer rubbed his back. "You're a tough cop with a huge heart. She's probably not good enough for you."

"It's the other way around for sure. But it doesn't matter." Daniel licked the salt from his lips. "I got a firsthand look at the kind of guy she dates, and I am definitely not that kind of guy."

Even if she had broken up with Brian Steel, there were plenty of other rich, good-looking, older men out there.

"So be it," his sister said. "You're moving on anyway."

"Yep. One more month of work, and I'm out of here."

"That's right. And you'd better go this time, promise me you will."

"I promise," he said, "no more false starts. I am taking my big adventure. And when I get back, whenever that might be, we'll sell this house and find a place for the three of us."

"Absolutely not. You are destined for a bigger life, and I will not be the reason you don't go after it."

"Stop with this bigger life crap. Lola needs us both, and she will even more as she gets older. Her dad hasn't been around in ages. Who even knows when he'll pop up again, creating all that upheaval in her life."

"Never, I hope," Jennifer said. "And please quit reminding me what a horrible choice I made."

"Sorry, but I always knew he was a scumbag." Daniel rested his chin on his hand. "Although he did give me my first beer."

"Yeah, you were like thirteen. I should've dumped him then. What's wrong with us, Danny? Why do we pick the wrong people?"

"Maybe we're destined to be alone. That's why we gotta stick together."

"Maybe." Jennifer leaned into him. "Not everyone can be like Mom and Dad."

Mom and Dad, not perfect, but close enough to give their children a secure, loving home.

Family photos adorned the shelves above Jennifer's kitchen desk. Daniel's favorite was one from a camping vacation they'd taken when he was six and Jennifer eleven. The four of them stood in front of a lake holding fishing gear. It had been the perfect trip. The Garretts had been the family every kid wanted. Until their father was killed in the line of duty.

"Do you still think about the what-ifs?" Daniel asked.

"All the time." Jennifer pushed around some pieces of popcorn, drawing lines through the salt at the bottom of bowl. "But I try not to dwell on it."

"What it would be like if Dad hadn't died?" Daniel allowed himself a rare moment of reflection. "Everything would be so different, especially with Mom." He wondered how she was. They hadn't spoken in months. She called on occasion, birthdays and holidays. Ten years after her husband died, she remarried and moved away. Their mother was uncomfortable with emotion, the kind of woman who probably never should have had children. Their father had been the nurturer, the anchor of the family. Daniel had worshipped him.

Jennifer rested her head on Daniel's shoulder and sniffled.

"Are you crying?"

"No." She sat up. "Maybe."

"What's wrong?"

She turned the empty bowl in circles. "I just know how much you miss Daddy, even after all this time. I should've stayed with you after he died."

For all her rough edges, Jennifer was the most loving person he knew.

His sister ruffled his hair. "Remember when you were five and broke your leg?"

"I do," Daniel said, recalling how his sister carried him around the house and helped him figure out how to walk with crutches. "You took better care of me than mom did."

"I loved you more than she did." There was a hint of bitterness in her voice. Their mother was so devoted to her social life that Daniel and Jennifer were often an afterthought.

"We had a good childhood, Jen. Don't overthink it."

"I guess." She draped an arm over his shoulders.

Daniel shook her off. "Can we not do this?"

Jennifer pulled back. "Do what?"

"Get all mushy. I know you love me." Daniel was being pulled in two directions. Maybe he should delay his departure a little longer. Mount Rushmore and Yellowstone and the Grand Canyon weren't going anywhere. Lola needed a father figure, and Jennifer, well, she needed supervision.

But postponing would open the door to countless excuses. There'd always be reasons to put off his cross-country adventure. A dream deferred was easily forgotten. He needed to quit second-guessing himself and take the leap before anyone or anything stopped him.

CHAPTER 21

*F*ive days after the event that went oh-so-wrong, Natalie was back at Mariano's.

Cece, Tessa, Patty, and Rebecca, plus Tessa's grandmother (Nonna to everyone) gathered at the antique table in the cellar at Mariano's. A separate room off the shop, the cellar was decorated like an old speakeasy, a place for intimate wine tastings where Tessa entertained her best clients. And where she welcomed her closest friends.

"I love our girls' night in," said Rebecca. "I've missed it."

"That's on you." Patty pressed a finger into Rebecca's shoulder. "We've been here, but you haven't come."

"Hey," Cece said. "Give her break. She's still a newlywed."

Natalie wrapped Rebecca in her arms. Part little sister, part mascot, the dog-walker turned small town advocate was beloved. "Look at our baby, all grown up and married now. And don't you pay any attention to Patty. You know how snippy she can be."

"I am *not* snippy."

"You are snippy," said Tessa. "Now please go get the Chardonnay out of the cooler."

126

"Fine, but don't talk about me until I get back," Patty said.

"So, Natalie, I hear you have news," Nonna said, her face open and interested. "A new man? I think that's—"

"Nonna!" Tessa interrupted her grandmother. "I told you that in confidence."

"Oh, I'm sorry. I didn't realize."

Natalie, unfazed, put an arm around Nonna. "Don't apologize, it's fine. But I do not have a new man. I wish I did, sort of. But I don't. The guy I brought to the wine tasting is only an acquaintance."

Patty set the bottles on the table. "I think you ought to get better acquainted then." She popped a piece of tuna sushi into her mouth. A drop of soy sauce dribbled down her chin. "Mmm, so good. Can you believe I went thirty years without eating sushi? Now it's my favorite food."

Cece, Patty's best friend since their college days, handed her a napkin. "Your brain is like a pinball bouncing from subject to subject."

"I'm so confused," Rebecca said. "Who are you talking about?"

"He's a cop," Patty said. "A gorgeous one, too. Nothing like anyone Natalie has ever dated."

"I'm not dating him. In fact, I'm sure I'll never see him again." Goodbye, flutters. Her phone screen lit up. "Oh my God, not another one."

"What is it?" asked Cece.

Natalie held up one finger. "A text from Brian. He's relentless. Texting me every day since the wine tasting."

"Let's hear it," Patty demanded.

"It's awful," Natalie said, embarrassed for him. "He's pleading with me, as if I were the love of his life, which I definitely am not."

"I think it's kind of romantic," Rebecca said, twirling the end of her long, red braid. "He wants to win you back."

Nonna patted Rebecca's hand. "It would be romantic if he weren't such an ass."

Natalie suppressed a laugh. Tessa's grandmother never insulted anyone.

"Excuse the colorful language," Nonna said. "That was unnecessary. But Brian Steel is a cad if I ever met one. And our Natalie deserves much better."

"That's what I'm saying." Patty stabbed a piece of yellowtail with a chopstick. "Natalie deserves better and different. Come on, Nat, out of all of us you're the most beautiful, and you're smart and nice. It makes no sense that you're the only one still single. You can't blame us for getting excited about you dating someone new."

"She's kind of right," Cece said. "We want what's best for you, that's all, and to see you happy."

"She means we want you to be in love." Rebecca, still moony over her recent marriage, had stars in her eyes.

"I don't care if you're in love or not," Patty said. "I just feel bad you're single when the rest of us are all part of a couple. It makes you the extra wheel."

Cece clapped a hand over Patty's mouth. "You need to stop talking."

"It is true, though," said Tessa. "Even Nonna has a boyfriend."

"What?" Natalie said. Nonna with a boyfriend was bigger news than her date with Daniel.

"I do have a new gentleman," she said. "We met at the senior center, and he's a lovely man. And he can drive at night, which at my age is a rarity."

"That's wonderful." Natalie reached across the table to squeeze Nonna's hand. The woman was like a favorite aunt. "I'm so happy for you."

"Thank you, dear. But it's relatively new, so don't expect to meet him anytime soon. In the meantime, the girls are right.

You need to get yourself out there more." Nonna spoke with a mix of authority and sympathy, and Natalie wasn't sure which she preferred less.

"This is supposed to be girls' night." Natalie pulled the sushi platter over and took all her favorite pieces. "So let's not focus on my love life, okay? We have way more interesting things to talk about."

The room fell silent. The women ate and drank and shrugged at one another.

"Seriously? Nothing more interesting?" Natalie turned to her right. "Tessa, how'd sales go after the tasting?"

Everybody perked up. Thanks to Tessa's over the top generosity and support of every cause in Clearwater, her success benefited all of them in one way or another.

"Funny you should ask," Tessa said. "One of our best nights ever, which unfortunately brings us back to Brian Steel."

Natalie slumped. "How is that possible?"

"Your ex-boyfriend purchased three cases of wine, placed a huge order, and bought several of the high-end auction items. Say what you will, but his fat wallet helped raise a lot of money."

"Money for the Lurensky Scholarship Fund," Cece said.

"And the animal shelter," Rebecca said.

"And the senior center," Nonna said.

Natalie leaned on one elbow and turned to Patty. "What about you, missy? What cause of yours does all this money support?"

"The 'Patty Sullivan gets a raise' fund. That's my cause."

They all burst into peals of laughter. Nobody could lighten the mood better than Patty.

"Ah, brutal honesty, a rare gift." Tessa dabbed her eyes with a napkin. "I knew it was a good move to hire you permanently."

Patty, the manager of Mariano's for almost five years, grinned. "I'd have to agree."

Natalie drank the last of her wine. "Tessa, I'm thrilled the event raised all that money, even if it did come from my embarrassing and annoying ex-boyfriend. I hope nobody noticed how I practically kicked him out."

"Oh, we noticed," Patty said. "Everybody did."

"Please say that's not true." Natalie knew it was not her finest moment.

"It's not," Cece said, shooting daggers at Patty. "Hardly anybody noticed. You were way over in the back anyway."

But Natalie believed Patty. Brutal honesty was her super power. "I'm sorry, Tess. I hope it didn't put a damper on the evening."

"On the contrary, it was merely a little excitement. And the gossip will die down soon. You know how quickly people lose interest."

"That's right, dear," Nonna said. "As soon as something more salacious happens, everybody will forget about your little spat with Brian Steel."

Natalie supposed they would. Still, she hated being the subject of gossip. "I think I'm going to head home," she said, pushing her chair away from the table.

"Please don't leave, it's barely nine," Patty said. "I promise I'll shut my mouth."

"Sorry, but I'm beat. And we have a busy day tomorrow. Our budding prima-ballerina is coming for her first real lesson with Cece."

Cece jumped out of her chair. "That's right, I'd better get home, too."

"Same with me." Rebecca began clearing plates. "Have to prep for the town council meeting next week. Oh, shoot, I forgot I don't have a car."

"Come on," Natalie said. "I'll drive you home."

"Really? Oh my God, that is so super totally nice of you."

"Don't go crazy," Natalie said, nudging her toward the door. "It's only a ride."

Outside, in the cool night air, they took a brisk walk across the park toward the studio where Natalie had left her car.

Rebecca jumped in and pulled the seatbelt across her lap. "I love love love your Mustang. It's so cute and fun and totally not you. I mean, you're so, well, sensible."

Sensible. Natalie was tired of being sensible. Would she ever get to be something else?

"And by the way, nobody meant to gang up on you back there," Rebecca said. "It really is true that we want you to be happy like we are."

Happiness, what an elusive desire. Maybe contentment was enough.

"I'm glad you're happy, Rebecca," Natalie said, backing out of the parking space. "You deserve it."

"You think so?" Rebecca faced her.

"Of course I do," Natalie said. "Why would you ask that?"

"I don't know. I mean, does anyone *not* deserve happiness?"

"If someone's a horrible person, they don't." Her thoughts returned to Brian. Did he deserve happiness? Maybe, as long as it did not involve her.

"Okay, then," Rebecca said. "If I, and most people, deserve to be happy, why don't you?"

Natalie slowed at a stop sign. The night sky was dotted with stars and a halfmoon glowed yellow. "I guess I deserve happiness. I just don't know where to find it." She picked up Rebecca's warm hand. "And you manage to find it everywhere."

"I don't just find it. I look for it."

Natalie contemplated Rebecca's wise words. "Maybe I'd better take a more proactive approach then."

"Good idea, and then when you—" Rebecca's cell phone buzzed with a text. "Oh no!"

"What?"

"There's an emergency at the animal shelter. I don't have time to go home and get the car. Can you drop me off there?"

"You bet." Natalie pulled a U-turn and sped down the country road.

CHAPTER 22

*N*atalie stopped in front of the main door to Furry Friends Animal Shelter.

"Thanks, Nat, see you later!" Rebecca flew out of the car and sprinted around the back of the building, a converted barn on the property of a small farm.

Natalie sat there, hands on the steering wheel and motor still running. What kind of emergency happens at an animal shelter? Curiosity pulled her out of her car.

Heading toward the back entrance, she hoped she wouldn't come across anything gruesome.

Florescent ceiling fixtures lit up the large space. Dogs in kennels barked and wagged tails when she entered. Rebecca looked up, her hands cupped around a tiny ball of blond fur.

"Natalie, hi. Did I leave something in the car?"

"No. I—I just thought you might need some help."

"Really? Great! Take this." Rebecca placed a newborn puppy in Natalie's hands. "We need to get these puppies into the warming box."

The fuzzy pup was the size of a small peach. She followed

Rebecca's lead, and they arranged the five babies together under a bright orange light.

"Is that Dr. Klansky?" Natalie pointed at the man hunched over an examination table a few feet away.

"Yeah, he's tending to the mom. She had to have a C-section. Soon as he's done fixing her up, we can get these pups nursing."

Natalie marveled at Rebecca's uncharacteristic calm.

"There's a puppy mill about thirty miles from here," Rebecca said. "Animal control raided it this afternoon and distributed the dogs. We got the pregnant mom. Nobody expected her to go into labor tonight."

Rebecca made sure they were snuggled against each other and positioned under the heat lamp. "If you don't mind staying a little longer, I could use an extra set of hands for a while."

"I don't mind," Natalie said, wandering over to say hello to her friend Dr. K.

"Hey there, Natalie. How you doing?" Dr. Klansky stitched up the mother's abdomen, yawning, as if an emergency C-section and the birth of five puppies were all in a day's work.

"I'm okay," Natalie said, taking a look at the groggy animal.

"I'm sure you miss your mom. I'm missing her, too."

"Yeah, I do."

"It was a nice service you had, very befitting a woman like her." The country veterinarian had taken care of Ilana's cats since Natalie was a little girl.

"Thanks."

He placed some surgical tools on a metal tray. "Takes time to adjust. I lost my mom over twenty years ago and still think about her every day."

Natalie wondered if she'd still be thinking about her mother every day in twenty years. "It's been a hard few months, few years, actually." She watched Dr. Klansky knot the surgical thread. "I can't believe this dog had five puppies. She's so small."

"Yep." He lifted her gums and checked her teeth. "Four or

five years old, no telling how many litters she's had." He stroked her reddish-brown fur. "Beautiful girl, a designer dog herself, born to do nothing but make babies. It's criminal."

"What'll happen to her puppies?" Natalie asked.

"They'll be fine. We'll have them nursing in a bit, soon as she wakes up a little more." Dr. Klansky packed up his medical bag then went to take a look at the puppies. "Give mom a few more minutes," he said to Rebecca. "Then bring her the pups. I'm gonna head home, but you call me if there's any problem. And Natalie, you take care." He gave her a fatherly hug before leaving.

Natalie remained by the mother, stroking the top of her head. A sense of peace washed over her. She stayed and helped Rebecca move the puppies to the mother's bed and make sure they were able to nurse. The tiny animal tended to her babies as if she had no idea her womb had undergone major surgery.

Natalie and Rebecca took turns monitoring the mother as the anesthesia wore off. They offered her small amounts of water through a syringe and nibbles of soft food every thirty minutes.

When Rebecca dozed off in the desk chair, Natalie managed on her own, caring for the mama while the mama cared for her babies.

It was two in the morning when Willy, the shelter director, showed up to take over. Natalie, although exhausted, left reluctantly. The puppies and their mother's well-being had taken on surprising importance to her. She dropped Rebecca off and drove home, thinking about the overworked, weary dog who knew nothing other than motherhood.

CHAPTER 23

*M*aura and Cece sat in front of Natalie in her office. Cece's arms and legs were crossed, her back stiff. Her bright blue eyes flashed with frustration—and a hint of worry. As for Maura, Natalie didn't know her well enough to read her expression. But she certainly did not look happy.

After the late night at the shelter, Natalie had hoped for a power nap before classes began. But then a disagreement between Maura and Cece arose, and she had no choice but to manage it.

"It's not unusual for two instructors working toward the same goal to have differences of opinion," Natalie said, feeling like a school principal. It was her inclination to agree with Cece on everything from how to run the dance school to how to navigate life. But Maura was a partner on this, and her opinion mattered. Natalie laced her fingers and leaned forward with authority. "We all want Ashley to meet certain benchmarks, of course. She's young, but she's late to the game."

"That's right." Maura interjected. "Which is why I want to make sure she, or we, adhere to a strict—

"I need flexibility." Cece faced Maura, her composure tested. "I need to see what's working and what's not. I've been in Ashley's shoes myself. You haven't."

Cece's confrontational tone threw Natalie for a loop. Her two "partners" in this venture, the ones who had come up with the grand plan in the first place, had hit a snag. It fell on Natalie to figure out how to unsnag them. She wasn't even sure what they were disagreeing about.

"I may not have been a ballerina at your level, Cece, but I know my student."

"Don't you mean *our* student?" Cece asked.

"Of course, I do. But Ashley was my—"

"Hold on." Natalie interrupted the back and forth. "I'm going to remind you both of a few things. First, Maura, you came to us with the proposal regarding Ashley. And Cece, you championed the cause. I didn't love the idea at first, but when the two of you brought the idea to me you presented yourselves as a team. And a team is what you need to be."

The women across from her shrank slightly, as if put in their place.

"There's no doubt that Ashley has what it takes to achieve greatness. But we all know that out of hundreds of potential world class ballerinas, only a handful ever get there." She glanced at the framed photos around the office. Over the decades, there'd been many Lurensky students talented enough to make it, but only a few had reached the pinnacle.

Cece's gaze turned inward, and Natalie knew exactly what she was thinking. If she hadn't quit, she would have been one of Ilana's prima ballerinas. Ashley was Cece's opportunity to prove she could do it—mold a ballerina as good if not better than she had been.

What would Mamma have said?

Her mind wandered, her mother's last words, spoken with a clarity Natalie thought she'd never hear again. Dementia had stolen her mother, but in the final moments a sliver remained. *Natalia, my greatest blessing. Now go.*

Now go? What did it mean? But minutes later, she was gone. Perhaps her mother knew she was about to die, that it was she who needed to go. Or did she mean it was time for Natalie *to go?*

"Natalie? Are you listening?"

She snapped to attention. "Of course I am. I was thinking about something my mother used to say."

Cece and Maura looked at her as if waiting for brilliance.

"You can lead a horse to water but you cannot make it drink." Natalie tinged her voice with her mother's Russian accent.

"That's what you were thinking about?" Maura clearly had expected more.

Even Cece couldn't hide her disappointment in the tired cliché.

"Well, it means more than what it sounds like." Natalie shook off the embarrassment of her trite remark and forced authority into her tone. "We all know how much work it'll take to get Ashley to achieve the ultimate goal. And it's up to the two of you to pave that road. How you guide her over the miles and through the years and in and out of endless, exhausting, physically brutal work that will wear her down, make her cry and want to quit, and push her to the brink—that's for you two to figure out. But in the end, it's up to her." Natalie waggled a finger at both of them and raised her voice. "So, solve your differences, get organized, and be the team leaders you promised to be. Because at the end of the day, we have businesses to run and hundreds of other students who require and deserve their share of our attention."

She puffed out a breath of air. Then in a polite yet firm way, Natalie dismissed them.

~

CECE HANDED NATALIE a glass of cold Chardonnay. They were sitting side by side on the sectional in Cece's family room after dinner. Upstairs, the best husband in the world was putting the cutest little boy in the world to bed.

Natalie propped her bare feet on the coffee table beside Cece's, both of them still wearing their dance clothes. A rare flash of envy made her squirm. Cece deserved her great marriage and wonderful family.

"That was some speech you made today," Cece said.

"I didn't mean to make a speech." She sipped her wine, and the sweetness tingled on the tip of her tongue. "I'm sorry if I came off as bossy."

"It's okay, you are the boss. But to be honest, you seemed kind of disconnected."

Natalie set her wine down. Had she been that transparent? "I'm connected, and I care about Ashley's progress. But not in the way you do. She's your project, your big goal."

"I get it."

"I know you do. I'll come around eventually. Do you have any cookies?"

Cece went to the cupboard then returned with a few mini-bags of frosted animal crackers. "Sorry, just Noah's lunch box snacks." She tossed one into Natalie's lap.

"I love these." Natalie ripped open the package and ate the overly sweet cookies as if they were peanuts.

"No offense, but you do look tired. You even have bags under your eyes."

"That's because," she said, licking her fingers, "last night when I drove Rebecca home, we were sidetracked by an emergency C-section at the shelter."

"Wait. What?"

"Believe it or not, I assisted Rebecca. And boy, is she good as what she does. Brand new tiny puppies the size of mice." Natalie finished her snack bag. "Do you want to go over there and see them?"

"Who are you?" Cece put her hands on top of her head. "First you lay into Maura and me like a drill sergeant and now you want to go check on a litter of puppies? You are not yourself."

Natalie groaned. "I know I'm not. Never mind the puppies. Did you and Maura work everything out after my reprimand?"

"Phew, you're back." Cece relaxed and curled her legs underneath her. "We did, actually. Despite our reaction to your pontificating, your point was well taken. Especially the part about, and I can't believe I'm saying this, the horse."

"The horse?" Natalie hardly remembered what she'd said.

"Yeah, it's true. We can take Ashley all the way to the edge, but at the end of the day she has to want this more than the rest of us combined."

Want, such a small word. So often misunderstood. An elusive desire for things large and small. Natalie hadn't spent much time with Ashley, but she'd seen the *want* in her intense eyes, the fixed position in her jaw the first time they met. She'd first seen that kind of determination years ago in her best friend.

"You know what that *want* feels like, Cece. I never did."

Cece studied Natalie's face.

"Why are you looking at me like that?"

"Because you did know what it felt like. We were fifteen years old, and you told me what you wanted."

Natalie sat back. "Are you talking about Adam Hawk? Because my crush on him lasted like a week."

Cece laughed. "No, not Adam. I can't believe you don't remember. We were sitting on the steps in front of the studio after dance class. Everyone we knew was at that party, the one at the ranch in the hills where no parents were going to be home."

"Oh, I do remember that. I was so mad my mom wouldn't let me go. But you didn't care," Natalie said, her memories taking her back to teen years fraught with angst, but a time when fantasies were still possible.

"*I couldn't care less about the party,*" Cece had said. "*I don't even want to go. I have to get my rest and be ready for rehearsal tomorrow.*"

"*You're lucky,*" Natalie said, picking at some chipping paint on the step. "*You know what you want. You always have.*"

"*Yep. And I won't let anything get in my way.*" Cece looked into the distance, as if she could see it unfolding before her eyes. "*I will be the next Lurensky prima ballerina, and I'll perform on the grandest stages around the world.*"

Natalie couldn't imagine wanting something with that much intention. She peered into the black sky wishing the stars would realign. Give her a dream a fraction of the size of Cece's. Show her what she might do, what she might become. "*All I want is to get out of this town. It's suffocating me.*"

Cece grabbed her best friend's hand. "*If that's what you want, Nat, you have to see it. Imagine every little piece of it. I see my dream day and night, and I cling to it as if letting go would stop my heart from beating.*"

Natalie envisioned her escape.

Over the next three years, she pictured it every day and dreamed about it every night. She saw herself riding into the sunset on a horse, driving in a truck headed to anywhere, going places where nobody knew her, cities like New York and Chicago. She visualized tossing her toe shoes and leotards into a box and taping it shut. Natalie heard herself say goodbye to her mamma, her papa, and her best friend.

"HEY, NAT, ARE YOU CRYING?"

Natalie sniffled. "No, I'm not. I'm fine. But it is sad that neither of us got what we wanted. We both quit on our dreams, didn't we?"

Cece sighed. "We did, but with good reasons. My family imploded and your father died."

The matter-of-fact tone Cece used made Natalie chuckle. Her logic was undeniable. "And you figured out a new path for yourself."

"Thanks to you," Cece said. "It's too late for me to become a prima ballerina but not too late for me to create one. Sort of the same dream but with a different spin on it."

"A different spin, good one." Natalie shook a few crumbs from her cookie bag. "I really admire you. When things go off the rails, you change. You go in a new direction. You never give up."

"You think you've given up?" Cece asked.

"I know I have." Natalie admitted it easily. It was the truth.

"Dreams don't have an expiration date, Nat."

"Maybe, but they do wither. Then they lose their appeal or become completely impractical." Natalie set her feet on the floor. "That's the thing about decisions we make when we're young. We think we can undo them, that the ramifications are immaterial."

Rarely did Natalie indulge in such introspection. The past was behind her. Far behind. She didn't care anymore. Didn't everybody want to get out of the town they grew up in? It's human nature to want something different. She'd had her chance to leave twenty years ago. It didn't happen then, and now it couldn't. The studio, her mother's legacy—that was her priority.

"Ugh, listen to me whining. I can't stand it. Thanks for dinner and wine and animal crackers. I'll see you tomorrow."

Cece walked her to the door. "You're a great woman, Natalie Lurensky. Don't ever doubt that."

"Thanks," she said, although she doubted it every day.

Outside, as Natalie got into her car, she lingered an extra moment to look through the big front windows of her friend's warm, welcoming house. Her home was always full of company and family and laughter.

Not Natalie's house. It never had been like that. It never would be.

She got in the car and slammed the door. The rearview mirror reflected her dreary face. "You're pathetic," she said to the woman staring back at her.

CHAPTER 24

The big barn doors were wide open, and loud barking could be heard even through her closed car windows. Rebecca's pick-up truck was parked out front.

Natalie wandered inside. Rebecca looked up, and a broad smile brightened her already joyful face.

"Hi! What are you doing here?" She sat cross legged on the floor, a puppy in one hand and tiny baby bottle in the other.

"Looking for you." Natalie joined her at the whelping box. "Thought maybe I could help."

"Oh my God, you totally can. Here, take this one." Rebecca practically dropped the puppy and bottle into Natalie's hands and jumped up. "I've got to mix up some more formula. The mama is doing her best to nurse, but it's taking so much out of her we have to supplement."

Rebecca went to the prep counter, shook up a few bottles of formula, then gave Natalie a full one and another puppy. "You showed up at the right time. This would've taken me all night on my own."

"Where's your wonderful husband?" Natalie knew Rebecca roped him into helping out whenever she could.

"He was here for three hours this afternoon. Then he had to go to basketball practice. He's the new assistant coach at the high school."

"Is he? That's great." Natalie's heart expanded. Her young friend's life had fallen into place. "Hard to believe you've been married eight months already."

"I pinch myself every day." Rebecca did little shoulder shimmy. "I have no idea how I got so lucky."

"It's because you're wonderful, and you deserve it."

"Well, you're wonderful and—"

"Don't go there," Natalie said, cutting her off. She wouldn't let Rebecca feel sorry for her or tell her how she deserved to be happy as much as anyone. It was a refrain she'd couldn't stomach. "Let me sit here in peace and feed puppies. It's oddly comforting."

"That's because it releases oxytocin. It's the hormone you produce when you're falling in love."

"Is that so?" Natalie couldn't deny how therapeutic feeding the puppy was. As if nourishing another life gave her a higher purpose. There it was again, that pesky word. *Purpose.*

"How's the mama doing?" Natalie asked.

"Dr. K checked on her earlier. She'll be fine, but after that C-section and hysterectomy, she's pretty worn out. Gotta hand it to her, she's a trooper. Doing her best to be what she is."

"A mama to her babies." Natalie nuzzled the pup to keep him awake and suckling.

"Dr. K said if we hadn't rescued her, she'd have died for sure."

"Really?" Natalie felt a surge of emotion over the thought of the poor little dog dying in childbirth.

"Yep. We got to her in the nick of time. Let's take the puppies to her. She's nervous when they're not with her."

They placed her babies inside the curve of her body. The pups scooched in as close as they could, smashing against their siblings. They had paws the size of peas and little pink dots for noses. Natalie stroked the mother's head, the soft fur between her ears. She seemed, somehow, contented by the soothing touch.

"What'll happen with them in a few weeks?" she asked. "Once the puppies are weaned?"

"If you can believe this, they're all spoken for. I sent a message out through the town council text alert, and four people stepped up. Some are even willing to take two pups. And one family wants the mom and a puppy. It's a totally happy ending all around."

As LATE AS IT WAS, restlessness had Natalie on edge. She didn't want to go home to her empty house. To prolong it, she stopped at the market and picked up some groceries. Shopping for one had to be the most depressing activity ever. She tossed this and that into her cart—some apples, a couple cans of soup, crackers, oatmeal—with no idea what might be in the cupboard at home.

A light poke on Natalie's shoulder startled her.

"Ma'am, sorry, but we're closing."

"You are?"

The young man tapped the edge of her cart. "Are you ready to check out?"

"Uh, yeah. Sure. Thanks." Natalie followed him to the register.

The conveyor belt carried her meager supplies toward the scanner. The checker avoided eye contact.

At home, she opened the cupboard and took inventory. Six canisters of unopened oatmeal stood side by side. The cheery Quaker Oats man winked.

Natalie brushed her teeth, plugged in her cell phone, then got into bed. She punched and flipped her pillow and settled into it. Sleep eluded her. She rolled onto her back and stared at the ceiling.

Finally, she drifted off. But the deep, dreamless sleep did not last long enough. The sun was barely up when her cell phone's annoying ring jolted her. She opened one eye and looked at the screen. She didn't recognize the number and assumed it was the mother of one of her students. Some of them were clueless when it came to respecting boundaries. Even Natalie deserved to sleep past six once in a while.

She almost let the call go to voicemail but then changed her mind.

"Hello?" she said, her voice raspy.

"Natalie?" A familiar voice, but she couldn't place it. Young, female, frightened.

"Yeah?"

"It's me. Kaylee."

Natalie bolted to a sitting position. "Kaylee?"

"Yes, I'm sorry to bother you."

"It's not a bother. Are you okay?"

The frightened teenager choked on a sob. "I'm in trouble, Natalie. Terrible trouble."

CHAPTER 25

Kaylee Robertson sat in a corner booth at a rundown coffee shop a few blocks from the apartment building where Natalie had gone looking for her. Other than the jagged shoulder length hair, ripped jeans, and tattered sweatshirt, Kaylee hadn't changed at all. She looked more like fourteen than nineteen, her face young and childlike.

Without a word, Natalie scooted into the booth and pulled her student into her arms. Kaylee collapsed against her and clung like a baby monkey. Natalie rubbed her back. First comfort, then questions.

A waitress came by with a cup and saucer and pot of coffee. She motioned to Natalie, as if to say *coffee?*

Natalie nodded and whispered, "please."

After two minutes of hugging, Kaylee released Natalie and sniffled. "Thank you for coming."

With a gentle touch, Natalie combed Kaylee's bangs—half black, half blonde—out of her eyes.

"Of course." She moved to the bench across the table and slid over, her leggings catching on a rip in the pink vinyl. There were hardly any other customers, only a man at the counter.

Heat blew on Natalie from the vent above the table. She pulled off her heavy wool sweater, the one she'd grabbed from a chair as she rushed out the door at the crack of dawn.

"I'm glad you called me." Natalie toyed with her coffee mug, tapping her nails on the porcelain. "I've been worried about you."

It was then she noticed the bluish, gray skin beside Kaylee's right eye.

Terrible trouble, indeed. Natalie contained herself. It was best to start slow. "Have you had breakfast?"

Kaylee shook her head. She looked as if she'd missed more than a few meals. Her face had lost its prior fullness and color.

"Let's order some food," Natalie said, signaling to the kind waitress.

The server took their order and topped off Natalie's coffee.

"How's my mom?" Kaylee asked as soon as they were alone.

"I haven't talked to her in a while, but I know she's been worried about you. And she has her hands full with your little brothers. It's not okay for you to be unreachable for weeks on end." Natalie didn't intend to make Kaylee feel guilty, but if she did feel guilty, it was with good reason.

Kaylee's eyes filled with tears. "I know. It's just that I was doing stuff." She dragged the sleeve of her sweatshirt across her face.

Stuff. Well, that explains nothing. Natalie didn't want to lose her patience or demand anything of her, but Kaylee had behaved like a petulant teenager. "You're almost twenty, Kaylee. You know better. And your mother has always had your back."

Their food appeared, breaking the tension. "Here we go," the waitress said. "Number four special for you, honey. And oatmeal for your mom."

"Thank you," Natalie said, not correcting the mistake. She easily could be the mother.

Kaylee stuffed a piece of bacon into her mouth. "I used to wish you were my mom."

Natalie's sympathy grew. It wasn't unusual for a child or teenager to wish such things, especially when their home life was unstable. And Kaylee's certainly was—an absentee father, a young mother struggling to make ends meet, and four little brothers to look after. "I understand, sweetie."

Natalie ate a spoonful of warm, creamy oatmeal sprinkled with brown sugar. She watched Kaylee try to cut her pancakes with the side of her fork. It slipped from her hand and clattered on the floor.

"Why are you eating with your right hand?" As a dance instructor, Natalie was always aware of a student's dominant hand. And Kaylee's dominant arm was resting in her lap. "What happened to your left hand?"

"Nothing. I tripped on the stairs at my apartment building."

Natalie reached across the table with her own knife and fork and cut Kaylee's pancakes into bite-sized pieces. All her restraint and intention to tread lightly evaporated. "Eat up. I'm taking you to a clinic for an x-ray. And tell me right now who is —" she hesitated to pick the right word, "who's *mistreating* you."

"Nobody." Kaylee focused on her plate and continued eating, awkwardly stabbing pancake pieces with the clean fork Natalie handed her. "I told you, I tripped."

If not for the bruise by her eye, Natalie might have believed her. "If that's the case, why did you call me?"

Kaylee wiped a drip of syrup off her chin then took a big drink of chocolate milk. Her little girl face was still there, hiding behind the face of a young woman who found herself in circumstances she had no idea how to manage.

"I heard you were looking for me."

"Who told you that?" Natalie asked, purposely being as vague as she was.

"One of the girls who works at the restaurant. She said a tall, super pretty woman from my past came by the apartment building asking about Kaylee Robertson. It kinda blew my cover."

"Oh, that's right. You go by Robin, now."

"Yeah, I didn't want anybody to know who I was, to look me up and see all my old ballerina pictures. I wanted to be somebody different."

"Fair enough," Natalie said. "I get that, but here we are. You have a sprained arm, or worse, and what looks like a black eye. You can't blame me for being concerned."

Kaylee sank deeper into her seat. "I know."

"Did Jimmy cause your injuries?"

Kaylee turned crimson. "How do you know Jimmy?"

Finally, a reaction. "I'm not sure I do. But I've been to apartment 249 on two occasions. And I met two creepy guys there. So, tell me, who is Jimmy?" Natalie could hardly wait to hear if Jimmy was the one she thought he was.

Kaylee rocked back and forth. "When I first moved into the apartment, he was just some guy who hung out at the pool with us. He was nice and cute." A slight smile, as if it were a pleasant memory. "We were part of a group, you know? Him and me and Mel and few other friends. Most of us worked at the restaurant. It was fun."

Innocent enough, Natalie thought.

"Anyway, we started going out some. He was kind of my boyfriend for a while."

"How old is Jimmy?" Natalie asked, trying to confirm if he was one of the guys she'd met.

"About twenty-two."

Twenty-two. That sounded more like the first guy.

"Does he have a bunch of tattoos?"

"Yeah." Kaylee frowned. "How'd you know that?"

"He answered the door the first time I came looking for you.

And for what it's worth, he might be cute, but he's definitely not nice. And any guy that would hit you is—"

"Jimmy didn't hit me."

Natalie took a beat and gave Kaylee a moment to realize she needed to reveal the truth. "Then who did, honey?"

Kaylee looked out the window, as if afraid of something, or someone, in the parking lot. "His older brother." She whispered it, despite the fact nobody was anywhere near them. "I did something stupid, and Colin, well, he got really pissed at me."

Questions flew at Natalie like a flock of lost birds. She had to choose them with care, like plucking information out of Kaylee with a tweezer. "What did you do?"

"I told someone something." Kaylee shrank into herself. "I thought it was no big deal. All I did was say that I thought Colin was, you know, doing some things that made me nervous and maybe we should stay away from him."

At least Kaylee used good sense on that thought. "And that got back to him, obviously," Natalie said.

Kaylee stared at her plate. "I guess." She raised her head, and her watery, innocent eyes met Natalie's. "Jimmy tried to calm him down, but he…he really lost it."

"I want to get you out of here today. Once we're back in Clearwater, we can report everything that happened." Natalie put her palms on the table. "I'm glad you called me. This will all get worked out, I promise."

"It's not that simple," Kaylee said.

"What do you mean?"

Kaylee fingered her black eye as if to remind herself it was there.

"Kaylee, I can't help you unless you tell me everything." Natalie leaned in closer. "Please, tell me."

Kaylee's teeth pushed into her lower lip. "Promise you won't tell my mom." It was a childish request, as if her infraction was little more than ditching class or failing a test. Natalie hoped against hope it was that insignificant.

"I don't know if I can promise that, honey. It depends on how much trouble you're in."

A slight nod, resigned to the truth of her predicament. Kaylee's eyes shifted toward at the counter where a few people sat. "There's a backpack under the table," Kaylee said, voice low. "Open it."

Natalie reached down and wrapped her hand around one of the straps. She pulled the backpack up. It was heavy, as if loaded with rocks.

"Whatever you do," Kaylee whispered, "don't freak out."

CHAPTER 26

atalie set the backpack beside her leg and unzipped it inch by inch, half expecting springy snakes to leap out at her. She glanced at Kaylee, then returned her attention to the backpack.

Sunlight filtered through the window beside the booth. Natalie positioned the opening of the backpack toward the light to see inside it. The contents glimmered and reflected in the sun. She stuck her hand in. It hit a plastic bag filled with something hard, like metal.

"It's not mine, I swear."

Natalie pulled the bag up toward the top of the backpack to see what Kaylee was hiding, what had her so terrified. "Oh my God."

Gold. *Gold?* She used the flashlight on her phone to get a better look. In the light, it glittered like pirate's treasure. Watches, bracelets, rings.

Not that simple. What an understatement that was.

"Where did you get this?" Natalie asked.

"It's a long story."

Natalie zipped the backpack up. More people entered the

coffee shop. Morning rush had begun. Four men took the booth behind them. Natalie pulled some cash from her wallet and put it under the salt shaker. "We're going to leave. Be casual. Let your hair fall forward. I'll take the backpack."

Natalie scooted out of the booth quickly, but not too quickly, with the backpack clutched to her chest.

Kaylee followed her outside. Natalie put one arm around her waist and guided her toward the car. "Get in." Natalie opened the passenger door, and Kaylee complied.

She closed Kaylee's door, hugging the weighty backpack full of contraband. Moving quickly, she popped the trunk, set the bag down, slammed the trunk, jumped into the car. Then she hightailed it out of the parking lot.

"Where are we going?" Kaylee's pale face was paler than before.

"I'm not sure. I need to call somebody first." Natalie tapped Cece's number on her cell. When her friend answered, she almost fainted with relief.

"Cece, I need talk to Brad."

"He's not here. Had an early flight this morning. You can reach him in a few hours. What do you need him for?"

Natalie glanced in Kaylee's direction, taking in her trauma-tized expression. "A legal question, but nothing to worry about. I'll see you later." She disconnected before Cece could pepper her with more questions.

Natalie merged onto the freeway and drove under the speed limit, feeling like she had a dead body in her trunk and doing her best to hide her trepidation from Kaylee.

How many crime shows had Natalie watched in which the cops pulled someone over and discovered drugs or weapons in the trunk? Her imagination went wild with crazy scenarios and ridiculous possibilities. They were nowhere near the California border, so at least she couldn't be charged with transporting stolen property across state lines. But what about driving into another city? Was there a law against moving stolen goods from city to city? Being in possession of stolen property, regardless of who'd stolen it, probably was a crime. What if Kaylee needed a lawyer? Her mother could never afford a criminal defense attorney.

Raspy, wheezy sounds came from Kaylee. She had tears running down her cheeks in rivulets. Her body shook as if she were having a seizure. "Kaylee, are you okay? Are you breathing?"

"I think I'm having a heart attack."

"You're not having a heart attack." Natalie squeezed her thigh as if that could comfort her. "But we should go to the emergency room and have your arm checked out."

"No, I have to get back to the apartment. If they find out I left with the backpack, they'll kill me. Last time I saw Colin, he terrified me." She pounded her knee with her right fist. "I can't believe I did this. I can't believe I let them talk me into it. It was nothing at first, I swear. Like little stupid pranks with Jimmy. It was—fun.

Pranks? Fun? The value of the jewels in that bag said otherwise.

Natalie's sweaty hands gripped the steering wheel. She needed someone she could trust to tell them what to do. Like it or not, she'd opened the door to Kaylee's troubles the first time she went snooping around the apartment building. And she'd walked through that door by agreeing to meet her this morning. She had no choice but to see it through. What happened to Kaylee from this point forward was entirely dependent upon Natalie's next move.

NATALIE PARKED on the street near the apartment complex but not directly in front of it. She checked the time, only 8:30. The buzz of cars passing by as people headed out to work or wher-ever normal people went filled her head. "This is not a good plan. You can't go in there."

"Please, you don't understand. I have to give it back to Jimmy."

Natalie wished it were that easy. "No. I'm not going to let you go back into any apartment where he or his violent brother might be. It's too dangerous now."

Kaylee dissolved into more tears, gasping for air.

"Calm down, or you'll hyperventilate. We'll figure this out together, okay?" She offered Kaylee a wad of tissues.

"Okay." She blew her nose and nodded.

"Now, how'd you get the backpack to begin with?"

"Jimmy gave it to me." Kaylee cradled her sore arm. "Late last night, he stopped by the apartment, a little nervous or maybe excited. It's hard to tell with him. Anyway, he handed me the backpack, told me to keep it safe, and that he'd be back to get it in an hour."

"You didn't ask him what was in it? Or peak inside?" How anyone could resist that, Natalie had no idea.

"I didn't. When it comes to Jimmy, and especially his brother, you don't ask questions. Over the last few weeks, they've gotten super secretive. I stay out of their business."

Thank goodness for that, Natalie thought. The more distance between Kaylee and those two criminals the better. "Then what did you do?"

"I hid it in a closet."

"Well, that makes sense." Natalie tried to sound encouraging, supportive of any move Kaylee had made that was at least somewhat sensible. "Whose closet?"

"The coat closet in my friend's apartment. It's in this same complex but on the other side of where Jimmy lives. It's where I've been staying."

Another wrinkle. Kaylee was crashing with a friend now. Her mother probably had no idea about this turn of events.

"Does your friend know about the backpack?"

"No. She's totally not involved in anything. And she's been out of town for over a week. She'll probably kick me out when she gets back and finds out what I've done."

"Probably." Natalie didn't want Kaylee going back to any apartment linked to a criminal enterprise. "Don't worry about that yet. Just finish the story. Jimmy said he'd come back in an hour?"

"Yeah, but he didn't." Kaylee's hyperventilating started up again. "I stayed awake as long as I could, fell asleep on the couch. When I woke up, I didn't know what to do. I called Jimmy's cell but he didn't answer. That's when I looked in the bag." Kaylee pulled her legs up, making herself small. "And called you."

"I'm glad you did." Natalie meant it. If she'd called her mother it would've been a disaster for them both.

Natalie wanted to tell Kaylee that none of this was her fault, but she couldn't. Her dire situation was a direct result of foolish decisions she'd made—starting with not listening to her mother about going to community college.

Now it was too late. Natalie's heart broke for this girl. Her life hadn't been easy. But what a colossal mistake she'd made. At Kaylee's age, Natalie didn't listen to her mother either, but at least it hadn't gotten her into trouble with the law.

"So, what should I do now?" Kaylee asked.

Natalie stared through windshield, considering her options. She had a huge decision to make on behalf of a nineteen-year-old girl whose life was careening off course like a runaway train.

CHAPTER 27

*T*he police station bustled with activity—a passed out kid on a bench, uniformed officers going in and out, and a line at the front desk ten people deep. It looked like an after Christmas sale at Target.

"Trust me," Natalie said. "We have to do this. And I know the person we need to talk to."

The line inched forward as random people reported incidents. One woman brought in a stray cat. Another was looking for her son, who had been arrested. A man in a suit was screaming about his car, which had been towed—unfairly, of course.

When they got to the front of the line, Natalie swallowed hard and set her shoulders back.

"I'm here to see Sergeant Fred White."

"What's it about?" The officer looked as if she'd been working twenty-four hours straight.

"Um, we have some information for him." Natalie didn't know how to make it sound critical without admitting to anything. "Please, tell him Natalie Lurensky is here. He'll want to see me."

The officer eyed Natalie (and the backpack) with suspicion. "You sure about that? He's a busy guy."

"I'm positive," she said,

"Wait here."

The backpack grew heavier every second. Kaylee clung to her arm like a little girl.

"It's going to be okay. Sergeant White is really nice. And he's kind of a friend of mine."

Kaylee moved closer, as if Natalie were a shield.

More people, officers in uniform and plain clothes, moved around in organized chaos. For a split second, Natalie wondered if Daniel Garrett was among them. It had been less than a week since the mortifying encounter with Brian at the wine tasting. She figured she'd never see the dashing detective again, and she certainly hoped she wouldn't today, looking as if she'd rolled out of bed and thrown on dirty clothes. Immediately, Natalie chastised herself for even thinking about such unimportant minutia in the midst of a crisis.

Finally, the clerk reappeared with Sergeant White in tow. He greeted Natalie like an old friend. "Nice to see you again, my dear."

Natalie almost cried with relief at the sound of his kind voice. "I need to talk to you."

"Follow me." Fred's friendly face turned serious. He led them through the crowd into the heart of the precinct. Natalie glanced to her right as they passed Daniel's unoccupied, messy desk.

"It's awfully busy here for so early in the morning," Natalie said.

"Always is. Besides, had a lot going on last night." Fred nudged a guy sitting in a chair, his head resting on the desk. "Wake up, buddy."

The handcuffed man raised his head.

"Oh my God!" Kaylee jumped toward him. "Jimmy! Are you okay?"

"What the hell are you doing here?" he asked, his voice hoarse. His expression went from confusion to realization in slow motion as he recognized Natalie and the backpack in her arms. His eyes bore into Kaylee's. "What have you done?"

Fred gave his chair a jolt. "Shut up, kid." He motioned to a uniformed officer who rushed over, lifted Jimmy by the forearm, and led him away.

"Natalie," Kaylee whispered. "What's going on? Why is Jimmy here?"

"My guess is he's in trouble," she said. "And I'm pretty sure it has everything to do with what's in this backpack."

Fred opened the door to a small room with a square metal table and four chairs. "Ladies, have a seat." His voice was gentle but serious. "I'll be right back."

As soon as they were alone, Natalie whispered to Kaylee. "Listen, I know you're counting on me, but I am not versed in criminal law. All I know is what I've seen on TV. And the TV lawyers would tell you to keep quiet."

Kaylee nodded in agreement.

"On the other hand, you haven't done anything wrong."

"Yes I did. I snuck into people's houses with Jimmy and took things, but I thought they were little things." She started hyperventilating again. "And now I've dragged you into this mess. I'm going to go to jail now. They're going to put me an orange jumpsuit and make me share a cell with drug dealers and murderers. And my mom will have to visit me behind the glass and bring me a cake on my birthday!"

Kaylee's hysteria took off, and Natalie tried to quiet her. There were cameras in two corners of the ceiling with small red lights that flashed on and off. "Shh, you need to stop talking."

She stopped talking but continued crying.

Natalie slouched in her chair. She rubbed Kaylee's back as

the teenager sobbed. The clock on the wall ticked. Almost ten. With her free hand, she texted Cece:

> Running late. Can't make the meeting with you and Maura. Fill you in later.

The door opened. Natalie lowered the backpack to the floor. She squeezed Kaylee's shoulder as Fred entered the room with another person, a woman in gray pants, white cotton shirt, and sturdy black shoes.

"I'm Captain Walker," she said, her tone even and cool. She glanced between Natalie and Kaylee. "You her mother?"

Natalie shook her head.

"Lawyer?"

It flattered her to be mistaken for an attorney. Although what lawyer would show up at a police station so unkempt?

"I'm a family friend," Natalie said, doing her best to use her authoritative dance instructor voice. "Kaylee called me for help."

"And you brought her here. Okay then." Captain Walker reminded Natalie of the hard-headed, sharp-witted TV show cops she admired. The imposing woman tossed her head in Fred's direction. "Sergeant White says he knows you. That you were here a few weeks ago regarding a missing person."

Fred gave Natalie a reassuring nod, as if to say *go ahead, respond to her.*

"Right. This is Kaylee," Natalie said, pointing at her. "She's not missing anymore."

"Well, that's good news." Captain Walker warmed up about one degree. "Let's get a few things straight. Nobody's under arrest, at least not yet. But Kaylee, it appears you are associated with one Jimmy Spencer. And he has been arrested. How do you know him?"

She might as well have asked Kaylee to open the encyclopedia of her life. Kaylee started talking, the words poured out faster than water released from a dam, starting with her move to Oakland and job at the restaurant and the fun, single life of the young and the reckless. Natalie thought she should stop her, but Kaylee spoke with earnestness and a most sincere desire to be truthful. When she got to the part about the backpack, Captain Walker interrupted.

"Where's the backpack now?"

Fred and the captain exchanged a look that Natalie couldn't read. Her trust wavered.

"Hold on." Natalie said, motioning to Kaylee to keep quiet. Of course they knew where the backpack was—Fred had seen her walk in with it. He saw how Jimmy reacted at the sight of it. "May I speak?"

"Go ahead." Captain Walker granted permission, annoyance in her tone.

"I, um, I think it might be in Kaylee's best interest to have a lawyer present."

"Do you now?" The captain showed no reaction other than the slightest smirk, although Natalie couldn't be sure.

"Yes, I do." Natalie sat taller. The stern police captain may be frustrated with her, but Natalie had every right to interfere. Or so she thought.

"Ms. Lurensky, your *friend* is an adult. You are not her representative."

"You're right, Captain Walker. I was dragged into this at zero-o'clock this morning. I don't want to be here. I'm missing work. I'm exhausted. And I'm completely ill-equipped to advise Kaylee. However, she has asked for my help." Natalie grew obstinate. She and Kaylee both were in possession of stolen property. Whether that was against the law or not, considering the way it was obtained, she had no idea. "And now that I've gotten myself entangled in this mess, I want a lawyer. Kaylee, do you want one too?"

"Um, I guess so."

"Say it."

"Say what?"

"Say: *I want to speak to a lawyer.*"

"Okay. I want to speak to a lawyer."

Natalie looked directly into the camera tucked up in the corner of the room. "I think we're done for now."

"I think we are." Captain Walker stood.

"Oh, one more thing," Natalie said. "Could I get a cup of coffee?"

CHAPTER 28

*D*aniel stood with crossed arms watching the video. When it got to the part where Natalie looked directly into the camera and said: *I think we're done for now,* his heart stuttered. He fell for her all over again. Damn, just when he thought he could move forward.

"You gonna go in there?" Fred asked.

Daniel turned toward the interrogation room where Natalie and Kaylee sat on the other side of the one-way glass. He could tell how concerned Natalie was, but she exuded confidence. It was in the way her head tilted toward Kaylee's, the way her hands rested on the table. Cops were versed in reading body language, and Daniel was better than most. "It's not my case," he said. "Walker would bust my balls if I stepped in."

Fred laughed. "That's never stopped you before. Besides, what's she gonna do? Fire you?"

"Too late for that, isn't it?" Daniel wandered away from the glass and into the break room for coffee. A fresh pot was brewing. He took off his Giants cap and scratched the back of his head, waiting for it to finish. A week ago, he'd run from Natalie and her boyfriend, or ex-boyfriend, like a kicked dog, certain he'd never see her again. Now here she was, only a few feet away in his house, so to speak. Would poking his head in the room be a bad idea? And what would he say?

Natalie, fancy meeting you here!

Natalie, what brings you into my neck of the woods?

Natalie, got yourself into a little mess, did ya?

The coffee pot beeped, and the last few drops dripped. Daniel filled a paper cup, hoping whoever made it had measured correctly. There was an art to making decent coffee, even at a police station.

"Well, Detective Garrett, how are you?"

He turned to see Walker standing by his shoulder. "Captain. Good morning."

"Do me a favor," she said, fingers flying over her cell phone.

"Sure."

"Someone in interrogation room two wants a cup of coffee." Walker didn't look away from her screen. "Can you deliver it? I got some calls to make."

She turned and left before he could answer. Daniel went to his desk, grabbed his one mug from the bottom drawer, then returned to the kitchen. He scrubbed it clean and rinsed repeatedly before filling it with hot, black coffee. Although he knew she drank it with a little cream, he wouldn't dare taint it with the powdered crap.

Carrying it with a folded paper towel underneath, he headed to interrogation room two, silently thanking Captain Walker for granting him this gift.

Slowly, he opened the door, hoping his professionalism hid his anxiety.

Natalie audibly gasped. "Daniel. Hi."

Kaylee Robertson blinked between them, her red-rimmed eyes confused.

"I heard you asked for coffee." Okay, not the best line, but not the worst either.

"Thank you." She accepted the mug, a slight smile formed. *"World's Best Uncle.* That's sweet."

"Lola gave it to me."

"I figured." She sipped. "Ooo, strong. Better than I'd hoped."

"It's not Nutmegs though, is it?" Daniel gripped the back of the chair across from her.

"Natalie," Kaylee whispered. "What's going on? Do you know him?"

Daniel had almost forgotten the teenager was there. He redirected the conversation, pushing away his fantasy of returning to Nutmegs. "Kaylee, I'm Detective Garrett. Ms. Lurensky and I are acquaintances. I, um, I had information to give her last week about, well, that's beside the point. Anyway, just bringing you coffee. I got to get—"

"Daniel, wait." Natalie stood. "May I speak to you in private?"

"Oh, well, yeah. We can step out for a minute."

Natalie leaned over Kaylee's shoulder. "I'll be right back. And don't worry, Cece is tracking down a lawyer for us. We need to be patient and stay calm."

Kaylee nodded. "Okay."

Daniel could tell how much faith the young girl had in Natalie, how she was depending on her. It didn't surprise him one bit. Natalie wore certainty like a charm on a necklace.

He opened the door and let her cross in front of him, imagining her pulling him into the janitorial closet and pressing him against the wall—brooms and mops and buckets falling around them. Instead, they lingered in the hallway by the door of the interrogation room. Loud conversation, bustling bodies, handcuffed suspects all around.

"I wanted to tell you how sorry I am about last week," Natalie said. "I had no idea my ex was going to show up. It was, well, terribly embarrassing."

Daniel didn't think she had any reason to be embarrassed. He was the one who hightailed it out of there. And the last thing

Daniel wanted at this point was to revisit the event. "Nothing for you to apologize for."

"Thanks." Natalie fiddled with a button on her oversized sweater. "Um, if I had known I was going to run into you, I would've dressed a little nicer."

Whoa. That was unexpected. He wanted to tell her she was beautiful in anything. A sexy red dress or old jeans and sneakers.

"But the last thing I thought when I got up this morning was that I'd be here in your police station again." Natalie wound her hair into a bun, exposing a smooth, creamy neck. "I'm already afraid I've messed this up."

"Messed what up?" Daniel asked, aching to nuzzle her neck and inhale the sweetness.

Natalie glanced through the glass at her young friend. "For starters, this whole thing with Kaylee. I mean, I don't know what the hell I'm doing. And now I've asked for a lawyer—" she laughed in a self-deprecating way. "I probably made a total fool of myself."

"Believe me, you didn't. And it was smart." Daniel lowered his voice. "I saw the video. A lawyer's a good idea."

"Thanks for saying that," she said, relief bringing some color back to her cheeks.

"And since you've requested one, nobody can ask you or her any more questions. So sit tight and wait." Daniel wished he could be more encouraging, but he had no idea what that back-pack contained—money or drugs or both, most likely.

Natalie moved a half-inch closer to him. Or had he imagined it?

"But also, I, well, I thought taking you with me to the wine tasting might've been—"

"I told you, no apology necessary."

Her emerald green eyes affixed to his. "I wasn't going to apologize. I wondered if—"

"Garrett!" Walker marched over like a drill sergeant. "I told you to deliver coffee. What the hell are you doing?"

"Nothing, Captain, just a…" he stopped and flipped a switch, trying to clear his brain of what Natalie was about to say. She was hoping they could—what?

Walker, the most authoritative short person he'd ever met, stepped closer. "You may have given notice, Detective, but you still work here. No slacking off, you hear me?"

"Yes, Captain."

"As for you, Miss Lurensky, your lawyer is on the way."

"That's good. Thank you."

"Right." Captain Walker glanced through the one-way glass. "Now why don't you go back in there to where your young friend is chewing her nails to the point of drawing blood."

"Yes, ma'am, I mean Captain. I mean, um, never mind." Natalie backed her way back into the interrogation room.

Daniel started toward his desk.

"Garrett!" the captain stopped him. "A moment, please. In my office."

He followed her down the hall, certain she was about to read him the riot act for chatting in the hallway like a high schooler hanging out by some girl's locker.

She shut the door and sat at her gigantic, scratched up wooden desk. It was hard to tell how old the captain was, maybe fifty or so. There were a few photos on the credenza. In one of them she was smiling proudly at a young man in a graduation gown. Daniel didn't exactly like her, but he did respect her tremendously.

"Daniel," she said.

"Yes, Captain?" He'd never heard her say his first name before. It was weird.

"Regarding your departure date. It's in less than a month, right?"

"It is." Here it came. She was letting him go now. Firing him for fraternization with—with a woman in the hallway. Okay, that was no reason to fire him. Maybe it was all the pistachio shells he dropped on the floor.

"I need you to postpone it if you can." She softened her tone. "We're going to be a little shorthanded with Fred taking leave."

"Fred? What are you talking about?"

"Oh, shit." The captain shook her head and frowned. "Forget that part. I just need you to stick around a few extra weeks, maybe a month. Think about it, let me know."

Daniel stared at her, his mind a whirl with disconnections. The shock of Natalie showing up, Fred taking leave, and Captain Walker being nice? His mind shot in too many directions, like an explosion gone wrong.

"Any questions, Detective?"

"Um," his jaw hung. "No, I don't think so."

"Very well. You're dismissed."

Daniel raced to find Fred. He wasn't at his desk or in the break room or any of the interrogation rooms. He texted with frantic fingers. *We need to talk!*

CHAPTER 29

aylee's head popped up when Natalie returned to the room. She hid her fingers in her lap. "What did he say? Did you tell him what was in the backpack?"

"I didn't tell him anything, Kaylee." Natalie sat and rubbed her back. "Don't worry. Our lawyer is on the way."

"We have one? Who is it? What am I supposed to say to him?"

Natalie rubbed her palms together. "I don't know who the lawyer is, probably someone from Cece's husband's office."

What attorney would have time to dash over on such short notice? Probably some child fresh out of law school. "Let's go slowly. I won't let you say anything you're not supposed to say."

Natalie's confidence in her ability to know what one should say to one's lawyer was about a two out of ten. She prayed the lawyer, whoever it was, would have at least some experience.

Ten minutes later, the door flew open. A commanding woman with a chic pixy haircut wearing a cherry red pantsuit, blew into the room. "Good morning!"

"Elaine?" Natalie jumped, and her knee hit the table leg. "Ouch. You're the lawyer?"

Elaine Cooper, the most scatterbrained but brilliant person Natalie knew, grinned.

"Lucky for you, I happened to be available when the text-tree beckoned: *Lawyer needed asap – call Cece!* Well, I thought, most divorces aren't that urgent so it had to be something much more interesting. And lo and behold, it is." She looked over her shoulder at the cameras in the corner, then yanked open the door. "Hey! These cameras and recording devices had better be off!" A pause, then she shouted down the hall. "Okie-dokie, thank you."

Kaylee scooched as close to Natalie as she could. Despite the length of time they hadn't seen each other until this morning, she had glommed onto Natalie with desperation.

The pillar in red fabric dropped her brief case on the floor, planted herself in the chair across from them, and reached for Kaylee's hand. "I'm gonna take good care of you, honey."

Kaylee's lower jaw trembled. "I don't have any money. And my mother is poor."

"Pro-bono, dear. That means it's free."

Natalie cleared her throat, still in shock to see Elaine and not some underling from Brad's office. "But you're a divorce lawyer."

Elaine wagged a finger. "I'm a *family law attorney*. Sounds much better. But I started out in criminal defense. And since I made my fortune with divorces and never-ending fights over houses and boats and portfolios worth millions, I have returned to my true passion. I now spend most of my time representing the down and out. And Kaylee, you appear to be somewhat down and out, not to mention landing in a situation through no fault of your own. Would you say that's right?"

"I guess." Kaylee glanced at Natalie as if to get her permission to speak.

Natalie gave her a nod and then relaxed. Elaine was the perfect choice. She could take over.

"Alright then. Tell me what happened. Start at the beginning. Leave nothing out."

The family law/criminal defense lawyer listened with keen interest as Kaylee spilled her story in painstaking detail—names, dates, places. She talked non-stop for so long Natalie wondered if she'd ever finish. Finally, Kaylee caught her breath and took a sip of water. "And that's when I called Natalie. I didn't know what else to do."

"And Natalie brought you here to the police station." Her head twitched. "Interesting move."

Natalie balked. "Are you saying I shouldn't have?"

"Nope." Elaine tapped her fingertips together. "Okay, so, to sum it all up and make sure I understand your story," she paused, squinting in various directions as if synapses in her brain were clicking into place.

Natalie checked her watch. Almost noon. They'd been at the police station for hours now. Her stomach rumbled.

"I heard that." Elaine switched gears like race car speeding around a track. "You kids must be hungry. Sitting around here for hours without so much as a snack." She opened her gigantic satchel as if she were Mary Poppins. "Let's see, I have granola bars, packs of dried fruit and trail mix, and a few apples."

Elaine displayed her impressive array of healthy treats along with a stack of napkins.

Both Natalie and Kaylee ate a granola bar while Elaine summed up Kaylee's fifteen minute confession in fifteen seconds.

"You moved into an apartment, met a group of friends and started hanging out. Then you followed the pack, innocently enough, as they snuck into houses. A bit of fun and mischief, you thought. Fast forward to last night. One of your "friends" asks you to watch his backpack for an hour. He never returns. This morning you get curious, so you look inside and discover what appears to be stolen jewelry. So you call your former dance instructor, an old friend, for help. And here we are. Accurate enough?"

Natalie couldn't believe how succinctly the lawyer wrapped up the whole story in a tidy box.

"That's pretty much exact," Kaylee said. "Especially the part about sneaking into houses." She lowered her head. "I really thought it was, like, just us having fun, you know?"

"I do, honey. Believe it or not, Elaine Cooper was a teenager once upon a time. And I bent plenty of rules."

Natalie did not find it surprising that Elaine had been a wild child.

"Okie-dokie, let's let this cat out of the bag." She snapped a pair of latex gloves on her hands. "Show me the backpack."

The moment they'd been waiting for. The big reveal. Natalie hoisted it onto the table.

"Oops, hold on a sec." Elaine bolted to the one-way glass and lowered the blinds. "I don't want to show off our evidence before we're ready."

Kaylee glanced between the two women who were her protectors. Her jaw quivered as she placed the backpack on the table. "I'm nervous."

"It's gonna be fine, Kaylee. I promise." Natalie had no idea if she could make such a promise and regretted adding it. Thankfully, Elaine confirmed the platitude.

"Of course it's gonna be fine. You've got the best lawyer in town, lucky girl. Well, one of the best. There's a guy in the city. Hands down, if I ever committed a crime, he'd be my first call." Elaine pulled a white towel out of her giant Mary Poppins bag and spread it on the table.

"Why do you have a towel?" Natalie asked, wondering what else might be in that bag.

"It's part of my emergency supplies." She gave them a concerned look. "You should never be without an absorbent cloth in case you spill something or get a sudden bloody nose or heaven forbid have an embarrassing accident of some kind."

"I'll make note of that." Natalie offered a thin smile at the eccentric and somewhat nutty lawyer.

"Be sure you do. Both of you." With an air of expedience, Elaine reached for the backpack and opened it as wide as it would go. She released a long, low whistle. "Boy oh boy, now we're talking." With her gloved hands, she removed the contents and placed everything on the towel. Watches, bracelets, jewel encrusted rings, chains, charms, brooches, strands of pearls, and more watches. Natalie spotted a few Rolexes and a Cartier covered in diamonds.

"Do you think all this is real?" Natalie asked.

Elaine pulled an old fashioned magnifying glass out of her bag of tricks. Like Sherlock Holmes, she studied the underside of the band on one of the gold watches. "It certainly appears to be."

Then, in one brisk move, she folded the towel up with the loot inside and returned it to the backpack. "All good. I'll have you two out of here in no time."

CHAPTER 30

From the moment Elaine opened the door and hollered for the captain to come back, everything progressed at lightning speed and with mind-blowing efficiency. The clever lawyer had been given an indecipherable recipe, whipped up the ingredients, and turned out a perfect cake.

Captain Walker thanked Natalie for bringing Kaylee to the station, then Kaylee for turning in the stolen jewels. She said the evidence would likely help them solve a series of burglaries. Not to mention, the theft victims would be ecstatic to have their valuables and heirlooms returned.

Elaine, who towered over the captain, stood straight as a rail, as if she were the one in charge. "We need an escort to the apartment building where Kaylee's been staying. She's going to pack up her stuff and go home to her mother's house."

"I'll arrange it," Captain Walker said. "The DA will contact you about next steps."

"Okie-dokie, good plan!" Elaine's gaiety seemed out of place under the serious circumstances, but her buoyancy gave Natalie hope that Kaylee's troubles would soon end.

"Garrett!" Captain Walker called as they exited the room.

Natalie's chest did an annoying flip.

"Here, Captain," he said, jumping from his chair.

"Our witness and her lawyer," the captain eyed Natalie, "and her friend need an escort to the complex where we think the gang of thieves has been hanging out."

Natalie took note of how Captain Walker referred to her as a *friend*, as if she were doubtful of the connection.

"Kaylee needs to gather her stuff and get out of there asap. We should have our search warrant in a couple of hours."

All the talk about search warrants, witnesses, and police escorts made Natalie feel as if she were in an episode of *Law and Order*. It was a little bit thrilling. And soon she'd be back in Clearwater delivering Kaylee to her mother. What a day.

Elaine took Kaylee in her car, so Natalie drove alone, keeping an eye on the rearview mirror where Daniel trailed her in his truck. Her mind danced in a million directions. Would she get back in time to teach her afternoon classes? Would Kaylee have a criminal record? And what was she going to say to Daniel?

Once they arrived at the apartment complex, Elaine took charge of going with Kaylee into the apartment. If they bumped into anyone, the lawyer could claim to be her mother.

Natalie waited in her car.

Daniel lingered by the gate, looking like an ordinary guy hanging out in jeans, sneakers, and backwards baseball cap. Nobody could tell he had a serious weapon under his sweat jacket.

As the minutes ticked, Natalie grew anxious. Daniel leaned against the wall, texting or perhaps pretending to text. He glanced up at her every now and then, a little lift of his head in acknowledgement.

Finally, she couldn't stand it anymore. Natalie got out of her car and approached him with trepidation, as if waiting for him to wave her back. But his expression was open, curious.

"I hope it's okay if get out of my car. I'm a little antsy."

Daniel glanced around. "Sure. It's fine."

Natalie rubbed her clammy hands together. Her feet grew sticky in leather flats. "It's taking them a while, isn't it?"

"Only been six minutes. Don't worry."

"Huh, it feels longer." Natalie had lost her train of thought. Any minute now, she'd lose her opportunity to speak with Daniel alone. He was the first man to spark her interest in ages. She straightened up to her best ballerina posture. "I wonder, detective, if we might see each other again, socially. Get to know each other a little better."

Daniel's eyebrows rose so high they practically disappeared.

Natalie didn't know what to make of his reaction—shock, which could be good or could be bad. It was hard to tell.

"Unless it's not appropriate for some reason, being that you're a detective and I'm a—a, hmm, not sure, a friend of a material witness in an ongoing investigation?"

Daniel stifled a laugh. "Spoken like someone who knows her crime shows."

"Oh, I do. I definitely do." Natalie glanced toward the courtyard to see Kaylee and Elaine coming down the stairs. Only seconds left before the conversation was cut short and they'd have to part ways. "Listen, if you don't want to, or if we shouldn't—"

"I do want to. I mean I would, but I don't want to start something I can't finish."

"I'm not sure what that means," Natalie said. She could tell he was attracted to her, that they'd formed a connection.

A regretful smile darkened his face. "It's about me making a change, quitting my job. I have this plan to—"

The gate squealed on its hinges as Elaine ushered Kaylee, with a deer-in-the-headlights expression, out of the courtyard.

"Okie-dokie. Let's get out of here." The lawyer handed Natalie one of the duffle bags. "You're in charge of her until I know the next step. Kaylee, do not under any circumstances come back here or speak to anyone from this unfortunate misstep in your life. These people are not your friends. They are criminals. And get yourself off every social media app under the sun. You are going underground for a while. If you want me to handle your case and see you through this, you must follow my instructions to a 'T.' Understand?"

"I understand," Kaylee said, her voice quivery. "Thank you."

"Don't thank me, it's my job. Thank your friend Natalie here. She's the one who really got you out of this sticky-wicket."

Natalie hardly thought she deserved any credit. After all, wasn't it just common sense?

"She's good." Daniel gestured toward Elaine. "I'm putting you in my Rolodex in case I ever need a lawyer."

"You should, although I hope you never need me." She removed a business card from her blazer pocket and handed it to Daniel. "Detective, nice to meet you. If possible, please keep me informed on the results of your search warrant."

"I'll do my best."

"Let's wrap this up. Kaylee, I will be in touch. Go get in Natalie's car."

The teenager's relief was palpable. She practically ran from them, jumping into the car as if zombies were chasing her.

"I need a private moment with Natalie," Elaine told Daniel.

"Fine, but be quick. I can't leave until you do." He walked away, texting as he went.

"Two things, Natalie."

"Okay," she said, hoping Elaine would tell her that once she got Kaylee home her responsibility would be over.

"You have to stay involved. Well, technically you don't have to, but I'd like you to. Kaylee is going to need support, and from what I gather, her mother is ill-equipped to deal with something this serious."

"That's not what I was hoping you'd say." Natalie balked. "I have a lot on my plate. You know—so many things I've neglected these past months. I'm kind of overwhelmed."

"I understand." The stalwart pillar of strength put her hands on Natalie's shoulders. "But I'll guide you. None of this is going away quickly. And I'm not sure yet how it will unfold."

Natalie sighed and groaned. "Alright, I'll do what I can. What's the second thing?"

"Second thing?" Elaine cocked her head. "Oh, right, the second thing is that sexy detective over there. He likes you, and you like him."

"How do you know that?" Natalie began to think her wacky lawyer friend was psychic.

"Oh, please, a divorce lawyer reads relationships like a first grade primer. I can tell the minute a husband and wife walk into the room if there's any chemistry left between them, any hope of reconciliation. It's kind of a gift. Any-hoo, he's adorable, and I can smell the attraction. Thought I'd let you know."

Elaine's shoes clicked on the sidewalk like a stop watch as she marched to her car.

CHAPTER 31

hey drove in silence. Once again, Natalie's mind flipped and flopped in all directions. What would she say to Kaylee's mother? What did Daniel mean by starting something he couldn't finish? All the distractions and over-thinking set her on edge.

At a red light, Natalie turned to Kaylee. "I always feel better about things when I make a plan. So do you want to talk about a plan for telling your mom what's happened?"

"I'm not sure." Kaylee chewed her nails. "But I'm sorry I dragged you into my problems."

Natalie had lost her patience with apologies. "Let me tell you something," she said as she merged onto the freeway. "A true apology means making a change. Correct your mistakes. You put your mother through hell, and you need to fix that. So, if you want forgiveness, from me or your mom, you'd better follow Elaine's instructions. Make a smarter plan for what you're going to do moving forward. Got that?"

Kaylee's soft whimpers made Natalie feel as if she'd spoken too harshly.

"Don't worry," she said, softening her tone. "I'm not going to leave you at the doorstep. If you want me to help you explain things, I will. And I'll help you move on from this. You're only nineteen, and thank God everything at this point is fixable. It won't be easy, but as long as you make a plan and stick to it, your life is still full of possibilities."

Possibilities, dreams, roads that lead to something new and different and exciting. It was not too late.

"Do you really think so, Natalie? You think I can start over?"

Natalie stared at the long stretch of highway in front of her. "I do, honey. I absolutely do."

~

THE CONVERSATION with Holly Robertson went better than expected. Kaylee poured out her story in fits and starts and round-about explanations. Holly took it all in with extraordinary patience, asking a few questions but mostly listening.

Natalie could hardly believe that Holly, who was her same age, had so many burdens. Ever since she and her husband split up, she lived in a tiny, rundown apartment, struggling to make ends meet. By comparison, Natalie's life was a piece of cake.

After Kaylee admitted and revealed every detail, including how her arm was injured and her eye bruised, Holly broke down.

"God knows I've made my share of mistakes," she said, wiping her tears with the back of her hand. "So the last thing you'll get from me is a lecture, at least for now. Natalie, I can't thank you enough for bringing Kaylee home to me."

"You're welcome." Natalie stood.

Holly touched her daughter's cheek. "Kaylee, give me and Natalie a minute. Why don't you take a shower and change? Then we'll go to the clinic to get your arm checked out."

"Okay." Kaylee pressed herself against Natalie with such

force it almost knocked her over. "I can't believe you saved me again."

Natalie held the teenager tightly. *Again?* What did that mean? "I'll be in touch, honey. I promise."

Kaylee nodded and smiled. Natalie had forgotten how bright and engaging her smile was. She had been such a special girl.

Once Kaylee closed the door to the bedroom she shared with her little brothers, Holly walked Natalie outside into a sunny afternoon. "I'm sorry," she said, grabbing Natalie's hand.

"It's okay, Holly. I'm just glad we got this—"

"No, it's not only about this. I've been a terrible person. A terrible mother. You tried to be my friend, and I rejected you."

"I'm not sure what you're talking about," Natalie said, backing up. It was starting to get weird. And when did she try to be Holly's friend? So many dance moms were in her life, some of them friendly and helpful, some nasty and controlling, some distant and uninvolved.

"You don't remember?"

Natalie racked her brain for some memory of an interaction or argument.

Holly squeezed her eyes shut. "Well, I wish I hadn't brought it up then. I'm ashamed of what I said, what I did. You were only trying to help Kaylee—and me."

The recollection struck like a splash of ice water. "Oh my God. I was right, wasn't I?"

Holly's face flushed. "You were. My husband was abusive. And I denied it."

"And I called Child Protective Services." Natalie leaned on the porch banister, her legs weak. It had been years ago, around the time Ilana had started losing her memory and Natalie's world was shattering. Kaylee, only eleven or twelve at the time, came to her with a secret.

My step-father is mean. He hurts my mother. I'm scared of him.

When Holly denied it, Natalie had no choice. It was her

responsibility to protect her student. She regretted none of it. And then it was over. Natalie's own problems consumed her, Holly divorced her husband, and Kaylee seemed fine after that. Fine, until now.

Natalie let out a huge, loud breath, almost a groan. Why did everything have to be so hard? "I really don't know what to say. Except that we need to move on. You don't need to apologize. And Kaylee is an adult now. If she wants my support, she'll have it."

"I appreciate that," Holly said, her shoulders folding forward. "Kaylee has always adored you."

"And I've always adored her. I'm glad to be back in her life, although under regrettable circumstances." Natalie stepped down one step. "Let me know what's up with her arm. I hope it's not serious."

Holly nodded, her gaze vulnerable and defeated.

CHAPTER 32

The studio was in mayhem when Natalie arrived.

Her beginning ballet class had been combined with the intermediate. One of their more experienced instructors was teaching it with a new assistant—a young woman whose name Natalie couldn't even recall. The main studio looked like a painter's palette with thirty tutus spinning around like colored pinwheels.

At the doorway to the smaller studio, Natalie watched Cece teaching the advanced class. When she caught Cece's eye, she motioned to her with one finger.

"Okay, dancers," Cece said, turning off Tchaikovsky, "let's take a break. You've got five minutes."

The ballerinas scurried down the back hallway toward the bathroom.

"Where have you been?" Cece's hair was askew, and she had mascara under her eyes. "At the risk of sounding like your mother, *being tardy to class is unacceptable.*" She tapped the top of her wrist.

"Didn't you get my voicemail?" Natalie sat and put on her ballet slippers.

"No."

"I left you a message hours ago."

Cece scrolled her phone. "No voicemail."

"Things got crazy," Natalie said. "I'm sorry."

"Forget it. And I'm dying to know what happened with Kaylee." Cece retied her messy, curly ponytail. "But Nat, we need another fulltime instructor, especially if you're going to be preoccupied with other—other stuff."

Natalie bristled at her friend's sharp tone. She and Cece were the best colleagues, they agreed on almost everything. And when they didn't, they worked it out. But her friend had carried the heaviest part of the load for more than six months.

"You're right. And with all the extra work that's fallen on you, I'll figure out a way to give you a raise, okay?"

Cece's blue eyes widened. "Are you serious? This is not about money!"

Natalie knew it wasn't about money; it was about her—the distractions and excuses and disinterest. And now she'd offended her oldest friend, the person who had been by her side for over seven years now. Without Cece, the Lurensky Academy would've shut its doors long ago.

"Do you want me to take over the class?" Natalie offered. "It's already after four. You can go pick up Noah early. Spend time with that gorgeous little boy of yours." Natalie hoped she sounded magnanimous and not desperate.

"No. I'll stay," Cece said. "You should pull the beginners out of the intermediate class. It's a circus in there."

The advanced dancers filed back in from their break. They greeted Natalie with respect, a kind of reverence, the way students had always treated Ilana. There were six of them today —five girls and one boy. Natalie moved around them with an authority she didn't feel.

"Sounds good," she said to Cece as if they'd been in a friendly discussion. Then she turned to the students. "Remember, the summer show is only a few months away. And I'm hopeful several of you will be ready to dance the primary roles."

"Yes, Miss Natalie," a few of them said, including Ashley Clark. Natalie had forgotten she was coming to Clearwater twice a week to work with Cece.

Natalie turned on her confidence with a smile and strong back, hiding the fact she was mortified by what she'd said to Cece about giving her a raise.

"Let's meet after class," she said to her colleague. "We'll go through the applicants for the open instructor position."

Cece nodded in agreement.

Natalie left the room, hopeful she would find the right words to make up with Cece. If she didn't set her priorities straight, she'd lose everything. Her business would suffer, her friendship with Cece would be irreparably damaged, and her mother's legacy would fade like a disappearing rainbow.

THEY DIDN'T EXACTLY FIGHT, but it was unpleasant to say the least. Natalie owed Cece room enough to unload her frustration.

"...and it has nothing to do with what you pay me. You know I'm as devoted to this studio, this business, as you are." Cece paced around the office in circles. "But lately it's as if you don't even care."

Natalie lowered herself onto the loveseat and curled her legs underneath. "Can I tell you what terrifies me?"

"Of course you can." Cece sat beside her.

"I feel like I don't care about anything—it's as if I've gone numb, lost my ability to have any emotion at all."

"That's ridiculous."

"It sounds ridiculous, but it's true." Natalie pulled a cushion onto her lap. "I miss my mother desperately, but I can't cry. I broke up with a boyfriend, and I could not care less. We've got a prima ballerina in the making at our school, and the sense of excitement I should feel bubbling in my chest isn't there. I don't know what's wrong with me."

For a moment Natalie thought she might be able to cry. This would be a good time for it, with Cece here to comfort her. But the urge passed and settled into the dull nothingness that had plagued her for what felt like forever. The only things that stirred any emotion in her now were the Kaylee situation and the mama dog with the puppies. And maybe Daniel Garrett.

Cece reached for Natalie's hands and held them tightly. "I'm no therapist, Nat, but if nothing in your life is inspiring or exciting or gives you a reason to wake up every morning, that's a problem."

Natalie eyed the ballerina photos on the wall, landing on the one of her at seventeen years old, the year she performed in Swan Lake. The Odile Variation, one of the most difficult and iconic solos of any ballet. She had been good but not even close to magnificent. The applause had bordered on polite with some enthusiasm sprinkled in. Not the response Natalie, or Ilana, had hoped for.

"Odile," Cece said, "Swan Lake. Look how gorgeous you were."

"Gorgeous, huh? An elaborate costume and tons of make-up, that's all it was. Beauty is meaningless, and it's certainly not what makes a ballerina shine." Natalie scooched back on the couch, freeing her hands. "I have a lot of thinking to do. This dance school is my life, and it has been since the day I was born. I need to take better care of it and of the people who work here. I'm sorry I let you down."

"You didn't let me down. Well, maybe you did today. But Natalie, you can be a business owner and still be something else. Look at Rebecca, she has like four jobs and ten hobbies. Tessa has the most demanding business in all of Clearwater, and she's always doing other stuff. Even our dear Patty has figured out how to do multiple things, sort of."

Natalie did not enjoy being compared to her friends. In that picture, she was always the odd woman out. "Easy for you to say, with your perfect life."

The cruel words popped out accidentally. Nobody's life was perfect, not even Cece's. And Natalie knew it. The hurt on her friend's face ripped into her.

"I'm sorry," Natalie said. "I didn't mean that."

"Doesn't matter." Cece rose from the sofa and held herself ramrod straight. "But just so you know, I was only trying to help."

"I didn't ask for your help." Natalie hadn't meant to snap at her, but snap she did.

"You may not have asked for it in words, but you sure as hell have needed it. I've been propping you up for months. And I'm not complaining, not at all. But this—" Cece drew a circle in the air in front of Natalie's face with one finger. "This is not working. Not for me, and definitely not for you."

Natalie was stunned. She'd never seen her friend so heated. Cece snatched her bag off the chair and stomped to the door.

"There's only so much I can do, Natalie. You need to figure out how to care again—about this studio, about all our students, and about me." Cece pointed at her. "Especially me."

Natalie shuddered when the door slammed. If there was one thing in the world she cared about, it was Cece. Her lifelong friend, in some ways her hero. She might not be able to fix much of anything at the moment, but repairing the damage she'd caused with Cece was not optional.

CHAPTER 33

*I*t wasn't until Monday that Daniel was able to corner Fred in the break room by the coffee maker. "I texted you all weekend. What the hell is going on? You're taking a leave of absence?"

Fred poured coffee into his chipped mug and stirred in a few shakes of powered creamer. "Minor surgery, that's all. Prostate. Now, you mind not asking me any more questions? The whole subject makes me queasy."

"I get it." Daniel had no desire to discuss his friend's prostate either. "And hey, whatever you need."

"Well, what did you tell the captain? Can you stay on a few extra weeks?"

"Absolutely."

"Good. Thanks," Fred said. "We work on most of the same cases, and there's no way I can get anyone else up to speed."

"Yeah, I'll stay as it long as it takes." Daniel clapped both of Fred's shoulders. The man had been his mentor and friend since he started at the precinct, a father figure. He'd do anything for him.

"I appreciate it, Danny. Just need to get this behind me. Sorry it puts your plans on hold."

"It's not like I've set an adventure kick-off date. Happens when it happens."

"You're a good friend." Fred leaned against the counter and sipped the hot coffee. "And please don't mention the details of my, uh, procedure to anyone. The fewer people who know the better."

Daniel turned his fingers in front of lips, locking them shut. "Won't say a word. And now I'll be here to see how the jewelry heists pan out. I heard they struck gold, literally, when they served the search warrant. People are coming in from all over town to claim their valuables."

"Hard to believe that sweet young girl got herself mixed up with a bunch of bad guys. And who brought us the break in the case? The beautiful Natalie Lurensky." Fred winked at him.

"What's that wink supposed to mean?" Daniel gave him a sidelong glance.

"Don't be an idiot, Danny-boy. I saw you with her in the hall the other day, trying to be subtle. Which you failed at miserably."

Daniel cringed at the idea that anyone would have noticed them. If Fred saw them, so did everyone.

"You oughta ask her out."

"Listen to this." Daniel leaned in close. "She sort of asked me out."

"What? Are you kidding? That's terrific. What'd you say?"

"Something idiotic. I said I didn't want to start something I couldn't finish." As he repeated the unfortunate words, they sounded even worse. The first woman to catch his eye in years, an incredible woman, suggested a date. And he turned her down?

"Why'd you say that? Are you out of your mind?" Fred

dumped his coffee in the sink and trudged toward his desk. "I'm gonna call her."

"You are not," Daniel said, rushing after him.

Fred spun around. "Then you will. Man, the things I gotta do for you. I'm going into surgery soon. And you need to ask that woman out before they put me under. On the off chance I don't wake up, I wanna rest in peace knowing you gave it your all. Y'hear me?"

Daniel turned his baseball cap around. "Yessir. I'll give it my best shot."

"Good man." Fred slapped the side of his arm and marched out.

Daniel groaned, returned to his desk, and opened a new bag of pistachios. How the hell could he back-peddle on his stupid excuse when it still was true?

He cracked open one pistachio after another reading through paperwork. His cell phone lay on his desk, taunting him. He grabbed it and scrolled for her number. Should he call or text? Oh, God, texting was such an immature, millennial fall back. He was a grown man. Calling a woman to ask her out was the proper, gentlemanly thing to do. Fred would approve. Besides, she probably was teaching a dance class and his call would go straight to voicemail. He quickly wrote out the message he'd leave her. *Hi Natalie, this is Daniel. I'd like to take you to dinner. Please give me a call. Thanks, bye.* A little stiff, but not awful. Direct and to the point. What's the worst that could happen? She shuts him down and says no thanks and then they both move on. He'd suffered worse.

He tapped dial before he could change his mind. And then the last thing he expected to happen, happened.

"Hello?"

"Natalie?"

"Detective?"

His brain went blank.

~

"IS EVERYTHING OKAY?" Natalie asked, suddenly worried. "Does this have something to do with Kaylee?"

"Oh, no. It's about the other day when we, uh, we were at the apartment complex."

Natalie stood in the hall by the bathrooms at the studio, waiting for a bunch of four-year-old girls to pee. Getting them back into their leotards and tutus would take forever.

"The apartment?" Natalie did not understand how that wasn't about Kaylee. "Do you have news?"

One little girl emerged, her tutu by her ankles and her pink leotard twisted around her waist. Natalie set her phone on a bench and tapped speaker. "Here, sweetie, let me help you pull that up."

"Excuse me?"

"Oh, sorry, not you," Natalie said. "I'm talking to one of my students."

"Sounds like I caught you at a bad time. Should I call later?"

"No, no, hold on a sec." Natalie waved over her assistant. She was anxious to know whatever he had to report, especially since Elaine hadn't returned her call yet. Plus, the details of the jewelry thefts still fascinated her.

"Help the girls with their leotards," she whispered. "I'll be right back."

Natalie scurried into the office with her phone. "Okay, sorry about that. So, what news do you have about the case?"

"It's not about that, although there is news. But that's not why I called." He coughed then cleared his throat. "To be honest, I didn't think you'd answer."

Finally, it dawned on Natalie why, perhaps, he was calling. Her suggestion that they see each other socially had caught him off guard the other day. And then he'd had such a strange response. Maybe he was reconsidering. She smiled inwardly. "Would you have left a message then?"

"Well, yeah. You want to hear it?"

"I do." Natalie grinned widely this time.

"Okay, here's the message. *'Hi Natalie, this is Daniel. I'd like to take you to dinner. Please give me a call. Thanks, bye.'*"

"That's it?" Natalie twirled a strand of hair, something she never did.

"That's it. This is actually saving us both time. Maybe. Unless you want to call me back, or text me, or tell me to—"

"I'd love to go to dinner with you."

"You would?"

"If I'm not mistaken, it was kind of my idea. So, yes, it's a date."

"A date, right. How's this Saturday?" he asked.

"Perfect. I'm looking forward to it already."

"Me, too. I'll pick you up at seven, okay?"

"You don't have to drive all the way out here. Why don't I meet you someplace that's—"

"If you don't mind, I'd like to pick you up. I'm kinda old-fashioned that way."

Natalie's insides turned to warm honey. "Then seven o'clock it is. I'll text you my address."

"Great. Um, thanks. Bye."

"Bye." Natalie's finger hovered over the end-call button. To her amusement, she overheard Daniel shout before the call ended. "Fred! She said yes!"

CHAPTER 34

*F*or the next few days, Natalie doubled down on work, staying focused and as motivated as possible. She hired a new instructor, one that Cece had flagged as the best candidate. She got a few estimates on repairs around the studio. And she checked in on Kaylee daily.

By the end of the week, the tension at the studio had dissipated. She and Cece had tip-toed around each other for a few days, but gradually, to Natalie's tremendous relief, they worked their way through it.

Friday afternoon, they picked up coffee from Nutmegs and strolled back to the studio through the park.

"Hey," Cece said. "I'm sorry about the other day. I really overreacted."

"Don't be sorry. You were absolutely right. I've been disconnected for months. I'm trying to fix that."

"I can tell," Cece said. "But I should've been a little less hard on you. Noah's going through a fussy stage, Brad is overwhelmed with a case—everybody has something going on, you know?"

"I do. And I'm sorry, too. Super sorry." Natalie faced her friend. "Nobody's life is perfect. I know that."

"I know you do," Cece said. "And apology accepted."

There were dozens of people strolling through the park, sitting under trees, tossing bread to the ducks. All of them had ups and downs, worries, challenges, maybe even crises. They passed the gazebo and turned toward the studio.

"I do have a bit of interesting news," Natalie said, a slight skip in her step.

"Yeah? What?"

"The detective is taking me to dinner tomorrow night."

Cece halted "Seriously?"

Natalie lifted her shoulders to her ears. "Seriously. I thought he wasn't interested in me. Then I thought he was, then not. Then out of the blue, after we kind of rescued Kaylee together, he called."

"That is so exciting!" Cece skipped around her as if they were teenagers again. "Oh my God, I cannot wait to hear every detail. Where are you going? What's the plan?"

"Slow down," Natalie said as they crossed the street. "I don't know the plan, only that he's driving all the way out here to pick me up."

"I love a man who goes out of his way." Cece released a romantic sigh. "Remember how Brian always had you meet him the city."

"I do. His time was more valuable than mine. But it was my choice, too." Natalie gripped the railing on the steps up to the studio's main door. "It's empowering to accept that I made my own decisions, whether I regret them or not. Every one of them, as far back as I can remember."

"Wow. Profound thought there, Miss Natalie."

They walked into the studio. "Just common sense, Miss Cece. And the truth."

NATALIE WATCHED Cece and the instructor from Maura's studio work with Ashley on the specifics of her solo for the upcoming recital. She tried to ignore the butterflies in her stomach, which fluttered every few minutes. In a matter of hours, she'd be going out on a real date for the first time in months, and with a man she really liked.

"Natalie, what do you think?" Cece asked.

Oh-oh, her mind had wandered into another realm. She took a stab at it. "Um, actually, it's good. Ashley, if you could set your shoulders back a tiny bit more, that would—"

"Yes, right!" the instructor from Maura's studio blindly agreed. While Maura revered Cece, her associate, who had idolized Ilana, now worshipped Natalie.

Cece restarted the music, and Ashley danced Sleeping Beauty's *Aurora's solo* again. For a few minutes, the enchantment of the music and Ashley's magnificent interpretation of her part pulled at Natalie's heart. *Mamma would have loved this.*

After rehearsal, which went remarkably well, Natalie ducked into her office. Her cell, which she'd purposely left on her desk, pinged at her with a text from Daniel.

> Hey there, confirming our plan for tonight. Pick
> you up at seven. BTW, casual works.

The butterfly flutters returned.

At six-thirty, Natalie was still deciding what to wear. Chastising herself for being ridiculous, she settled on dark jeans, suede ankle boots, and a flowery, low-cut peasant blouse.

When Daniel knocked at one minute after seven, she was ready.

"Hi," he said. "You look great."

"So do you," she said.

"Thanks." He wore jeans and a button down shirt with the sleeves rolled up to his elbows.

"Would you like to come in?" Natalie asked. She'd cleaned the kitchen, vacuumed, and plumped every cushion and pillow several times.

"Uh, actually," Daniel said, gesturing toward his truck. "We should go. I made a reservation."

"Okay, then." Natalie slung a small cross-body bag over her shoulder. "Let's go."

Daniel opened the passenger door. She hoisted herself up into the seat, noting the fresh, lemony scent.

"I went to the car wash earlier," Daniel said as he got in on the other side. "And they hung this lemon thing on the mirror." He removed it and tossed it over his shoulder into the back seat.

"It appears they vacuumed up all the pistachio shells," Natalie said.

"Oh, they did, thousands of them." Daniel winked at her. "You do like pistachios, don't you?"

"Of course. Doesn't everyone?"

"I have a big bag of them if you want some."

Natalie laughed. "Maybe later."

Their repartee continued as they drove out of Clearwater and onto the main highway toward Oakland.

"I really hope you didn't come all this way only to drive back to Oakland."

"No ma'am." Daniel exited the freeway and headed North into the hills. "We're not going anywhere near where I live. We are going to a place you've never been before."

Natalie pulled on her seatbelt and turned slightly. "How do you know where I've been? I've lived here my whole life and been to a lot of places."

"I kind of doubt you've been to this one. But if you have, I hope you loved it enough to go again."

Natalie settled into her seat, fully intrigued.

The drive was pleasant, better than pleasant. They caught up on Kaylee and the substantial progress made on the case. Daniel said it was all moving quickly, thanks to the backpack full of jewels as well as Natalie's management of the primary witness.

"That's quite the lawyer you found for Kaylee. I asked around about Elaine Cooper, and wow, she's the real deal."

Natalie laughed. "She certainly is. Nutty as can be, but brilliant."

"That's the way I like my lawyers," Daniel said.

"Me, too," Natalie teased. "Look at us, same taste in lawyers. That's got to mean something."

"I hope so," he said.

They turned up a country road with no homes or businesses or structures of any kind. Like the middle of a forest.

"I have no idea where we are," she said.

"Don't be nervous. You're perfectly safe."

"I'm not nervous. Not really."

Daniel made a sharp turn into a parking lot full of trucks and motorcycles. "Now, don't jump to any conclusions."

Natalie leaned forward as a huge barn like structure came into view. "Hmm, a biker hangout. I like it."

Daniel leapt out of the truck and came around to her door. She accepted his hand and landed on both feet.

"Believe it or not, the food here is excellent. And the music's pretty good, too."

Inside the converted barn, strings of white lights hung across the ceiling. They sat at a roughhewn round table in the midst of noisy conversation and upbeat background music.

"How on earth did you ever find this place?" Natalie asked.

"We busted the owner a few years back for money laundering. The assistant manager, who testified against his old boss, was a real go-getter. Soon as the place went into foreclosure, he bought it from the bank, fixed it up, and reopened a year ago. Been one of my favorite hang-outs ever since."

"I can see why," Natalie said, already thinking she should bring her friends here.

The hamburgers were the best ever, the beer smooth and icy cold, the conversation easy and light.

"This is so delicious," Natalie said, her mouth full. "I never eat like this. It's such a treat."

Daniel grinned as he dipped a French fry into barbecue sauce. "Thanks for going out with me."

Natalie licked ketchup from her thumb. "Thanks for asking me," she said, lowering her chin and searching his eyes. "But what changed your mind?"

Daniel ate another fry. "My mind about what?"

"Going out with me."

He rubbed his clean shaven cheek, and Natalie wondered again about the scar.

"Fred."

"Fred?"

"Yep, Fred. He saw us talking in the hallway, said I was an idiot, and then kind of threatened me." Daniel balled up his paper napkin. "Plus, my situation has changed a little since the last time I saw you. I'm staying on the job a while longer."

Natalie dusted invisible crumbs off the surface of the table. "What does that mean, exactly?"

"A month, maybe more. The captain has to, uh, shuffle some things around, and she asked me to be flexible. Which I can be. I've been trying to figure things out for a while. Another month or two of figuring won't matter."

"I get that. I'm figuring things out myself." Natalie sensed they were headed into a more serious conversation. Half of her wanted to deflect it. The other half wanted to dive right in. She reached out and touched his cheek with her palm. His skin was smooth and warm. "Where'd you get this?"

He leaned into her hand as if it held some kind of magic.

"First year on the job. A suspect pulled a knife. I was too close. Fred shot him."

Natalie sat back. "That's quite a story."

"Yeah, it was a bloody mess. Sixteen stitches. Fred got the guy in the shoulder, so he's fine. Still in prison though."

"A good outcome. I like that. My mom's favorite show was *Law and Order*, so I have a firm sense of what justice looks like."

"You know," Daniel said, the corners of his mouth rising, "it's just a TV show. Cases usually aren't solved so neatly. And the wheels of justice turn a whole lot slower than you'd think."

"Yes, but it's human nature to want stories to wrap up. People don't like to be left hanging—in fiction or in life."

Daniel took a pause. "You are right about that."

The server came by and cleared their plates.

"Can we get two more beers, please," Daniel said. "Oh, sorry, I didn't mean to presume. Would you like another beer?"

"Actually," Natalie glanced at the table next to them. "I'd love one of those hot fudge sundaes."

"Yeah? Great idea." Daniel showed the enthusiasm of a kid. He looked at the server. "The biggest one you make and two spoons."

The ice cream set the mood for fun. Natalie couldn't remember ever enjoying a date this much. They chattered about ice cream and their favorite childhood treats before Natalie circled back to the more serious topic.

"What is it you're trying to figure out?" she asked him, scraping a drip of fudge off the side the dish. "I mean, are you starting over in some way?"

Daniel shifted in his seat. "That's the plan."

Natalie leaned on her elbows. She spoke in a soft, even tone. "Remember the first time we met? The day I drove you to your sister's house?"

"How could I forget?"

"Lola said something, or asked me, actually, that was both adorable and intriguing."

"Oh, God. That little girl never knows when to stop talking. Go ahead, tell me," he said with a grimace.

Natalie thought twice. If Daniel was offended or embarrassed, it could put a real damper on the night. On the other hand, she was really starting to like him. She needed to know what baggage there might be. "She asked if I was the woman who would heal her Uncle Danny's broken heart."

Daniel burst out laughing. "Oh, that's my Lola. There's nothing that gets past her. It's my sister's fault. She talks way too much, and Lola hears everything."

"I'm glad you're laughing," Natalie admitted. "I thought it was sweet, that she's concerned about you, I hope it's not too personal a question."

"You didn't ask me a question." Daniel turned serious. "But feel free, if you want."

Natalie swallowed. "Do you have a broken heart?"

He leaned back and hooked an arm over the back of his chair. "Not anymore."

Natalie raised her eyebrows expectantly.

"I had a long relationship that crashed and burned. It was, well, unexpected. So, my sister and my niece think I'm still struggling to get over it. But believe me, I'm over it. Probably dodged a bullet—so I'm good."

"Okay, then."

"Now my turn," Daniel said. "Are you and that Steel guy done? Or is he still trying to win you back?"

Natalie leaned in. "Yes, and yes."

"Interesting," Daniel said, his eyebrows sinking. "But fair enough. There's no way I can compete with him."

A competition, how romantic. The flutters roared back. "Are you saying you wish to win my affections?"

Daniel snickered. "Perhaps."

"Tell you what," Natalie said, needing to get a grasp of where they were going. "Let's see where this leads us. I'm still getting back on my feet since my mom passed away. I let too many things slip by the wayside, so that's my focus. And you, well, sounds like you might be moving on soon."

It was a statement and question.

"Yeah, maybe." Daniel gave her a sorry smile. "I guess we're both in limbo, at least for a while. So, you're right—let's see where this goes. I can tell you one thing for sure though."

"What's that?" Natalie asked, enjoying their banter more and more.

He pointed toward the front of the dining room. "Live music is about start."

Natalie turned to see a four piece band setting up on a small stage. "That'll be fun."

"Music," Daniel said, rising and taking her hand. "And dancing."

The band jumped right in with Luke Bryan's "That's My Kind of Night," so loud and rhythmic it made Natalie leap to her feet, her hand squeezing Daniel's.

"You did not mean to take a dancer dancing!" She laughed, her hips already moving.

"Didn't I?" Daniel backed up with her toward the dance floor, couples already moving in that direction. "When was the last time you danced just for fun?"

Natalie rested her hands on his shoulders and pulled him closer. "I have no idea."

"Well, let's see what you got." Daniel took the lead and held her close with one strong arm around her waist.

"You don't think you can really keep up with me," she twirled under his arm and did a quick two-step, "do you?"

"We'll find out."

CHAPTER 35

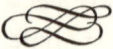

*K*eep up, he did. And then some. Dancing for fun was so out of her wheelhouse, Natalie hardly knew how to do it. But song after song, she danced with an abandon she'd never experienced. Pure, unadulterated delight. She perspired, her pulse pounded. She cast off her inhibitions and left them behind.

Another round of beer, more music—Daniel clearly was having as much fun as she was.

Two hours later, he opened the passenger door for her. Natalie's body still vibrated with the beat of the music blasting out the barn doors and into the crowded parking lot. She was about to put a foot on the running board to lift herself into the truck when the music changed, and one of her favorite songs, "My Eyes Adored You," cut through the voices and laughter. The lead singer sounded exactly like Frankie Valli.

Daniel tugged her away from the truck. "I love this song," he said.

"I do, too." Natalie lifted both arms over his shoulders as he leaned into her, his heart thumping against her chest. They swayed side to side. He sang softly, his lips so close to her ear that goosebumps rose on her skin. They danced in the moonlight, oblivious to everything. The volume increased, and the band's harmony wrapped around them as if they were sharing a blanket.

As the chorus swelled, Daniel slipped a hand up the back of her neck and into her hair. His eyes locked on hers, pupils large and black. Natalie moistened her lips, inviting his. He lowered his mouth onto hers, his lips soft and searching, as if unsure, waiting for her to respond. And she did, parting her lips as if to say *yes, please, more...*

AT EVERY STOP LIGHT, they made out like sixteen-year-olds. Natalie could barely catch her breath.

At her doorstep, under the porchlight, the kissing continued, deepening with an intensity she wished would never end.

"Where did" (more kissing) "you learn" (deeper kisses) "to dance like that?"

After one more swoony kiss, Daniel loosened his hold on her. He, too, was a bit out of breath. "Kevin Bacon."

"Kevin Bacon?"

"Yep. My sister was obsessed with 'Footloose.' We must've watched it a hundred times. Plus, I went to a lot of Bar Mitzvahs."

Natalie burst out laughing. "I love it. Kevin Bacon and Bar Mitzvahs. Perfect combo."

"It did the job," Daniel said. "I'm not only an excellent detective, I'm a damn good dancer. Not sure how those two skills complement each other though."

"I'm sure you'll figure it out," she said, tilting her head back for another kiss.

She wanted more, she wanted all of him. What was she waiting for? Why not throw caution to the wind, and let whatever was going to happen, happen? The house belonged to her alone now. It was her private sanctuary, and she could do whatever she wanted.

Then again, it was only a first date. And the practical side of her didn't want to give the wrong impression.

"If you're thinking of inviting me in," Daniel said, his arms still tight around her. "I'm afraid I have to say no."

"You're kidding, right?"

"Dead serious. Rule number one. I never sleep with a woman on a first date."

Natalie appreciated his rule. "Good to know, because I have no intention of inviting you in."

"Come on, you didn't even think about it? The way you danced with me told a different story."

Natalie's cheeks heated up, and she hoped he couldn't see her blush.

"For a cop, you are quite the dancer."

"For a ballerina, you have some racy moves." Daniel brushed her hair off her face. He placed one hand on the back of her neck and coaxed her into another luxurious kiss—slow and warm. His tongue wrapped around hers as if they were in a dance all their own. Good God. Whoever thought the straight-laced detective could kiss like this?

His lips trailed from her ear down her neck to the supple spot where neck meets shoulder, giving her a shiver. "When can I see you again? Please say soon."

"Soon," Natalie replied.

"How soon?"

"Very soon." She stepped back and checked the time. "Oh my God, look at that. It's almost midnight."

"Someone gonna turn into a pumpkin?"

"Go to your car."

"Are you sending me away?" Daniel asked.

"Go to your car," she said with playful insistence.

"As you wish."

He backed down the steps, holding the handrail, as if waiting for further instructions.

"Keep going," she said.

"Okay," Daniel said, sounding like a disappointed kid. He turned and walked reluctantly toward his truck. Natalie chuckled. She removed her cell from her bag and started texting.

> I had such a good time tonight.

Daniel jumped when his phone pinged. He faced her, barely ten feet away.

Natalie laughed. In the moonlight, she could see his broad smile as he texted back.

> I had a great time too and I'd love to take you out again

> May I ask you out?

> Of course

> Are you free Sunday?

> As in tomorrow?

> Yes, tomorrow, at say twelve-ten?

> Lunch?

> Not lunch, twelve-ten AM

Daniel's laughter reached through the darkness.

> That's in eleven minutes

> Time is of the essence

> I happen to be free – see you then

Natalie giggled, rushed into the house, and closed the door. She moved the curtain to the side and watched him jump into his truck and drive away. Natalie dashed to her room, threw open the closet, and grabbed a long red dress draped carelessly over a hanger. She brushed her teeth, freshened her make-up, and wound her hair into a loose bun with wispy tendrils framing her face. Then, a quick spritz of perfume.

Thanks to Tessa, her wine rack contained good wines. She selected a Cabernet and pulled the cork. The moment she had the cookies plated and two wine glasses on a tray, the doorbell rang.

∾

DANIEL WAITED for her to appear, convinced she was the most incredible woman on earth. Whoever would have thought up such a surprising and titillating second date? It made him rethink his entire life, as if every wrong turn and disappointment were part of a grand plan to bring him to this moment, this place.

The woman who opened the door made his heart stop. He sucked in a breath, holding onto the doorjamb for balance. The red dress. It was even more stunning and sexy in person. It pooled on the floor around her bare feet.

"Hello, Daniel," Natalie said as if meeting at midnight were an ordinary, everyday event. "Welcome to our second date."

He thrust a few wildflowers toward her. "I picked these from your neighbor's bush."

"They're lovely," she said with a flourish that beckoned. "Won't you come in?"

Daniel pulled himself together. He needed to regain at least some control, but Natalie Lurensky was in charge, and he loved it. He stepped over the threshold into her warm, cozy house. It took him a minute to get his bearings. His first of impression of her fell by the wayside. She had seemed like the kind of woman who would live in a high rise condo in the city with a view of the Golden Gate Bridge. But her home was simple, unpretentious, welcoming.

On the coffee table in front of a sofa, a few candles burned. She took him by the hand and led him into the kitchen

"Could you hold these?" Natalie handed him the flowers, filled a vase with water, and arranged his pathetic attempt at chivalry into a colorful display. "I love wildflowers, thank you."

Then she picked up a tray with a bottle of red wine and two stemmed glasses. Her soft smile nearly tore him to pieces. The woman he'd danced like crazy with only a few hours ago had become a gentle, alluring mystery.

"Are those cookies from my new favorite bakery?" he asked, nodding at the plate on the tray.

"They are."

He followed her into the living room. Natalie set the tray alongside the candles.

"May I pour the wine?" he asked as they sat.

"Please, do."

They clinked glasses. "To our second date," he said.

Although he was no expert when it came to wine, the taste and feel of whatever they were drinking was like nothing he'd had before.

"Do you like it?" Natalie asked. "It's one of my favorites."

"It's excellent." He took another sip.

"You can't live in Clearwater, or be friends with Tessa Mariano, without becoming an amateur expert on wines. May I show you how to really taste it?"

He would never in a million years say no to this woman. "Yes."

She broke a cookie into pieces. "These aren't ordinary chocolate chips. They're chunks of dark chocolate bark made by an order of monks in Oregon."

Daniel didn't care of it were true or not. He hung on her every word.

Natalie nibbled around the chocolate. He did the same. The cookie alone stirred his appetite—for chocolate and for her.

"Now, place the chocolate on your tongue and kind of massage it in your mouth. It'll melt slowly and smoothly. Don't rush it."

Oh, the innuendo. Did she have any idea what she was doing to him? He moved his legs to the side and adjusted his position.

"I might be messing up the order of how this is supposed to be done, but it's close enough." She laughed lightly and licked a tiny spot of chocolate from the corner of her mouth. "Okay, do what I do."

She swirled the wine in her glass, then held it close to her nose, but not too close. Daniel copied her every move. She inhaled deeply, and he did the same.

"Take a generous sip and hold it in your mouth." Her eyes fixed onto his, everything in tandem, each step simultaneous.

The wine filled his mouth, it reacted with the chocolate. The taste was earthy, a pleasant bitterness. Natalie's eyes closed and her lips pressed together as she combined the flavors. He watched her swallow. It was the sexiest thing he'd ever seen.

"You can swallow now," she said, looking slightly concerned.

Daniel had been so entranced, he'd nearly forgotten his mouth was full of wine. He swallowed hard, and did his best not to choke. "That was, um, incredible."

"It's a bit much. But I thought we'd give it a try. After all, on our *last* date—"

"You mean the one when we went dancing?"

"That's the one. You impressed me with a skill I never expected you to have."

"I got moves, don't I?"

"You do, indeed." Natalie curled her legs underneath her. "So

I wanted to impress you with my wine tasting skills. Although, in all honesty, I'm not that proficient."

"Then you fake it well." Daniel leaned closer and kissed her tenderly. He had no idea where the night would lead. Since it was their second date, he'd be willing. More than willing. But she was in charge, and he was man enough to have no problem with that.

The red dress clung to her body, a peak of cleavage inside a soft fold of fabric that gathered across her breasts. He ached to peel the dress off her body.

"I saw a photo of you in this dress." He touched the fabric where it draped around her bent knees.

"You did? Where?"

Time was of the essence. No games, no equivocation. He was falling for her more deeply with every passing minute. "Shortly after we met, I looked you up and found an article online. There was a photograph of you at a fancy show or something. You were with your fiancé."

Natalie lowered her chin. "Ah, the paparazzi, they followed me that night as if I were royalty."

"Photographers chase after you?"

"Not usually, no, but I'd gone to the ballet for a special event where they were honoring my mother. She was too frail to attend, so I stepped in for her. I was front and center for about two minutes. Don't know why they identified Brian as my fiancé. We were hardly even a couple at that point." Natalie paused with a slight smile. "Why were you looking for me online?"

"Curiosity, intrigue, attraction." Daniel hoped he didn't sound like a stalker. "But not in a weird way, I promise."

"I'm not concerned."

"So, he was never your fiancé?" Now he sounded jealous, which was the most unattractive emotion. "Not that it would matter, I mean, as long as—never mind."

"He was never my fiancé. And now he's barely a distant memory." Natalie took a sip of wine. "Okay if I ask a question?"

"Go right ahead."

"What's your plan?" she asked.

"For tonight?" he teased. "Thought I'd play it by ear, see where things go. Follow your lead."

She laughed. At least he'd amused her. "You know what I mean, Daniel. You told me you weren't going to be a detective much longer. That sounds like a big career change for someone so—so young."

"I'm not *that* young." He figured she was a year or two older at most. "But you're right, it's a big change."

How could he tell her he'd be going away just when they were getting started? When they were falling into lust and infatuation. When all he wanted was to be floating in her orbit.

"I'm taking some time off," he said honestly. "I'm not sure of my exact plan yet. But two years ago, after I was unceremoniously dumped, I decided I'd work a few more years then take a break and travel. I've been saving money, living cheap, eating at my sister's house. It's finally doable."

"Where are you going?" she asked.

"Somewhere, anywhere, everywhere? You know, embrace my free-spirit like the guys in 'Easy Rider.' Now's my chance to do it." Daniel sobered. In a few more years, he wanted to be established, to put down roots, maybe start a family.

The expression on Natalie's face puzzled him. Part joy, part sadness, part disbelief—he didn't know what to make of it.

"I think," she placed her hand on her chest. "I think that's the most wonderful, exhilarating idea in the world. Good for you. You must be so excited."

Natalie filled their glasses with more wine. She handed him his and took her own. "To adventure," she said. "To taking risks, exploring the unknown, and seizing opportunity."

They tapped their glasses and sipped the wine. It tasted even better as it aired, just like she became more intriguing and alluring with every word and touch. What did she mean by risks and unknowns and opportunities? Those words applied to every aspect of life.

There was so much to unpack when it came to Natalie Lurensky. He wanted to figure her out, to discover her secrets, her dreams, her life. The proverbial clock was ticking.

CHAPTER 36

*T*hree nights after her date with Daniel, Natalie and her best friends were gathered around the table in Tessa's cellar drinking wine and eating pizza.

She took a bite of her slice, pineapple with ham. Nobody except for Natalie ate pineapple pizza, so Tessa always ordered a small one just for her.

"No, we did not sleep together, Patty. But thank you for asking the question so bluntly."

"Everybody wanted to know," Patty said. "Not just me."

Rebecca's jaw dropped. "I didn't want to know. It's not my business."

"Well, I admit I was wondering," Tessa said, filling the wine glasses. "What about you, Cece?"

"I already knew. Natalie tells me everything." Cece winked at her. "Almost everything."

Natalie paused to decide how much to share with the group. "I will tell you that we had a wonderful time. He's a phenomenal dancer, which was quite unexpected."

"Did he kiss you?" Rebecca could hardly contain herself now. "I mean, if you don't mind my asking."

214

"He did." She wasn't about to go into minute detail about the way he kissed her or the depth in his eyes or how she'd longed to invite him into her bed. But before anything went that far, Natalie had pulled away. What was the point? His life was taking him in a new direction. It wouldn't be fair to either of them to start something they, as he had said, couldn't finish.

"How did you leave it then?" Cece asked "Are you going to see him again?"

"I don't know." Natalie ignored the emotion welling inside her. "He's about to take off on a long adventure of some kind. So, I'm not sure what will happen."

Eight eyes trained on her.

"Okay, what?" Natalie tried to decipher their reactions.

"I just want you to be happy," Rebecca said. "I want you to be in love."

"Forget about love!" Patty shouted at her. "A wild fling with a hot cop is exactly what you need. I'd spend every night with him from now until he leaves. You have any idea how much sex you could bank?"

Natalie practically spit out her wine.

"Patty!" Cece flicked her friend's arm. "That's not Natalie's style. She's much too sophisticated to be some guy's nightly booty call."

"Thank you," Natalie said, bolstered by her colleague's support.

"However," Cece continued, "I think you're making a mistake cutting it off this quickly."

Natalie turned to Tessa. "Do you have an opinion here? Because I'd really like to change the subject."

Tessa tapped her red nails on her wine glass. "I do. But you're not going to like it."

"That means I will," Patty said with excitement. "Let's hear it!"

"Go ahead, say what you must." Natalie prepared herself for more advice she'd undoubtedly choose to ignore.

"Very well. As the oldest and wisest in this group, I shall speak." Tessa straightened up, as if pleased with her authority. "Natalie, I've known you your whole life. I've known every man you ever dated. And every relationship you've had has been with a divorced, significantly older, emotionally distant man. True?"

Four heads turned toward Natalie.

"I guess." Natalie was not unsettled by Tessa's assessment. Her dating history was no secret. "So what?"

"So for the first time in your adult life, you're attracted to a new kind of man—not divorced, not only not older but actually *younger*, and, from what you've told us, the opposite of distant. Frankly, he sounds pretty perfect for you."

Natalie sat back. Tessa had her pegged. Daniel might be perfect for her, but she wasn't about to risk falling for a man who would not be sticking around.

"Do you really know how committed he is to this adventure?" Tessa asked.

"I would never in a million years suggest he change his plans. Never."

"What if he came to that decision on his own?" Cece asked.

Natalie's jaw clamped shut. The memory of the day she shoved her suitcase into the back of her closet flooded her mind.

"He won't." She cleared her throat. "Daniel is not going to set aside a dream on my account. It might sound romantic at first, but you all know infatuation doesn't last. Real life sets in, then the 'what if' questions, and then the regrets. That's how life works."

"Sounds like you've made up your mind," Tessa said.

"I guess I have." Natalie hadn't meant to disappoint her friends. And why they had to be so invested in her romantic life she didn't know. Except the weak explanation that they wanted her to be happy, to find love, to be fulfilled like they were. She finished her last bite of pizza. "Nonetheless, I thank you all for the therapy, and I gotta go. Rebecca, you need a ride home?"

"Oh, yes I do, I almost forgot." Rebecca said. "Goodnight everyone."

They exited the side door and headed to Natalie's car.

"That was a quick departure," Rebecca said. "Is it because everybody gave you advice?"

Natalie let out an exasperated breath. "Yes, partly, I'm tired of advice and of people telling me they want me to be happy. It's so trite."

"Fine, I won't say it anymore." Rebecca scurried after her. "But I know you're texting with him."

Natalie halted. "How do you know that?"

"You left your phone on the table when you went to the bathroom." Rebecca curled her hands under her chin like a little kid caught stealing cookies. "It vibrated, so I looked. I swear I didn't read the whole thread. Just, um, one or two texts. Maybe three—sorry."

"It's okay." Natalie could never be mad at Rebecca, the one person in the world who truly had a heart of gold. "We're figuring things out. Between you and me, I'm not closing the door on him quite yet. Maybe Patty's right for once. I should seize the day, have that hot fling, live in the moment, and then let him break my heart."

Rebecca gasped. "You think he'd do that?"

"Not intentionally, but that's probably how it would end." She unlocked the car. "Anyway, we have something more important to talk about."

"We do?"

"We do. Get in, and I'll tell you about my plan. You're gonna love it."

Rebecca hopped into the car and buckled her seatbelt. "Tell me tell me tell me."

Quickly, Natalie explained Kaylee's situation to Rebecca—how she'd fallen in with a bad crowd and needed to stay out of trouble. "She has to find purpose in doing something meaningful. I think you're the perfect person to help her do that, and the shelter with those new puppies is a good place to start. I'm hoping she can perform her community service hours with a project she'll enjoy. And who wouldn't enjoy puppies?"

"Oh my God, I totally love it! And boy, could I use an extra volunteer. But why didn't you talk about it at dinner tonight? I bet everyone would—"

"The fewer people who know about Kaylee at this point, the better. You know how gossip runs rampant around here."

"Do I ever!" Rebecca practically shouted. Then she whispered, "So it's a secret between us?"

"Yes, for now." Natalie knew Rebeca would love sharing a special connection with her. She also wanted to keep her involvement with Kaylee quiet around the others, especially Cece. With everything they had going on at the studio, Natalie didn't want her Kaylee project to be a topic of conversation.

Since their argument, Natalie had taken as much off Cece's plate as possible. Last night she'd worked until one in the morning, planning the summer recital, budgeting the scholarship funds, and sending emails to the parent volunteers.

But Rebecca didn't need to know any of that. She only needed to help her keep Kaylee busy and out of trouble.

When they pulled up in front of the apartment, Kaylee was already outside waiting for her.

"Hi," she said in a shy voice, crawling into the backseat.

Natalie was pleased to see her looking like her old self. Her hair had been trimmed and bleached back to its natural color.

Rebecca glommed onto Kaylee as if they were old friends. "Do you remember me? I totally remember you! I was working at Nutmegs one time when you came in with your brothers. Oh my God, they were so cute, just little boys. I gave them cookies, and—

"Slow down," Natalie said to Rebecca. She caught Kaylee's attention in the rearview mirror and winked at her.

"I remember," Kaylee said. "Do you still work at the bakery?"

"Oh, I kind of work everywhere," Rebecca said.

Natalie interjected before Rebecca launched into another subject. "Rebecca's in charge of the volunteers at the animal shelter. If you like it there, maybe you can volunteer regularly. It'll probably satisfy your community service hours."

Kaylee pulled on the seatbelt strap. "I need to get a real job though, one that pays."

"That's a good plan, too," Natalie said. "But let's take this one step at a time, okay?"

"I guess," Kaylee said. "I'm getting really nervous about talking to the prosecutor."

Natalie didn't blame her. It was a situation one should be nervous about. "I'm sure it'll be fine. Elaine Cooper is the best lawyer for this kind of thing. Plus, getting set up with community service work ahead of time is going to reflect well." Natalie stopped at a red light. "Rebecca, why don't you tell Kaylee about the puppies and the shelter."

The exuberant everywhere girl practically broke into song describing all the wonderful and exciting projects at the shelter.

Kaylee asked a few questions and seemed enthusiastic. Natalie would have to stay involved to make sure the arrangement worked not only for Kaylee but for Rebecca, too. It was another obligation on top of so many others, but no way would she abandon Kaylee at this point. Like everything else, she needed to see it through.

CHAPTER 37

*W*ithin twenty minutes, Kaylee had taken to puppy care as if she'd been trained for weeks.

"It's probably because I helped with my brothers when they were babies. I loved feeding and changing and snuggling them." She held two puppies against her chest. "They are so cute and tiny. How old are they?"

"Two weeks today." Rebecca mixed formula in bottles. "Here, I'll take this one, you feed that one. Let's sit over there."

The two young women bonded instantly. If there was one thing Rebecca loved, it was a new project. And how wonderful for Kaylee to have someone like her to look up to. Natalie prayed her idea would work. That Kaylee would turn her life around and get a chance to start over with a clean slate. There was no telling what might go on her record if the DA decided to press charges. Elaine had explained all the possibilities to Natalie, including the worst case scenarios.

As her young friends tended to puppies, Natalie sat on a blanket on the floor beside the whelping box, where the mama licked her other puppies, all of them pushing against each other trying to latch onto a nipple. Her milk supply was dwindling, according to Dr. Klansky, despite her babies' desperate demands for nourishment.

Natalie stroked the top of the mama's head. "Pretty soon you'll go to your forever home, sweetie. You'll be spoiled and given treats and have a cozy bed all to yourself. I'll bet someone will put you in one of those silly front packs and take you everywhere they go. You will have the best life. You've certainly earned it."

The dog blinked her sleepy eyes, kissed Natalie's hand, then returned to grooming her babies.

THE TEXTS from Daniel came at regular intervals, as if he were setting an alarm every few hours. Natalie answered him, trying to ignore the broken heart looming in the not-too-distant future. She'd survive it. She'd been through worse.

One week after their 'second' date, Daniel returned to Clearwater. And this time, he brought Lola.

"Uncle Danny says there's a place where they have the best coffee in the world here. Is that true? The best in the whole world?" The precocious seven-year-old scampered ahead, then circled back as the three of them strolled the park.

"I think it's true," Natalie said.

"Can we get some?"

"Aren't you too young to drink coffee?" Natalie asked.

"My mom gives me coffee milk every morning before school. She says it'll keep me alert when my teacher gets boring. And my teacher gets boring a lot."

"Seriously?" Natalie asked Daniel.

He shrugged. "That's my sister. Her mothering decisions are sometimes questionable."

"They really are," Lola said, bolting toward the pond. "One

time she let me drive the car, well sort of. Oh, look, ducks! Danny, did you bring bread to feed the ducks?"

"No."

"I got ya, Lola." Natalie withdrew a sack of bread heels from her bag.

"You've thought of everything," Daniel whispered.

"Yes, I have," Natalie said, her shoulder brushing against his.

As Lola tossed tiny pieces of bread into the water, squealing with delight every time a duck snapped up the snack, Natalie and Daniel sat on a bench in the shade of an Oak with sprawling branches. Spring blossoms and damp earth filled the air with a subtle, musky scent.

"Does this qualify as our third date?" Daniel asked.

"Hmm, not sure. Does it count as a date when you bring a child along?"

"I don't see why not. We're together. We're holding hands, sort of, although somewhat surreptitiously." Their hands were side by side, his fingers touching hers. "I want to spend every free moment I have with you," he said, his voice low.

Natalie allowed her fingers to toy with his. "Is that so?"

He nudged her. "Yeah. What do you say?"

"I'm thinking."

"Thinking is good." Daniel sounded hopeful.

Natalie focused her attention on Lola, the adorable little girl who was worming her way in. The advice from her friends echoed, especially crazy Patty's suggestion that she throw caution to the wind and jump into a whirlwind fling. She turned and faced him. "I can feel things getting complicated already. I don't know if we should slow things down, speed things up, or end it all here and now."

"All kidding aside." Daniel flashed his wry smile and scooted closer. "If speeding things up is an option, I vote for that."

A short fling with a hot cop. Would she regret it? Probably.

But neither one of them was going to end it yet. And slowing things down, well, that was a non-starter, a waste of time

She stood and pulled him up off the bench. Lola was busy with the ducks. Nobody was nearby. She touched her lips to his ear and whispered. "I vote for that, too. But right now we need to get your niece a decaf coffee milk."

They shared a Nutmegs sticky bun and a giant chocolate chip cookie. Lola declared her coffee milk with cinnamon and sugar for sure the best in the world. After the bakery, they wandered up and down Main Street. Daniel bought his niece a caramel apple to take home and a yellow *Lake Clearwater* sweatshirt she said she 'could not live without.' Every chance he got, he planted a quick kiss on Natalie's lips or neck.

By the time their day together ended, the sexual tension was thick as peanut butter. The worries, concerns, doubts clouding Natalie's decision-making capabilities were tossed aside.

Five days later, her passionate affair with Detective Daniel Garrett began.

CHAPTER 38

*D*aniel appeared at her door clean shaven, in a gray t-shirt that stretched across his chest and shoulders. His cologne was a faint woodsy, masculine scent that Natalie inhaled as he crossed into the house and handed her a single red rose.

"One red rose," she said. "The symbol of passion."

"I know." Daniel took her into his arms and kissed her. "I googled it."

"You are so good at that."

"Kissing or googling?"

"Both, obviously." Natalie guided him by the hand where she'd set the table with her mother's china, crystal, and sterling cutlery. Cloth napkins, a variety of tea lights and candles in various sizes. The flames flickered in the low light.

"You cooked?"

"Goodness, no. I don't cook, but Tessa does. She makes the best Bolognese ever, so all I had to do was boil the pasta according to the directions." She brought an oval platter to the table. Layers of wide noodles covered in the rich, aromatic meat sauce. "Tessa suggested tagliatelle."

"I don't think I've ever had tagliatelle," he said, pulling her against his body.

She luxuriated in another sensuous kiss and shivered when his warm hand slipped under her blouse and rested on her lower back.

"They call it ribbons of pasta," she said, slightly breathless. "You'll love it."

"I'm sure I will." He tightened his arms around her, a hand trailing upward.

Natalie laughed. "Are we talking about pasta?"

"Of course we are. And I'm starving." He pulled out her chair. "Shall we?"

Natalie took her seat. He leaned over her shoulder and dusted the side of her neck with feathery kisses.

"If you don't stop, we'll never have dinner."

"You're right." Daniel sat in the chair beside her and raised his fork. "Smells divine."

"You have no idea." Natalie dished up generous servings and poured the wine, an Italian Barolo, into the cut crystal goblets. In the candlelight, it shone with a dark red hue and orange reflections.

Natalie watched him eat. Even the way he chewed intrigued her, as if every bite were an experience. If delicious food gave him this much pleasure, she could only imagine what lay ahead of them.

"This is insane," he said. "The flavor and textures and perfect amount of spiciness. Did you say Tessa the sommelier made it?"

"I did. She is a woman of many talents. And for some reason very invested in my romantic life."

Daniel raised his glass. "I'm liking her more and more."

They ate and drank and chatted with ease. As the minutes ticked by, anticipation grew. Natalie knew she'd be inviting him into her bed. She just didn't know how—or when. She hadn't been this nervous about sleeping with a man in years. In truth, she hadn't had many lovers. Her relationships tended to be drawn out over long periods of time. And they never overlapped.

After dinner, they cleared and cleaned up together. Natalie did her best to appear composed, but she couldn't stop her hands from shaking. Whatever Daniel might be feeling, he exuded an easygoing air of confidence

"Would you like to take a walk?" Daniel asked.

"A walk?"

Daniel removed the towel from her hand. "I like taking a walk after dinner, and it's a beautiful evening."

His calm was contagious. It settled her trembling hands. "That sounds lovely."

Outside, in the spring breeze, they strolled along the sidewalk under the street lamps. Daniel talked about his parents, the loss of his father, how much he loved his sister and niece. Natalie shared how devastating it was to watch her mother fade away over the years. They circled the block, then wandered into a public garden where a full moon cast a path of golden light.

Daniel took her into his arms and placed a warm kiss on her lips. "We don't need to rush this, Natalie. I want to be with you more than anything, but it's not only about that."

With those words, a little more of her fell for him. But at the same time, a tiny piece of her heart ached. Was there anything more foolish than falling for someone who'd be leaving her behind?

On the other hand, Natalie's life had shifted when her mother passed away. Her priorities had changed. Decisions were seen through a different lens. She didn't need to weigh every choice as if it were life and death. She wanted to take a chance now and then, consequences be damned.

"I think a lot about firsts," Daniel said, taking her hand as they walked deeper into the garden. "My first Giants game with my dad, my first Christmas after my dad died, my first day at the police academy, the first time I held Lola in my arms. The first time I set eyes on you—I tried to be so, I don't know, controlled."

"If I recall," Natalie said with a poke on his shoulder. "You seemed aloof, and definitely unimpressed with my non-situation."

"It was all a cover. I was spellbound. And I can't believe I'm here with you now. It's turning my life upside down. You have changed everything."

Natalie caressed the faded scar on his cheek. She would never let him undo his plans for her. But where she stood now, under the moonlight, his hands encircling her waist, she had no power to resist him.

CHAPTER 39

"*D*etails!" Patty demanded. "I want specific details. After all, the fling was my idea."

"No. I'm not sharing details." Natalie sat on a barstool at her favorite spot at Mariano's Cheese and Wine—the counter in front of a giant charcuterie board that Patty had put together. Cece sat beside her, cutting slices of smoked Gouda and arranging crackers. Tessa was at some function and Rebecca was at home, so it was just the three of them.

At least Natalie had two fewer friends asking questions. Her fling with Daniel Garrett was one week old. They'd spent the entire weekend together. Every waking moment was filled with giddiness. Adrenaline soared.

"I will tell you, though," Natalie said, choosing her words carefully, "that I haven't been with a man in his thirties, like, ever. My last two boyfriends were at least ten years older than me."

Cece did a little shimmy. "Now I want details."

Natalie laughed. "Let me put it this way—I have a new appreciation for younger men."

"Don't I know it!" Patty said. "When I lived in Santa Monica,

I had this thing with a kid at work who was barely out of high school. Whoa, that was fun fun fun."

Cece looked horrified. "Oh my God, was he even eighteen? He'd better have been eighteen."

"Come on!" Patty pushed a small spoon into a jar of fig jam. "You know me."

"Yeah, that's what worries me."

"He was twenty-two, at least twenty-one." Patty wrinkled her nose at Cece. "So there."

Natalie delighted in her friends' banter and the relaxed atmosphere with just the three of them. They were drinking a fruity, smooth merlot that went perfectly with Patty's artful presentation of finger food.

"But seriously, Nat," Cece said. "You're really okay with something that's not going to last?"

"I am." As Natalie said the words, a prickle of uncertainty flickered, but she brushed it aside like a pesky mosquito. The last week had been electrifying, every nerve in her body on fire with passion. Their *first* had led to a second and third and beyond. It was turning out to be exactly what Patty had suggested—torrid, steamy, irresistible.

"At the risk of sounding like Rebecca," Patty said. "What if you fall in love with him? Or worse, what if he falls in love with you?"

Natalie lowered her face into her wine glass and took a long, slow drink. It wasn't like she hadn't considered it. But nobody was falling in love. Real love took time—months, at least, probably longer. She and Daniel were in the throes of infatuation and passion that increased with every encounter.

"I don't want to think about it." Natalie licked jam off the edge her thumb. "I just want to enjoy myself without second guessing every detail."

"You're absolutely right," Cece said. "No more analyzing."

"Fine. Whatever." Patty raised her glass. "Let's drink to Natalie and her new lover that has the whole town talking."

"Wait. What?"

Cece glared at Patty. "Big mouth."

Patty clasped her hands in front of her lips. "Oops, sorry, never mind."

"Don't oops-sorry-never-mind me. Why is the whole town talking? It's not like I'm the first woman around here to have a—a romance!"

"Now it's a romance?" Patty downed her wine and poured more into her glass. "I can't wait for the next town council meeting. I'll make sure Rebecca puts 'Natalie's Romance' on the agenda."

Cece groaned. "She's kidding. I think."

"I know." Natalie laughed, sort of. Naturally people would be talking about her. She was a fixture around town. Almost everybody knew, and cared about, Natalie Lurensky. "I guess I can't escape small town gossip. But I'm warning you both, especially you, Miss Patty, do not be a part of it. And if anyone asks you about my *romance*, you know nothing. Got that? Nothing."

While Cece offered a firm nod of agreement, Patty groused as if she'd been punished.

"You really are a buzz-kill." She slid the charcuterie away from Natalie.

"Right, buzz-kill. That's me." Natalie retrieved the board and stabbed a toothpick into three green olives, which made her think of an icy cold martini. *I wonder if Daniel likes martinis.*

CHAPTER 40

$\mathcal{N}$atalie's office was packed with parents for a meeting about the upcoming show. She stifled a yawn. Yesterday's discussion with Patty and Cece had weighed on her all night. She'd slept fitfully, awakening multiple times, anticipating the pain of loneliness once Daniel was gone.

She excused herself and slipped out. In the bathroom, she splashed cold water on her face and drank half a Diet Coke before returning to her office.

"Let's get started," she said, trying to sound enthusiastic and wide awake.

The summer recital was only seven weeks away, and the most demanding dance moms had lined up to take charge. One in particular, Suzi Parks, had been driving Natalie nuts ever since Ashley joined the studio. Suzi's daughter, a very good dancer but by no means extraordinary, had been whining and stirring up trouble for weeks.

"Before we start the meeting," Suzi said, her black shoulder length hair swishing with every turn of her head, "there's something we need to discuss."

"Alright." Natalie glanced at the clock. "What is it?"

"Well, I, or we, actually, we think that your new student has disrupted things around here."

Ah, yes, of course it was about Ashley. She was a shining star, and perhaps she was shining a little too brightly. "Disrupted?" Natalie kept her tone in check. "How do you mean?"

"It appears," Suzi said, eyeing the other mothers, "that Cece is spending more time with her, to the detriment of my, I mean the other dancers."

Natalie braced herself and channeled her inner Ilana. What had her mother taught her about dealing with demanding parents? Listen, learn, stay firm.

"I don't think that's true, Suzi." Natalie kept her tone polite. "Although we have made changes to the schedule, all students are getting the attention they deserve. And I'm always more than happy to show any parent the current breakdown of who teaches which classes and what our instructor to student ratio currently is."

"It appears you're not hearing me, Natalie!" Suzi raised her voice, which was both inappropriate and offensive.

"I believe your issue, Suzi, has more to do with the fact that somebody might be feeling uncomfortable with the competition."

"Are you suggesting my daughter is jealous of Ashley?"

"I'm not suggesting it," Natalie said. "I'm informing you of it. I've seen it first hand, and if you'd like to discuss it further, we should do so in private."

The other mothers stared wide-eyed. Few people had the nerve to put Suzi Parks in her place. The ultimate queen bee, she often manipulated and provoked dissension between the dance moms. Ilana had never allowed overly competitive mothers to gain control, and Natalie wouldn't either.

"But today, we're here to get to work on the summer recital, which is for the benefit of all our students."

Most of the mothers voiced their agreement.

"So let's get started on—" Natalie's cell buzzed in her hand. The screen flashed Daniel's number. "Excuse me, I need to take this call." She ducked out before answering.

"Hey there," Natalie said, moving into to the empty locker room.

"Hi." His voice never failed to make her heart skip a beat. Oh, she was definitely a lost cause. However long this affair lasted, it would be worth it.

"I can't see you tonight," Daniel said. "Captain plugged me in on the late shift."

Her swelling balloon of anticipation deflated. "That's too bad."

"I'm really sorry," he said in the low, breathy voice he used when they were in bed. "Maybe we can—"

Noise coming from the hall stole her attention. It sounded like arguing. "Daniel, I'm sorry but I've gotta go."

"Wait! What about tomorrow?"

"Maybe. Or yes, I think so. Let's talk tonight." Natalie ended the call then marched into the hallway where parents had spilled out of her office, some of them bickering like children.

Natalie put two fingers into her mouth and let out a high-pitched whistle.

Instant silence.

"What is going on here?"

Several of the mothers exchanged glances, and Natalie could tell something was amiss. "Well? Is somebody going to speak?"

Suzi stepped forward. "Natalie, you dismissed my concerns, so be it. But you should know that many of us are invested in certain aspects of your business."

"I don't know what you're talking about," Natalie said, her agitation growing.

"The old Mayfair Hotel, for instance," Suzi said with a flourish of her hands. "The place where your parents established the Lurensky Academy back in the eighties. "This building is on the historic registry. And you know it's owned by a community-based organization that has the authority to approve, or disapprove, any requests for renovation and repairs. And then of course, there's the town council, of which I am a member, who also has a vested interest in, well, everything." Suzi inclined her head as if to make it clear she held a degree of power over Natalie.

"Are you saying you will prevent repairs to the studio if I don't do your bidding?"

Suzi's response was a mere shoulder shrug.

The dance moms drew back, as if in retreat. Should they follow their dictator or break rank?

"You know..." Natalie began formulating her response. Even in flat ballet slippers, she towered over the women facing her. "I'm truly sorry if anyone is unhappy with me. And, Suzi, I'm aware that you will do whatever you feel is in your best interest. If that means punishing all the families this dance academy benefits, that's up to you. My concern is my students, every single one of them. Therefore, because I can see dissension in the ranks, I'm disbanding this planning committee." Natalie spoke with the kind of authority Ilana had demonstrated for decades.

"Natalie, hold on," one of the mothers said, jumping in. "We don't all agree. Sorry, Suzi, but let's face it. You're a mean girl, and I'm not. And I genuinely want what's best for our school."

A shy father with two little girls in the beginner class also stepped up. "I agree with her."

"Thank you. I appreciate that," Natalie said. "But I stand by my decision to reevaluate the committee. The summer recital is a huge production, not to mention a tribute to my mother. I won't allow it to be subverted by one individual's own selfish interest."

At that moment, Cece entered through the back door. "Hey,"

she said, obviously unaware of the friction filling the hallway. "What's going on?"

"We're having a little chat about the direction our studio is taking." Natalie put an arm around her Artistic Director's shoulders. "But now that you're here, it reminds me of an incident that took place a long time ago, a real learning experience for me." Natalie paused to gage the interest of the women and one man in front of her. All of them tilted forward, even Suzi. "Many years ago, Cece and I were dance rivals. Yes, we were best friends, but when it came to dance, we were fierce competitors. At the age of fourteen, we both auditioned for the role of the Sugar Plum Fairy for the Christmas production of Nutcracker. Everyone thought I would get it. After all, I was Natalie Lurensky. My parents owned the studio. My mother was in charge of every decision. Well, one night she sat me down and said: '*Natalia, here is zee truth,*' (her imitation of her mother's accent made everyone's eyebrows rise). '*You are good ballerina, but Cecilia Rose is better. You work hard, but Cecilia Rose work harder. I am sorry, but she will be Sugar Plum Fairy. Not you.*'

The women gasped.

"And you know what happened?" Natalie asked. "I sucked it up. Despite my disappointment and anger, I congratulated my friend on winning the role. And I accepted the truth. I was not as good a dancer as Cece, and my dedication to ballet paled in comparison. What I am now, however, is the headmistress of an elite academy that turns out ballerinas who will dance professionally and keep my mother's vision alive. And I will not be bullied by self-centered stage mothers who think their children are more deserving than others."

Suzi Parks turned three shades of red. "Well then, I guess my annual five thousand dollar donation won't be missed."

Natalie's chest rose, and she suppressed a derisive laugh. "Is that a threat, Suzi?"

"Please, Natalie. Don't misunderstand." Suzi spread her arms wide. "We all want to support this school and you, especially after everything you went through with losing your mother."

Suzi's voice dripped with empathy, genuine or not.

"That's not what I'm hearing." Natalie stepped closer. Intimidation was not her go to reaction, but she couldn't stop herself. She'd spent almost twenty years keeping dance moms happy, preventing disappointment and bitterness, balancing the needs of every dancer and family—that was her job, her responsibility. But she was worn out. All that appeasing had taken its toll. She stepped even closer to Suzi. "You talk a big game. You flattered my mother endlessly over the years, but I wonder if it wasn't just you ingratiating yourself in order to have influence."

"That is not true. I held your mother in the highest esteem." Suzi looked like she was about to cry. "You must know that!"

Suzi's emotional outburst softened Natalie and brought her ire down a notch. She took a breath and summoned the stamina she needed to put this entire episode to rest.

"I don't know that, but I'll take you at your word. The bottom line is that my mother was respected. And I believe I've earned that respect as well." She eyed the parents standing in front of her. "So here's what we're going to do. Cece and I will form a new committee to plan the summer recital. We'll tap some parents who have been excluded in the past. As for you, Suzi, you're gonna sit this one out."

CHAPTER 41

*I*t was after eight when Natalie closed her laptop. She rubbed her face, exhausted. Friday night, Daniel was at work, and her friends were scattered.

And she was starving.

No stranger to eating alone, Natalie considered taking herself out for Chinese food. If she went local, she'd probably run into one of the mothers she'd tangled with earlier in the day. Natalie had no regrets for anything she said, but that didn't mean she wouldn't be criticized for it. Her love life already was trending in the Clearwater gossip circles, why not her professional life as well?

Going home was her best option. Another quiet night in her empty house, the television flickering with an old episode of *Law and Order*.

As she pushed her chair away from her desk, her cell buzzed. She smiled, a fleeting rush of hope that it might be Daniel saying he'd gotten off early and they could rendezvous as planned.

The screen flashed: *Elaine Cooper.*

"Hello?"

"Natalie, hi, Elaine Cooper here." The succinct lawyer spoke quickly, as if she were walking at speedy clip. "Are you busy? Can we meet?"

"Oh, um, yeah," Natalie said, completely caught off guard. "Is everything okay?"

"Is everything ever truly okay?"

Natalie didn't respond to the rhetorical and disturbing question.

"There's a little bistro nearby," Elaine said, "about halfway between us. I'll text you the address."

NATALIE PARKED a few blocks from the restaurant and wound her way through the crowd. Friday night on a warm spring evening in a trendy area full of art galleries, tasting rooms, expensive shops. Café tables lined the sidewalks for pleasant outdoor dining.

She'd managed a quick change out of her ballet instructor costume. She'd done it a million times—jeans over her tights, a cropped vest on top of her black leotard, and high-heel pumps. As usual, heads turned when she walked into the bistro. Natalie always attributed the attention to the fact that in heels she was well over six feet tall.

Elaine waved from a table in the back.

"Well, this is a nice surprise," Natalie said, taking her seat.

"I didn't expect you to be available." Elaine wore her signature outfit, a monochrome pantsuit, this time a subtle shade of olive green. "What with your new romance in full swing."

"How do you know about that?" Natalie asked.

"Are you kidding? I keep up with everything, including Clearwater gossip."

The waiter set two cocktails on the table.

"I ordered your drink—vodka martini."

"Exactly." Natalie sipped the icy cold liquid. "You have quite the memory, don't you?"

"I do. I can recall testimony from years ago. It's one of those weird left brain things." She drank, then asked, "How's it going with the hot detective?"

"Is that why you invited me out? To get the scoop on my love life?"

"Not really." Elaine drank again. "Maybe a little. But let's order, and then we'll talk."

Clearly, the attorney had an agenda.

Natalie scanned the menu, curious about what inspired this last minute invitation. Elaine was such an eccentric, one never knew what she was up to. And while Natalie had known her for years, they weren't exactly friends. In fact, she was under the impression Elaine didn't have many friends. She had family in Los Angeles and spent much of her time there. Other than that detail, Natalie didn't know much about her. Of one thing she was certain, though. Elaine Cooper was whip-smart, and when it came to representing a client, she was a relentless advocate. Which was what Kaylee needed.

After they ordered, Elaine jumped right in.

"So, *the dancer and the detective*. Sounds like a romance novel."

Natalie stirred her martini. "We're seeing each other, for now anyway. But it's not going to last. He has big plans."

"Plans change," Elaine said. "Trust me, every divorced couple had plans to stay married forever. You know, *until death do us part*? Ack, fast forward a decade or two and they can't stand each other."

"Such a cynic." Natalie laughed as she buttered a warm roll. "But I'm a little cynical myself these days."

"Life will do that to you. So many people are disappointments. We expect them to be gracious and do what's right, and they fail every time. It's one of the reasons I'm cutting back on divorces. People are at their worst when dissolving a marriage. I'm too old for it."

Old? Natalie wasn't sure how old Elaine was. Fifty, maybe? But age had no bearing here. She was a kind and generous person who stepped up when called upon. The more they interacted, the more Natalie liked her.

"So, your detective has big plans?"

"He does. He's going to leave his job and go off to explore the world, or the country, or some such thing."

"That's bold. Good for him." Elaine sipped her cocktail. "Mmm, best Old Fashioned around. I discovered this drink when I was nineteen and backpacking through Europe. I met a man, and oh, did he teach me a lot."

Nineteen and backpacking through Europe. Natalie shook off the sting of envy. "You've had an exciting life, haven't you?"

"Very," Elaine said. "It helped that I come from a wealthy family and have a ridiculously high IQ. I was able to accomplish a lot in a short time."

Natalie laughed. "I don't know how you do it, but somehow that didn't sound like bragging."

"Nothing to brag about when you're born to parents who are smart and have money and by some miracle stay together. It's just dumb luck."

"I guess you're right."

"I usually am. And that is me bragging." Elaine ate her maraschino cherry. "So, where were we? Daniel has big plans, but hey, maybe he'll change his mind now that he's met you."

"His plans are not going to change," Natalie said. "At least not on my account."

"Fair enough." Elaine reached across the table and patted her hand. "You know, I think you and I have a lot in common."

Natalie scoffed. "I'd say we have virtually nothing in common. You're a lawyer with umpteen degrees, and I never even finished my bachelor's. And our lives, our situations, could not be more opposite."

Her friend grew serious. "I'm not talking education or the way we live. I'm talking about strength, independence, decisiveness. I admire your certainty. And by the way, Kaylee and her mother think you walk on water."

"Well, that's silly. I'm just trying to help a young woman get back on track. She deserves another chance."

"I agree."

Natalie tapped her nails on her martini glass, eyeing the stalwart woman across from her. "As much as I'm delighted to have dinner with you, I assume you have something you want to talk about."

"Obviously, Kaylee." Elaine said without hesitation.

The waiter set their dinners in front of them. Natalie's stomach gurgled, but she made no move to begin eating. "Is there a problem?"

"I'm afraid so. It appears this theft ring is a whole lot bigger than originally thought. Break-ins all over the place, mostly jewelry but guns, too. It's serious. The district attorney is coming down hard. Kaylee might be charged with aiding and abetting."

Aiding and abetting? Natalie rested a shaky hand on the table. "Have you told her this?"

"Of course. But I'm not sure she fully understands." Elaine cut into her rare filet and took a bite. "Oh, delicious. Would you please eat your dinner? It's getting cold."

Natalie complied. The whitefish drizzled with lemon butter sauce and capers was tasty, but it stuck in her throat. She was prepared to help Kaylee with community service work, happy to be a friend to her and Holly, but beyond that she wasn't so sure. "Go on," she said to Elaine.

"We're seeing the DA next week. I'd like you to be there. Her mother, although quite lovely and sweet, can't handle it. She's exceedingly immature and a little flighty. I want the DA to see that Kaylee has support from an upstanding person like you."

"Oh, okay, I'll try. When?" A surge of anxiety struck. She was barely managing her schedule as it was. "We're in the midst of planning the summer recital, and I am up to my eyeballs in—"

"Seriously?" Elaine put her knife and fork down with a clatter. "A young woman's life is hanging in the balance, and you're worried about a dance recital?"

Whoa. Natalie was not expecting to be reprimanded. Nor was she prepared for how concerned Elaine was. Up until a minute ago, she thought Kaylee was in the clear, or would be soon. But she didn't like Elaine's implication that her work was frivolous by comparison.

Natalie patted her lips with her cloth napkin. "I'm doing my best for Kaylee. But do not diminish my work, Elaine. It's much more meaningful than just teaching children to plie and pirouette. It shapes them, disciplines them, gives them confidence. It's what I tried to instill in Kaylee over the years, but the instability of her life at home was too weighty."

Elaine's stern expression faded. She broke eye contact. "You're right. I apologize."

Natalie's respect for her grew. That the woman could apologize readily and not follow it up with an excuse was a testament to her character.

"Thank you." Natalie swallowed the last drop of her vodka martini. "Apology accepted."

"Another drink?" Elaine offered.

"No, one's enough." Natalie returned to her fish, ruminating. "What exactly did Kaylee do that might be considered aiding and abetting?"

"Allegedly do," Elaine corrected her.

"Right, allegedly. I thought she was just, you know, a follower. That she didn't know what they were really up to."

"Her *ex*-friend Jimmy claims she knew everything, and that she drove the getaway car, not once, not twice, but three times."

Natalie choked, took a sip of water, and coughed some more. "The getaway car? Jesus, it sounds like Bonnie and Clyde. Could she go to jail for that?"

"If convicted." Elaine sliced her filet with the precision of a surgeon. She was nothing if not exacting. "That's why it's 'let's make a deal' time. I don't want this to go to trial. If I put her on the stand, she'll get ripped apart on cross."

Natalie rearranged the roasted vegetables on her plate. If only her responsibilities, her burdens, could be moved around so easily.

Elaine cleared her throat. "Look, Natalie, if I'm asking too much of you, tell me now."

Too much of her? It was Elaine doing all the heavy lifting here. "You're not. Besides, I was the one who dragged you into this mess."

"It's my job. It's what I do. You, on the other hand, sort of fell into it because you care about our young lady and because you found this whole foray into the investigation, dare I say, exciting."

"Have you been talking to Tessa?" Natalie asked.

"No. Well, yes. I talk to her all the time. We're great friends you know. And she might have mentioned how, hmmm, how'd she put it? How much the *Kaylee situation* has stirred something in you."

"It has." Natalie looked at her plate. "I admit it."

"No shame in that," Elaine said. "People aren't meant to stay in one place, literally or figuratively. It's human nature to want to break free. Some people do it, some don't. But from what I've seen, everyone indulges in 'what if I'd done it differently' fantasies at some point in their life."

What if... a question Natalie could never get out of her head. "Even you?"

Elaine looked almost wistful. "Especially me. I've made my share of mistakes, God knows. Have a few regrets, too. Not a night goes by when I don't wonder about changing my life."

Change. Such a small, simple word.

Suddenly, a recollection of that first conversation with Maura flashed through her mind.

Promise me you'll reach out if anything changes.

The only thing I can promise, is that nothing is going to change.

But it wasn't true. Everything was changing. Everything had changed.

CHAPTER 42

*D*aniel bounced Lola on his knee, then gave her a tight hug. "I gotta go, Lola-granola."

"Aww, Uncle Danny, why can't you stay for dinner?" She moaned with great drama. "Mommy's cooking something special for the company."

"Company?" He glanced at his sister, who was running the vacuum with earbuds in her ears. "You're having company?"

"Yep," Lola said with a firm nod. "His name is Gordon."

"Gordon?" Daniel tip-toed into the subject carefully. "Just Gordon?"

"We met him at the paint store. He's nice."

The vacuum went silent, and Jennifer came into the kitchen. Daniel settled back onto a stool and rested his elbows on the counter. "Who's Gordon?"

"Lola!" Jennifer removed her earbuds and dropped them into a small dish.

"Sorry, Mom, I forgot." Lola's giant blue eyes widened even more. She played the 'innocent little girl' like a pro. "But don't you want Uncle Danny to meet your boyfriend?"

Daniel choked. "Boyfriend?"

245

"He's not my boyfriend. We've only gone out a couple of times."

"Uh-huh." Daniel didn't like the sound of it. Jennifer never dated, which was how it should be. Lola didn't need strange men coming and going. It was disruptive, and she needed stability. "I thought you decided no men until Lola was at least twelve. Or twenty."

Jennifer removed Lola from Daniel's lap. "To your room, young lady."

"Noooo! I want to stay. Uncle Danny, tell her I should stay. I know what you're going to talk about."

"Sorry, Lola," Daniel said. "Your mom and I need to have some grown-up talk. But don't worry. I'll fill you in." He winked at his niece and scooted her toward her bedroom.

Once he heard the door close, he turned to Jennifer. "What the hell? Why didn't you tell me you were seeing someone?"

Jennifer let out an exasperated grunt. "Because I knew you'd react this way, all *I don't like the idea of a man in Lola's life.* And I wasn't looking to meet anyone. It just happened."

"At the paint store? As in where you buy paint?"

Jennifer groused at him. "Uh, yeah. That is what 'paint' and 'store' imply."

"So, Gordon works at a paint store?" Daniel tried to keep his agitation in check. "That's his job? How old is he? Where does he live?"

"Wow, *daddy*, got any more questions?" Jennifer pulled her hair up and secured it. "Gordon is a good guy. He's forty-three, a house painter, and lives a few miles from here. He's never been married and has no children."

"That he knows of," Daniel remarked, not hiding his sarcasm.

Jennifer laughed. "That's exactly what he said."

Daniel puffed out a breath of air. What if his sister got serious with this guy? It would upend Lola's life, maybe not a in a bad way, but still a drastic change. And what about his relationship with his big sister? The way they'd relied on each other for most of their lives.

"I have to take care of you, sis."

"No you don't, Danny," Jennifer said, taking his hand. "Look, I don't know what's going to happen with Gordon, but that's not the point. I don't want you to plan your life around me and Lola. You're a young, totally hot, wonderful guy. You can do anything and go anywhere you want. Don't let anyone tie you down, especially not me."

"It's not about being tied down, Jen. We—we're just really close, you know, as far as siblings go."

"That will never change," his sister said, ruffling his hair. "But let's be real. In forty years, we don't want to be one of those scary brother-sister couples who live in a creepy old house on the edge of a cliff."

Daniel laughed. He'd seen a horror movie like that once. "I guess."

Jennifer stood and nudged him off his perch. "Get up. Go have a fun time tonight. Don't worry about me. If things get more serious with Gordon, I promise you'll be the first to know."

Daniel had no choice but accept her assurances that the guy in her life was a good man, and that he had nothing to worry about. So he said goodbye to his sister and turned his thoughts to Natalie.

It was his first night off all week, his first time seeing her since the weekend they'd spent together, the weekend that changed everything. People say it takes time to fall in love, but not in this case. Someday he'd tell her that it was love at first sight. Followed by an almost desperate need to be in her presence. And then, the passion, an all-consuming desire. It blew up everything—as if he'd hit the reset button his life.

~

DANIEL PULLED her closer and swept her hair out of her eyes, her skin warm against his. "Are you okay?"

"Of course." She kissed him, caressing his cheek rough with whiskers. He was such a beautiful man. She was beginning to wish they'd never met. "Are you hungry?"

"I don't know," he said. "What time is it?"

"About ten," Natalie said as he nuzzled her neck. "We skipped dinner, you know."

"Did we?"

"We did."

"Food was low on the priority list when I got here," Daniel said.

Natalie laughed. "It was."

He stroked her shoulder and ran his hand down the length of her arm, then under the covers and around her waist.

"Well I'm starving." Natalie rolled away, breaking the moment. "I have a loaf of homemade sourdough, some of Mariano's finest cheese, and a bottle of savory Sangiovese. Come on, we'll pretend we're in Italy."

He pulled her back. "Let's stay in bed a little longer."

Natalie acquiesced. She turned over and cozied her back to his front. They fit together so perfectly it made her eyes burn. Damn, exactly what wasn't supposed to happen. A slow, painful crack was winding through her heart.

After a few minutes of spooning, she unwound herself and set her feet on the floor, taking a quick glance back at the man in her bed. "My stomach is rumbling. I'll go set up our Italian style supper."

Although the days were warm, the nights were cool. Daniel built a fire in the fireplace, and Natalie spread a blanket on the floor. The flames provided the only light in the room, and they threw shadows against the walls. Natalie talked about her continued involvement with Kaylee, and Daniel told her about his sister's new beau.

"Well, good for Jennifer," Natalie said. "As long as Lola likes him."

Daniel tore off a piece of crusty bread and ate it with a slice of cheese. "Lola's a tough one to please. And probably more discerning than my sister. I'll have to follow her lead, I guess. But the whole situation makes me nervous. I don't like the idea of not keeping tabs on them."

"I understand. But, well, who knows? A lot can happen between now and when you leave."

"You mean like he might be out of the picture by then?" Daniel asked.

"Maybe." Natalie realized how that paralleled their trajectory. In a month's time, she would be out of the picture, too.

Daniel stared into the fire. "Are you trying to tell me something?"

"No." Natalie responded too quickly, as if defensive. "Well, what do you mean?"

He turned to her, a slight smile, firelight reflecting in his eyes. "I don't mean anything." He cupped the back of neck and kissed her with lips that tasted like wine. "Let's go back to bed. We have a date tomorrow morning with a couple of espressos and a sticky bun."

"We do," Natalie said, relieved he'd pivoted and turned the conversation away from anticipating the future. She chastised herself for overthinking their relationship. It wasn't even a relationship—it was a hot fling, a torrid affair, a tingling romance that would burn as bright as the sun and then end as quickly as it started.

CHAPTER 43

The District Attorney, a formidable woman in a black pencil skirt and leopard print blouse, came down so hard on Kaylee that Natalie wondered if the poor girl would end up traumatized. As it was, she could hardly hold it together, but Elaine, swooping in like a super hero, made it clear how much Kaylee had done for the DA's case.

"If my client hadn't brought that backpack full of jewels to the authorities, putting herself at great risk, you'd have nothing. The victims' heirlooms would be somewhere in South America by now. And the theft ring would still be operating with impunity. Thanks to her, you have enough evidence to convict ten times over."

The opposing lawyer argued back, throwing around words and legal mumbo-jumbo that Natalie didn't understand. The lawyers lobbed balls at one another for over an hour. Elaine had a comeback for every argument her opponent threw at her.

It appeared that Natalie's presence made no difference to the DA. The aloof lawyer never once made eye contact. But if Elaine thought her attendance was important, Natalie believed her.

In the end, a deal was struck. The DA pushed for jail time,

but Elaine pushed back harder. In exchange for a lengthy probation and five hundred hours of community service, Kaylee
would not serve time.

"You're very lucky, Miss Robertson." The DA stood and
gathered her papers. "If not for your lawyer, you'd have left this
room in handcuffs. Make no mistake, this is your one and only
second chance. Don't blow it."

Kaylee didn't budge. Natalie nudged her shoulder and whispered. "Stand up. Say thank you."

Kaylee followed her instructions.

The DA gave her a curt nod. Her harsh expression turned
friendly as she shook Elaine's hand. "Good to see you, Elaine. I
appreciate a strong adversary."

"You're quite the opponent yourself. Good luck with the rest
of the case. I hope the other defendants get what they deserve."

"Oh believe me, they will." The DA opened her office door
and stood to the side as they left. Natalie felt like she'd been
released from jail herself.

As they rode the elevator down to the lobby, Kaylee leaned
against Natalie as if she needed help staying upright.

"Are you okay, sweetie?"

"I'm just so thankful," she said tearfully.

Elaine led the way down the steps from the courthouse
toward the parking lot. They stopped beside Natalie's car.

"Kaylee," Elaine said, "listen to me very carefully. You need to
do everything by the letter of the law going forward. Make sure
you have a schedule for performing your community service
hours at the shelter and that all the paperwork is completed and
sent in on time. You'll have your first meeting with your probation officer in two weeks. Show up early. Dress professionally.
Report back to me." Elaine put her hands on Kaylee's shoulders.
"The DA was right. You are incredibly lucky. Even I'm surprised
she let you go without serving time. Your former friends are in
a world of trouble. They'll be incarcerated. And believe me,

those pretty young men will not fare well in prison. Promise me, swear to me, you will never interact with any of them again."

"I promise," Kaylee said, brushing away tears and falling into Elaine's arms. "Thank you for helping me."

Elaine drew Kaylee into an embrace, before putting her in Natalie's car.

"Well, good job, my friend," Elaine said to Natalie. "Dare I say, you saved that girl's life."

"I don't know about that." Natalie dismissed Elaine's assessment of her impact.

"Believe me, without your intervention she'd have gone down with her idiot friends."

"It's you who deserves the credit. All I did was guide her in the right direction."

"Yes you did, and that's the most important part of the process." Elaine took a beat. "I thought more about what you said to me the night we had dinner together."

Natalie shook her head. "What did I say?"

"You talked about how your work is much more than merely teaching children how to dance. That it gives them tools for life, encourages discipline, confidence, commitment. It's really quite astounding. And you are absolutely right."

"Thank you." Natalie appreciated Elaine's acknowledgement. "But it didn't work so well with Kaylee. To tell you the truth, I kind of feel like I failed her."

"Well, for some reason the universe gave you a second chance to change her life. I'm cautiously optimistic that Kaylee will stay the course."

Natalie hoped beyond hope that Elaine was right.

~

CECE WAS WAITING on the steps in front of the studio, sitting like a kid and scrolling on her phone.

"Hey there," Natalie said, sitting on the step beside her.

"How'd it go?" Cece asked.

"Better than I'd hoped. A year of probation and a boatload of community service. Thank God for Elaine."

"I'd say thank God for you," Cece offered.

Elaine had said as much. And a second chance to redirect Kaylee's life? Natalie didn't much believe in stars aligning or destiny. Most everything in life could be attributed to common sense—or the lack of it. Every one of Natalie's decisions had been made sensibly and with full awareness of what the consequences could be. Even the choice to stay with her mother all those years ago.

"What are you doing sitting out here anyway?" Natalie asked.

"Waiting for Ashley. Her mother's coming with her today, remember?"

"I do," Natalie said, although she'd completely forgotten. Her morning at the DA's office plus getting Kaylee home and situated had drained her body and mind. "I'll go clean up my desk. Let me know when they arrive."

Natalie climbed the steps with false enthusiasm for the afternoon ahead.

Despite her exhaustion, she rose to the occasion. Natalie greeted Ashley and her mother and Maura with charm and compliments, extolling the young ballerina's talent and the progress she'd made under Cece's instruction and guidance

Although she used all the right words and mustered an air of keen interest and zeal, she felt none of it.

CHAPTER 44

*D*aniel was unnerved by how quickly his plans were falling into place. Fred's recovery was speedier than expected, and he planned to return to work within the week. After several interactions with Gordon, including a family dinner, Daniel's concerns about him were alleviated. His sister's new boyfriend was a good man, solid and committed and adorably smitten with Lola.

Jennifer had assured Daniel that Gordon could never replace him, but he wasn't buying it. If they ended up together long term, and all evidence pointed to that outcome, Daniel's role in Lola's life would be drastically altered. But Jennifer and Lola deserved the kind of permanence a man like Gordon would provide. He wanted that for them, regardless of the fact that he'd be relegated to a lesser role in his niece's life.

His responsibilities and obligations were on the verge of coming to an end. Nothing to tie him down or hold him back or keep him from loading up his truck and hitting the road.

Nothing except for the fact that he'd fallen in love.

"Can't you say you're not feeling up to coming back to

work?" Daniel asked Fred in one of their frequent calls. "Get a doctor's note or something?"

"You want me to lie about my recovery and extend my disability leave, so that you can lie to Natalie and tell her you can't leave the job yet?" Fred said. "You have any idea how crazy that sounds?"

"Not that crazy." Daniel didn't see any other way around his predicament.

"Why don't you tell her the truth? That you're head over heels and can't live without her. Then you could move to her little storybook town and live happily ever after."

"It's too soon for me to drop that in her lap," Daniel said, although the idea wasn't half bad. He had no idea how he'd let it get this far without realizing what a sap he'd become. "I don't think she's ready for such a huge confession, even if it is true. I mean, we've only been seeing each other a month. If I could maintain the status quo through the summer I think I'd be in a more, I don't know, a more solid position."

Fred groused. "Well, you'd better make a decision soon. I have it on good authority that the captain's got her eye on someone to replace you."

"Already?"

"What do you mean already? You gave notice like four months ago."

"I did, didn't I?" Daniel recalled the day. He'd been excited, proud even, the moment he told the captain he was leaving. The adventure he'd been planning and anticipating was actually going to happen. He'd made it happen. Never in his wildest imagination did he think someone like Natalie would come along.

"Listen kid, the clock is ticking. Let the captain know you want to keep your job. Otherwise you'll end up lovelorn *and* unemployed."

And homeless. Daniel had to factor in that his lease was up in a few weeks. He could move in with Jennifer, but now with Gordon in the picture, that would disrupt his sister's life and make him the pathetic baby brother.

"Gotta go, Danny-boy. Time for my nap." Fred yawned audibly. "Have to admit I'm going to miss my afternoon siesta when I get back to work."

"See? You're not ready!" Daniel gave it one last push.

"Sorry, buddy, but I'm more than ready. Going stir crazy around here. And the wife can't wait for me to get out of the house. She's already told me to forget about retiring. Take it from me, old married couples are not meant to spend every waking moment together."

Daniel couldn't fathom it. Each moment with Natalie only made him want more.

It was just as she'd feared. Natalie wondered if someday she'd look back and decide it had been worth it. Would their love affair that rivaled the great romances in history be worth the heartache on the other side? She had no choice but to break his heart, and that, in turn, was breaking hers.

They'd returned to her house after a late dinner and were cuddled on the sofa listening to music.

"I need to talk to you about something," Daniel said. "Something important."

Natalie sat up. "Okay."

He broached the subject with the logic of a graduate student presenting his thesis. She half expected him to open a laptop and launch a power point. Most women would be over the moon to have a man like Daniel Garrett pleading his case for turning his life upside down to be with her.

But try as she might, Natalie Lurensky was not most women.

"I won't be the reason you give up on your dream, Daniel." Natalie ran a finger along the scar on his cheek.

"Did it ever occur to you my dream may have changed?"

"Dreams don't change. They get set aside, postponed, forgotten. But they're always there in the back of the mind. Trust me —I gave up a dream a long time ago, and not a day goes by when I don't think *what if.*"

She'd never shared with him her own derailed plans, the life she might have had if she'd chosen a different path.

Daniel's brow lowered. "I thought this was your dream, carrying on your mother's legacy and taking her place in the world of ballet."

"It wasn't."

"What was?" he asked. "Tell me."

"It doesn't matter anymore," Natalie said. "It's long past and irrelevant to the life I have."

"Then why the daily *'what if's'*?"

He'd caught her in her own confusion. But none of that mattered because her old, expired, forgotten dream from the past had nothing to do with his present.

"If I agreed and you changed your life for me now—in the throes of passion and infatuation and new love—you would come to regret it."

"You don't know that."

Natalie closed her eyes against the flood of emotion. "Then I would. I would regret that my life limited yours. I already do. I should never have let it get this far. I'm so sorry."

Daniel tucked her hair behind her ear and stroked her neck. "Don't say that. No matter what happens, the time we've spent together will more than make up for the heartache that lies ahead. If we're not destined to be together forever, I'm certain we are destined to be together for now."

Natalie stopped breathing. He was poetic, and the depth of his declaration moved her to tears.

"Then that's what we will do," Natalie told him. "We will be together for now."

~

"I DON'T UNDERSTAND you at all," Rebecca said, washing a large metal bowl in the oversized sink. She filled it with some kind of brown mash and set it in the corral with the puppies. "Last night he told you he's changed his mind about leaving? Why aren't you over the moon?"

Natalie stroked the soft fur on the mother's head. Pretty soon she'd be starting her new life. "It's complicated, Rebecca. You don't get it."

"I think it's you who doesn't get it."

Whoa, that was a mouthful. Why Natalie had confided in the starry-eyed Rebecca of all people, she had no idea. But her night with Daniel had been so intense she couldn't stop thinking about it. And for some reason, every time her emotions got the better of her, she ended up at the shelter. That was one thing Rebecca was right about—dogs definitely brought about a sense of calm, and an hour at the shelter was cheaper than an hour of therapy. Besides, she didn't have a therapist, at least not yet.

"You know what else, Natalie? You're totally stubborn, and getting more stubborn the older you get."

"That's harsh." Natalie lowered her face into the mama dog's neck and nuzzled her. "I've never known you to be so outspoken. It doesn't suit you."

"I'm just being honest." Rebecca's eyes went teary. "An amazing man is in love with you, and you're sending him away. It's like a gothic romance—star crossed lovers who no matter how much they want to be together are forced apart by forces they cannot control. Oh! It's so sad."

"You're being a bit dramatic," Natalie said. Her friend's declaration would have been funny if it weren't true.

"I don't care if I am being dramatic. I think you're wrong. And to make matters worse, you're getting too attached to that dog. She goes to her forever home soon. Then what are you going to do?"

"Cry, probably," Natalie said. "Yet another thing you're right about."

Rebecca's defiant expression turned sympathetic. "The first thing they told me when I started working here was not to get attached."

"How'd that work out for you?" Natalie asked.

"Not good, I always get attached. But at least I have Mila."

Rebecca did have the best dog in the world. In fact, on the surface, she had it all. A fabulous dog, a wonderful husband, and a loving mother up the road. Natalie had none of that—no dog, no family, and soon enough, no boyfriend. All those years dating men she had no intention of staying with, running away from relationships when they demanded too much of her, protecting herself, avoiding risk. Look where it had gotten her. Now she had the right love at the wrong time. If only she and Daniel had met long ago or sometime in the future. Shakespeare was right—timing was everything.

"Natalie? Are you okay?"

"Huh?" She raised her head. "Oh, sure. Here." She handed the mama dog to Rebecca and reset her mood. "Kaylee will be here tomorrow, so I'll check in with you, see how she's doing. Thanks again for taking her under your wing. Gotta go."

Natalie drove away, eager to return to the comfort of her rigid, empty life. Timing truly was everything. Had her father's death occurred only a few weeks later, who knew what her life might have been. But there had been events when timing had been on her side. Good timing brought Cece back into her life all those years ago. Even her mother's death had occurred at the right time—after Christmas—as if scheduled by divine intervention. She'd been there to attend one last Lurensky production of The Nutcracker. Although Ilana's brain was almost a blank slate by then, life flickered in her cloudy eyes as the music sparked memories.

But timing was tricky a thing. She had a clock following her, ticking in the background like a lingering ghost. Every night she and Daniel spent together carried the heaviness of an impending storm. It was a tragic ballet—two lovers with time running out. Daniel would soon become her undoing. Unless— unless she changed her mind. Unless she gave in. Rebecca was right—an amazing man had fallen in love with her.

Perhaps it was time to listen to her heart instead of her head.

CHAPTER 45

atalie watched Ashley with an eagle eye. The teenager had made strides in her progress that astounded almost everyone. But not Natalie. She saw how relentless and determined their young dancer was. Her physicality and mental acuity were outstanding. She could repeat one movement dozens of times without tiring. No doubt, the Lurensky Academy would be credited with presenting a prima ballerina who would dance on stages around the world.

"Leg a little higher, Ashley. That's right, strong arms, chin up." Natalie paid close attention despite her exhaustion. She'd hardly slept the night before as she see-sawed over Daniel Garrett. It was as if her heart and her head were in a race to the finish line. At the moment, her heart was a hair's breadth in the lead. She contemplated what she might say to Daniel, how she'd tell him that she'd changed her mind. That his declaration of love had won her over. Just thinking about it sent her adrenaline into overdrive, both the thrill of throwing herself into the relationship, as well as the nagging fear that it might be a terrible mistake.

The music stopped, and the abrupt interruption broke her trance.

"Miss Natalie." Ashley so rarely spoke that Natalie was startled to hear her soft voice. "Can I take a short break. I need to use the bathroom."

"Of course," Natalie said. "You're doing amazingly well, Ashley. Your pirouettes are stunning. I know how hard you've been working to improve your spotting. It really shows."

"Thank you."

"Cece should be here any minute, so take a break until then. We've got a busy afternoon ahead. The little ones are so excited to dance with you in the show."

"I'm excited, too." Ashley laced her slender fingers together and twisted them.

Natalie inclined her head toward her student. "Are you concerned about something?"

Ashley blinked, and her eyes grew watery. "No, well, I know some of the girls aren't happy about me training with Cece. I feel bad about that."

"Don't you give it another thought." Natalie placed her hands on Ashley's shoulders. "Dance is extraordinarily competitive. As you rise, the field narrows and the competition gets stiffer. Believe me, Ashley, you will surpass your friends, and some will resent you for it. But nobody achieves greatness without being tough and resilient."

"I don't like people being mad at me."

"I understand completely, but that's what your coaches are for. We train you physically and mentally. And there's nothing you can tell us that we haven't heard before. I promise you."

"Thanks." Ashley wavered a moment, then she hugged Natalie with fierce strength. "Thank you for believing in me."

The sweet and talented ballerina scurried toward the bathroom, leaving Natalie with a mix of pride and worry. No doubt,

Ashley would face plenty of mean girls on her way to the top. She needed to be prepared for it.

Natalie returned to her desk and opened her laptop, but before she could accomplish anything, one of the new instructors tapped on the open door. Natalie struggled to remember the young woman's name. Mandy? Sandy? Andi?

"Hi, Andi."

"It's Candy," she said shyly.

"Candy, right. Sorry. What can I do for you?"

"There's a woman out front asking to see you."

"Do you know who it is?" Natalie had been inundated with calls and texts from parents regarding the summer recital. Thankfully, Suzi Parks had quieted down since their run-in a week ago. But that didn't mean she'd stay quiet. "It isn't Mrs. Parks, is it?"

"No. It's someone I've never seen before."

"Okay, I'll be right out." Natalie slipped her feet into flats as she quickly scrolled through messages. There were at least a dozen texts in the last two days from parents with questions and requests. The unscheduled visitor could be any one of them.

Natalie hurried to the main studio, halting at the sight of a woman standing in the middle of the room gazing up at the ceiling. Natalie had no idea who she was. Blonde ponytail, dark jeans, a plain blouse, and white sneakers freckled with drips of brown paint. Wait. Not paint, dark wood stain.

"Jennifer?"

"Hi, Natalie, these are beautiful chandeliers." Jennifer turned her attention to the walls. "And the antique moldings are magnificent. When was this place built?"

"1925," Natalie said, slightly in shock. Daniel's sister showing up unexpectedly inspired a plethora of questions. "What brings you all the way out to Clearwater?"

"Well," Jennifer said, running a hand over the smooth wood of the ballet barre. "Lola hasn't stopped talking about some place called Nutmegs where apparently they serve the best coffee in the world. Thought I'd come see for myself."

"Long way to travel for a cup of coffee," Natalie joked.

Jennifer laughed and relaxed her broad shoulders. "And to see you. I'm sorry to barge in, but I was hoping we could talk. It won't take long."

"Of course." Natalie had maybe forty-five minutes before dozens of children showed up and afternoon classes began. "Let's go get coffee."

They walked through the park with little conversation. Every now and then, Jennifer commented on a something Lola had mentioned. The vegetable garden, the bridge, the duck pond.

At the counter in Nutmegs, Jennifer studied the menu on the wall. "Remember the days when coffee was just coffee? Now we've got too many choices. What do you recommend?"

"In the mornings I like a double espresso," Natalie said. "In the afternoons I go a little lighter, cappuccino or latte."

"Hmm, cappuccino then."

Natalie ordered two cappuccinos and a pecan sticky bun in a box. "For Lola," she said.

Jennifer set her credit card down, but Natalie pushed it away. "Please. My treat."

"Thank you," Jennifer said. "But I can't promise that decadent looking pecan thing will make it back to Lola."

"I wouldn't blame you if it didn't." Natalie guided her to a corner table where it was unlikely they'd be interrupted. The barista brought their coffees. Jennifer's foam was in the form of a heart and Natalie's a perfect ballet slipper.

"Impressive artwork." Jennifer sipped her cappuccino. "Mmm. This very well might be best in the world. Definitely close to it."

Natalie eyed her boyfriend's sister. How much had Daniel had told her about their relationship and its impending end?

Was Jennifer going to plead his case for him? No way would he have asked her to intervene on his behalf. She was here of her own accord.

"I'm here to talk about my brother."

Natalie tapped her mug, anxious to keep the conversation light and vague. "I figured there was more to your visit than the search for the world's best coffee."

She smiled, and the female version of Daniel's face flashed for split second. "I understand that your, um, your relationship is getting serious."

"Is that so?" Neither confirm or deny, she thought.

"It is. And I sense things have gotten complicated, what with his plan to head out on an adventure of a lifetime."

"Head out. Yes. I'm aware of his plan."

"You're not making this easy on me," Jennifer said.

"That implies you have something to tell me that I might find, well, objectionable." Natalie pressed on. She had no desire to intimidate Jennifer, but she wasn't about to be intimidated herself. "Either way, I don't think Daniel would appreciate your interfering in his—his love life." Natalie purposely used a gentle tone. She knew how close Daniel was to his sister and niece, and she didn't want to be the cause of any friction.

"He definitely wouldn't. I hope you won't tell him. But you'll do whatever you have to do." Jennifer picked at some stain on her fingernail. "I guess I should get to the point."

"I wish you would," Natalie said.

"I like you, Natalie." Jennifer lowered her voice, infusing it with authority. "I could tell the first time we met that you're a quality person. And you might remember, I hinted at the idea that my brother needed a girlfriend."

Natalie sat back. "I do recall."

"But now, it appears he's fallen in love with you. And he wants to turn his life upside down to be with you."

"Did he tell you that?"

"Not in so many words, but here's the thing. You have turned Daniel into a man I barely recognize. And I cannot sit idly by and allow you to ruin his life."

Natalie gaped at Jennifer. She certainly did get the point, finally. "Ruin his life how?"

"By derailing his plans. I'm sorry to be so blunt, but you need to let him go."

Natalie stiffened. Her head and heart both came to screeching halt. She'd been toying with the idea of agreeing to let Daniel abandon his dream in favor of her. Now Jennifer was pushing her back to her original stance.

"I have to admit," Jennifer said, "that this mess is partly my fault."

"Why would anything be your fault?" Natalie asked

"Because I pushed Daniel to pursue you. I thought he was so hung up on his ex-girlfriend that he needed a distraction." Jennifer laughed to herself. "I never expected him to fall so hard."

Natalie understood the sentiment. She hadn't expected to fall so hard either. And she really hadn't expected to be having this conversation with his quirky sister. "So let me get this straight. You want me to let him go. What exactly does that mean?"

"Don't see him again."

"I should break up with him right now, today, over the phone?"

Jennifer brightened. "That'll work."

"Daniel and I are not teenagers, Jennifer. I'm not going to do that."

"Then find some other way."

Natalie looked around to make sure nobody was eavesdropping. "I don't know why you've inserted yourself into this. Daniel and I have agreed to be together for now, enjoy the time we have. I know he's about to go away, and I don't—"

"That's just it! He's not going to go. I can tell. I know my brother better than anyone, certainly better than you do." Jennifer's words were coming out faster, almost frantically. "What you don't understand, Natalie, is that Daniel is destined for a bigger life." Jennifer pointed back and forth between the two of them. "We? You and I? We will hold him back."

To her embarrassment, Natalie's eyes burned. Jennifer's words hit too close to home. She, too, had been destined for a bigger life. What if someone had stepped in at some point and convinced her to leave her tiny world behind? Would she have had accomplished more, been more, lived more? Probably. Definitely.

Her cell vibrated on the table. Natalie glanced at the screen. Shit. She'd been with Jennifer for over an hour. The message from Cece was urgent:

> WHERE ARE YOU?!!!

Natalie jumped up. "I have to go, Jennifer. I will not mention our conversation to Daniel."

"But will you do what I've asked?" Jennifer looked up, desperation darkening her face. "Please?"

"I don't know, but please do not drop in on me unexpectedly again." Natalie moved toward the door, then she turned back and snatched the pink bakery box off the table. "If you give Lola a sticky bun, she'll know you were here. And if you want one for the ride home, you can buy it yourself."

CHAPTER 46

*P*andemonium greeted Natalie. A dozen little ballerinas splashed in the water spurting out of a broken pipe under the bathroom sinks. Cece was on her hands and knees trying to block the fountain with bunches of towels while Candy scooped up children two or three at a time to relocate them.

"What happened?" Natalie asked, although it was obvious.

"Where have you been?" Cece shouted, water spraying her in the eyes. Her brown curls were plastered to her face. "I don't know where the water shut-off valve is. Do you?"

"I think so. I'll be right back!"

Natalie ran out the back door and down the side of the old hotel in search of the shut-off behind a thick hedge. She squeezed in between the branches. Twigs and thorns scratched her hands and arms and face as she reached for the lever and turned it ninety degrees. When she crawled out from the bush, Patty was standing over her with an outstretched hand.

"Your day really sucks, doesn't it?"

"You have no idea," Natalie said, taking her hand. "How did you know where I was?"

Patty, wearing her *Mariano's Manager* apron, had a pained look on her face. "I was coming to help Cece when I saw you dashing over here. Thought you might need me. By the way, you're bleeding."

Natalie touched the scrape on cheekbone. "Ouch."

"Come on," Patty said. "I'll help with whatever's going on inside. I'm sure it's a disaster."

Natalie jogged back to the front of the building with Patty alongside her. The front studio had collected at least an inch of water. It was seeping into floorboards and up the walls.

First it was Jennifer demanding she exit Daniel's life and now an epic flood. It was almost funny that her first interaction with Daniel's sister occurred because of a plumbing problem, and now her own plumbing problem was made worse by their second interaction. If Jennifer hadn't dropped in on her, Natalie might have caught the leak before it exploded. Or at least been there to manage it.

The old wood floor in the main studio was absorbing water like a drought-parched field. No intervention at this point would save it. Natalie sloshed across the room without bothering to stop the youngest students from splashing around as if they were in a water park.

"What are you going to do?" Patty asked.

"Jump off the closest bridge."

"It won't do much. The closest one is over the duck pond. You'll only drop about three feet."

Thank God someone could still crack jokes.

Cece appeared, dripping wet with an expression Natalie had never seen on her before. Something between exasperation and fury. "We need to get the kids out of here. I alerted most of the parents."

"I'm sorry," Natalie said. "So sorry. I should've been here."

"Yeah, you should have been here. And you should've called the plumber last week like you said you would."

"You're right." Natalie vaguely recalled a conversation about a tiny leak but had forgotten all about it.

"I don't know how many more of your dropped balls I can pick up." Cece pushed a bunch of wet curls out of her face, shook her head, and walked away.

"Oh-oh," Patty said. "I think you're in trouble."

"Yep." Natalie watched a little girl spin through the water singing with delight. "Big trouble."

PARENTS SWARMED THE STUDIO. Some were sympathetic and showed up with mops and towels. Others whisked their kids away as if there were a leaking nuclear reactor in the building.

Rebecca sent a text through the town council emergency alert system that the studio needed clean up help. Within minutes dozens of people appeared to lend a hand.

"This is why I love this town," Patty said. "Everybody steps up, you know?"

"I guess." Natalie frowned. "Do you know where Cece is?"

"Um, I think she had to go get Noah."

Natalie eyed her best friend's best friend. "You're lying."

"Yeah, sorry." Patty offered a tight smile. "She walked out, didn't say anything. I think she needs to cool off. Don't worry, she'll come around. Cece has a huge, forgiving heart. She doesn't even know how to hold a grudge."

"That's true." Natalie's stomach roiled. She had let Cece down. She owed her more. Her partner deserved better.

Natalie's pocket vibrated with a text.

> Hey there see you tonight. Dinner at eight.

In all the chaos, Natalie had completely forgotten he was coming out after his shift. Her thumbs hovered over the keys.

There was no way she could see him now, not with the disaster at the studio. Not with the looming (and much deserved) denunciation from Cece. And definitely not while she was processing Jennifer's entreaty that she dump him.

"What's wrong?" Patty asked.

"Nothing. I was supposed to see Daniel tonight, but I've got to cancel."

"Why would you do that?" Patty gawked in disbelief. "Spending a few hours in bed with your hot detective sounds like a great way to end this terrible day."

Natalie rubbed her eyes, smearing mascara on the heels of her hands. She considered Patty's sage advice, but then dismissed it. "This place is a train wreck, and it's all my fault."

She returned to the clean-up crew and worked alongside her generous neighbors and friends. The wood floor along the hallway was already buckling. Her dance studio was in ruins. It would take months to fix the damage, and cost a fortune. Half her students would go to other studios or quit dance altogether. Her best ballerinas, the ones who stood a chance of earning spots with a professional company, would have no choice but to go elsewhere. Consistency at the highest stage of one's training was paramount. It required six days a week of intense work and practice. Natalie would need to refund thousands in prepaid tuition. Nobody understood the delicate balance she had to maintain to keep her studio afloat, the thin profit margin that allowed her to pay her employees and bills. Not even Cece knew that Natalie had gone without taking a paycheck for months.

Cece's dream of turning Ashley into the prima ballerina they knew she could become was all but finished. The Lurensky Academy would go down in flames. Her mother's legacy would be destroyed. And Natalie would forever be known as a failure.

The Fire Chief and several emergency workers converged

on the scene. They shut off the electricity and forced everyone to exit immediately.

"Sorry Natalie," the chief said. "Everyone's gotta get out. This is an old building, and there could be exposed wires."

"I understand." Natalie looked at the beautiful chandeliers, the bulbs now extinguished, leaving the Mayfair Hotel ballroom in blurry, dim light as the sun set on what was now one of the worst days of Natalie's life.

She thanked the fire chief and exited the building.

Everyone who had been helping had gathered across the street in the park. She joined them, wandering into the crowd to receive their whispers of sympathy and support. It was like a flashback to all the unwanted attention thrust upon her when her mother got sick, then sicker, then dying, and then dead.

In the distance, she spotted Tessa running toward her. As soon as her friend reached out, Natalie cracked. She gasped and balled her fists, trying to control the outburst. Lurensky women did not fall apart. But the flood had upended her. For months she'd been clinging to the side of a mountain that grew slipperier with every crisis. Her priorities were out of whack, she had too many distractions and responsibilities, and all she wanted to do was sit on the ground and cry.

So she did.

The tears she hadn't shed for her mother poured out. Angry, ugly crying that mortified her. But she couldn't stop. With no idea who was grasping her arms, Natalie allowed herself to be lifted like a child and guided away.

In Natalie's bedroom, Tessa helped her remove her wet clothes and wrapped her in an old chenille robe. The tears still hadn't stopped. "I—I can't b-b-believe I'm crying this hard." She blew her nose into a wad of tissues.

"Four months since your mom died," Tessa said. "That's a lot of pent up emotion. I'm not surprised today's disaster was the last straw."

Natalie sat on the edge of her bed, the bed she'd slept in all her life. "What am I going to do? Even with insurance, this is going to wipe me out." She wondered what the interest rate was at the moment. The house she inherited was her only real asset, that and her roster of students—and maybe the name Lurensky.

"Natalie!"

"What?" She jumped, startled by Tessa's tome.

"You looked like were about to faint. Come on, let's get you something to eat."

Natalie followed Tessa into the kitchen where her friend searched the cupboards. "You have a lot of oatmeal."

"I know."

"I'll make you some. It's good comfort food."

"What time is it?" Natalie asked. "Who's watching your shop?"

"Don't worry. Patty and Rebecca and Nonna have everything under control." Tessa put the kettle on the stove. She measured oats into a pot, added water, and stirred. When the kettle whistled, she made chamomile tea. She tended to Natalie with great care, as if she were reenacting their old relationship when Tessa was her babysitter.

They sat on the couch eating oatmeal with raisins and brown sugar and sipping their tea. Oatmeal and tea—something she'd made for Ilana a million times.

Natalie scraped her bowl clean and licked a bit of sugar off the back of her spoon. "Thank you for taking care of me."

"We all need a little taking care of from time to time," Tessa said. "No matter how strong and stubborn we are."

"Look at my hands. They won't stop shaking."

"I'll stay with you as long as it takes. All night if you want. We can snuggle like we did when you were a little girl."

That at least made Natalie laugh. "No, I'll be fine. I'm just exhausted. And scared. I need a plan, you know? I'm always better when I have a plan."

"Then here's the plan. You get a good night sleep, and tomorrow we will hash this out together. You need to let us help you. Sound good?"

Natalie nodded. "I guess."

"Okay," Tessa said. "I'll clean up, and you go take a bath."

"Absolutely not. You go. I can clean up." Natalie stacked their bowls. She walked Tessa out the door.

"Thank you for rescuing me today."

"That's what friends do—and old babysitters, too."

THE TEXT ARRIVED the moment she finished rinsing the dishes.

Almost there - see you soon

"Oh no." Natalie couldn't believe she hadn't cancelled. Now what? She needed more time to figure out how to break up with him. At least now she agreed with Jennifer. The relationship had to end, and not because Daniel needed to fulfill his destiny of a bigger life. It had to end because Natalie Lurensky had taken her eye off the ball, allowed herself to be distracted. If she didn't give everything she had to saving her business, it would cease to exist. She had no time for a relationship, no time for love, no time for happiness. She didn't deserve any of it.

CHAPTER 47

hen Natalie didn't respond to his first text, Daniel wasn't concerned. She usually sent back an *'ok'* or a *'great'* or at least a happy-face-emoji, but it had been mid-afternoon. She probably was wrangling a bunch of little ballerinas.

But when she didn't reply to the second text, he wondered if something had come up. Didn't matter though. He was only a few minutes away, and no matter what, he intended to plead his case one more time, exactly the way Fred had suggested.

When she opened the door in a bathrobe, Daniel could see something was wrong.

"Sorry," Natalie said. "I'm not ready to go. Can you give me like fifteen minutes?"

Daniel swept inside and drew her into his arms, touching his lips to hers lightly. "Of course. And hey, we don't have to go out. I could go pick up a pizza or something."

"Would you? I really need a quick shower after the day I had. A pipe ruptured at the studio."

"Oh, man. Did it cause much damage?"

"I'll tell you about it over dinner." She gave him a quick kiss then disappeared into her room.

He locked the front door on his way out and drove the short distance toward Main Street. Settling in Clearwater, making it his home, had grown on him. Sure, it would be a quieter life than he'd imagined, but the town had a small police department. There was even a bit of crime in the outskirts to keep things interesting. Only a week or so ago, some kids graffitied a wall at a community center. Graffiti was a misdemeanor, but it was a gateway crime, always leading to something worse like vandalism, breaking and entering, assault.

Daniel parked his truck in front of the pizza place. He went in but then realized he didn't know what kind of pizza Natalie liked.

He studied the menu.

"Can I help you?" a teenage boy asked. He had a name tag pinned to his white apron—*Kyle.*

"Um, yes, I just need find out what my girlfriend likes on her pizza." Daniel pulled his cell from his pocket.

Kyle laughed "You got a girlfriend, and you don't know what kind of pizza she likes?"

"To be honest," Daniel said, amused by the wise-guy kid, "we haven't been together that long. And we haven't gone out for pizza yet. I'll text her."

"Who's your girlfriend?"

"Huh?"

"Is she a local?"

"Yeah." Daniel wondered where the kid was heading.

"What's her name?"

"Natalie," he said, thinking Kyle might make a good cop one day.

"Wow, you are one lucky guy. My buddy was in love with her for like ten years. But she was so far out of his league it was hilarious. Anyway, she's a pineapple and ham pizza person."

"She is?" Daniel found that hard to believe.

"Long as I've been here," Kyle said. "And I been here a long time."

He stretched out the word 'long.' Daniel wondered if he meant the pizza place or the town. "Can you do half and half?"

"Sure can. What do you want on your side?"

"I'm a straight up pepperoni kinda guy."

"Gotcha," Kyle said, writing on a slip of paper. "One large half pep, half P and H. Be ready in fifteen minutes."

"Okay, Kyle, thanks. I'll be back."

Daniel wandered up the block in the charming, small town that would soon be his home, if all went according to plan. Before he knew it, he was standing in front of his favorite bakery. His taste buds came to life as he inhaled the scent of freshly baked dough. It was a little before seven, and the bakery was closed. He checked the door on impulse. It swung open, but nobody was behind the counter. "Hello?"

Nothing. Jesus, he could walk out with that fancy espresso machine or six trays of homemade bread. There were no cameras tucked into the corners by the ceiling and definitely none on the street. Crime would find this town like a slithering snake about to nab an unsuspecting mouse. And he'd be the hero to keep it in check.

"Anyone here?"

The door behind the counter flew open, and a tall woman with flaming red hair piled on top of her head popped out. "Hi!"

"Hi. Are you closed?"

"Technically, yes. I'm just in the back prepping some stuff for tomorrow."

"Why wasn't the door locked then?" Daniel asked.

"In Clearwater? We don't lock our doors, or hardly ever. Although I might lock up when I leave. Probably a good idea. Even though there's no crime in Clearwater."

Daniel had heard that before. "Okay, so the bakery's closed, but since you're here, okay if I buy something?"

"Sure, totally. If you want sticky buns though, we're out. But you're new here, aren't you? You probably don't even know about them, so pretend I didn't mention it. Although, to be honest, I set two aside to bring home. I should let you have them. I can get more tomorrow."

Daniel was practically out of breath listening to her. She certainly was amusing. "I don't know what I want to buy. The smell pulled me in here. Are you, um, the owner or something?"

"Me?" The woman burst out laughing. "Oh, gosh, no. I just work here from time to time when they need someone to fill in. My name's Rebecca."

"Nice to meet you." Daniel thought he might be able glean some interesting tidbits from this very talkative resident. "Have you lived here long?"

"Hmm, well, let me think." Rebecca leaned on the glass counter and twisted her lips in thought. "Yes! Well, not my whole life, but like ten years. My mom runs the cottages, which is a super nice place if you ever need lodging on the lake. I work there sometimes, too. And at Mariano's. Have you been there? It's the best cheese and wine shop in like, well, in the whole world as far as I'm concerned. Anyway, that doesn't matter. So, are you visiting for the weekend or just passing through?"

"Yet to be determined," Daniel said. "My girlfriend lives here."

First her eyes widened. Then her skin flushed. Then her mouth gaped. "Oh. My. God! Are you Daniel? You are. I know you are. How did I not guess right away?'

"I—I don't know," Daniel said, now recalling that Natalie might have mentioned her exuberant friend once or twice.

Rebecca came around the counter and threw her long arms around him. "I am so happy to finally meet you in person!"

Daniel returned her expression of affection with a modest hug. "I'm actually here to get a pizza."

Rebecca let him go. "Sorry. We don't make pizza."

"No, I meant here in town. I guess Natalie had a rough day."

Rebecca flailed her arms. "Did you hear? It's a disaster. The whole place is like totally ruined. I don't know what she's going to do. But the town council will help her. I've already started a campaign—that's my job, you know, proposing initiatives to improve infrastructure for residents and business as well as assisting with repair and maintenance of historic buildings. Well, we really only have one. The old Mayfair Hotel, built in 1925. Although I'm trying to get the gazebo on the register, too. Then there'll be money for its upkeep." The young woman inhaled some air.

"You have a lot of jobs, don't you?" Daniel asked, hopeful she was exaggerating about Natalie's dance studio.

"So many. That's why they call me the 'everywhere girl.' Everybody runs into me, well, *everywhere.*"

"I guess Clearwater is a special place," Daniel said. If he were going to be hanging out with Natalie's friends, this one would take some getting used to. "I'm going to go pick up my pizza. Could you box up some cookies or something? Whatever you think Natalie will like."

"Oh, for sure! I know exactly what she likes—chocolate chip pecan is her favorite, but she also likes peanut butter which is actually one of my favorites. And of course everybody loves—"

"Yeah, all of those." Daniel backed toward the door. "I'll pay for them after I get the pizza."

"Don't worry. I'll put it on your account."

"I don't have an account."

"I'm setting one up for you right now. Detective Daniel Garrett, right? You're a police officer. I know you're good for it."

"Yeah, okay. Thanks." Daniel left the crazy, red-headed

everywhere girl thinking he might need a nap after that encounter.

~

NATALIE'S CELL received a series of texts from Rebecca:

> Oh my God, he's gorgeous!

> I'm so happy you decided not to break up with him!

> Can't wait to have a double date!

> He opened an account at Nutmegs!

By the time Daniel arrived with pizza and enough cookies for the whole neighborhood, Natalie knew he'd been the recipient of Rebecca's overflowing, eager enthusiasm.

"You opened an account at Nutmegs?" she asked, pulling a gray sweatshirt on over navy leggings and winding her hair into a loose bun. She had never looked so unkempt in front of Daniel, but it was the best she could do.

"I guess so." Daniel dropped his Giants cap on the coffee table and handed Natalie the box of cookies. "Your friend Rebecca is quite the town cheerleader."

"That she is," Natalie said. "I'm so sorry about tonight. And I'm such a mess."

"Don't worry about it." Daniel set the pizza on the dining room table and pulled her into a tight hug. "You're not a mess, and we'll make up for tonight next week."

No, we won't, she thought.

Natalie looked up at him. His face was etched with concern. How would she ever do what had to be done?

Daniel, with one arm still around her, opened the pizza box.

"You got pineapple and ham?" She started crying all over again. "How did you know?"

"Kyle told me."

Natalie laughed and cried. "Do you like pineapple pizza?"

"No, but it's not a deal breaker." He smoothed her hair.

Natalie sniffled and held the back of her hand under her nose.

"And Rebecca picked out your favorite cookies, too. Now let's eat while it's hot, and you tell me what happened at the studio."

Natalie sat and took a piece of pizza from the box, a string of hot, melty cheese sticking to the paper. Ordinarily, she'd devour three pieces at least. But she couldn't eat. Her stomach was a jumble of nerves and anxiety. Plus, she'd eaten all that oatmeal. She nibbled at it so that Daniel would eat.

"I can honestly say this is one of the best pizzas I've ever had. And I've had a lot of pizza."

"We do have good pizza here," Natalie said, struggling to act normal.

"Between the pizza and the coffee and the sticky buns in this town, what else could a man ask for?" Daniel gave her an expectant smile. "Oh wait, just the most beautiful woman in the world."

Oh, God, he was making everything so much harder. "Do you want water? I'm getting water." Natalie jumped up and went to the sink. She gripped the edge as a wave of dizziness made her head spin.

Daniel came up behind and held her. "Are you okay?"

She turned, her body stiff. "We need to go to the studio."

CHAPTER 48

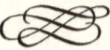

They drove in silence. Daniel kept glancing over at Natalie, unable to discern her grim expression. At a stoplight, he squeezed her hand. Thankfully, she squeezed back.

Once inside the old Mayfair Hotel, Daniel saw the utter destruction for himself.

Natalie nudged a warped floor board with her toe. "I can't believe eight hours ago, this place looked normal."

Water had seeped into every crack and crevice. Half of the wood planks on the gorgeous old hardwood floor had been torn up and tossed in a heap off to the side. All the way the down the hallway toward Natalie's office, he could see the plaster bubbling.

Daniel knew enough about carpentry and home repairs to see that it would take a lot of time and money to restore the historical landmark.

"Do you have insurance?" He instantly regretted asking the question.

"There's some, but it won't come close to covering it..." Natalie wandered into her office. She removed a photo from the wall. It was the black and white of her mother that Daniel had noticed the first time he'd been in her office.

She rested her hips against the desk and stared at the photograph. "I'm so sorry, mamma."

He could barely hear the words.

Daniel positioned himself beside her. "Natalie, sweetheart, please let me help you."

"No." She moved away from him. "I am a sinking ship. I will not take you down with me."

"You don't understand." Daniel's heart rate ticked up. "I'm not going away. I—I can't. I'm changing jobs though. That's really what my crazy plan was about all along anyway. Just needing a change."

Natalie squeezed her eyes shut and shook her head.

"Don't do that," Daniel said. "You have to listen to me. I know we've only known each like what, two months? But I am in love with you—hopelessly, insanely, desperately in love."

There, he'd said it, exactly the way Fred told him to.

"Here's the thing," he continued. "I can't leave. There's a whole other problem preventing me from going." The fabricated story came to him out of sheer panic. "Jennifer needs me to stay. She said so. Her situation is all, you know, up in the air with that new boyfriend. And Lola's been acting out. So—so they need me."

Natalie narrowed her eyes. It would've been scary if not for the saddest smile he'd ever seen.

"I'm no detective, Detective, but I think you're lying."

"I'm not lying, I swear I'm just being..." he couldn't keep it up. Natalie saw right through him. "What about a compromise then? We do a long distance thing—I go on my, whatever the hell I'm thinking it is, but we don't actually break up? Then when I come back, we pick up where we left off. I really need to get—"

"Daniel, stop. I'm going to tell you something, and you can't argue with me. You have to take me at my word. Can you do that?"

"Of course." If there were one thing he knew about Natalie, she was as genuine as they came.

THEY WALKED across the street into the park. Natalie couldn't take being in the studio another minute. It felt like a graveyard.

They sat on a bench facing the Mayfair Hotel. Stars blanketed the sky like pinpricks of light. With a quarter moon overhead, the inn looked untouched and undamaged. Like a woman hiding her grief, the devastation was buried inside.

Natalie had thought she'd hit rock bottom when her mother passed away. Little did she know how much worse it would get. She allowed Daniel to scoot close and wrap an arm around her.

"Please start talking," he said. "I can't stand not knowing what it is you need to tell me."

Natalie cleared her throat and summoned the last drop of strength she could muster. No more tears, she told herself. "First of all, you are one of the—no, scratch that—the most wonderful man I've known since my dad."

"Now you're going to tell me I'm a nice guy, right?" Daniel said, a hint of humor.

"I wasn't, but you are."

"Fine, I believe you. Is that what you wanted me to tell me?"

"It's not. I only wanted you to know how much I admire and…" she hesitated before choosing the next word.

"You don't need to say it. I believe you love me, too. You can deny it if it helps."

"See? You're so intuitive. God, I was such a fool."

"You're not a fool. You're amazing." He placed his hands on her cheeks and pulled her in for the most heart wrenching kiss, his smooth lips pressing hard against hers. She gave into it, one last surrender to him. It would have to sustain her forever. It tasted of pain, defeat, and loss.

Finally, he released her. Even in the darkness, she could see the smallest flicker of hope in his gaze. She needed to extinguish it.

"Even if you didn't go on your adventure, I can't do this anymore. There was a moment when I thought maybe I could, but I can't. I have failed at everything I was meant to do."

"But maybe you're not meant—"

Natalie placed a finger over his lips. "You promised to take me at my word, so you need to hear it. I let myself get distracted, to venture into things that were different and new. The whole Kaylee situation was horrible, but it was also exciting. And then you, a man I never dreamed of and a man I don't deserve. Even the puppies at the shelter threw me out of focus. Today has been the absolute worst day of my life. Worse than when my parents died, because today was my fault. If I'd been doing what I should be doing, this would not have happened. I have disappointed some of the most important people in my life. I can't do that anymore."

"Natalie, what I'm trying to explain, poorly I'll admit, is that this trip I've been planning, well, it's not important anymore. And it was never my life-long dream, not really."

"Wasn't it though? Daniel, you're meant for a bigger life."

His head twitched to the side. "Now you sound like my sister."

Natalie should have chosen different words. She would not reveal Jennifer's secret. It didn't matter anyway. The decision was hers. It had nothing to do with his sister's request.

Natalie stroked the scar on his cheek. "My life, me, this town —it's too small for you."

"It's too small for you, too. I know it is."

"It's not. It fits me just right. I made the choice long ago what my life would be, what I was destined to be—the guardian of my mother's legacy. And now I have to see it through."

"So that's it then?" His voice choked up.

Natalie willed herself out of any emotion, forced numbness into her heart. "That's it then. Everything I built with my mom is on the verge of collapse. If I don't devote a hundred percent of myself to saving it, I'll..." She paused. She'll what? Never forgive herself? Be cursed? Regret it for the rest of her life?

"You'll what?" Daniel asked her the same question she was asking herself.

"I don't know. All I know is that I have no choice."

Choices, options, possibilities—she had only one. Natalie was one of the millions of people in the world who had limited her own life because of fear—fear of venturing out, taking risks, exploring the unknown. By the time she was ready to tamp down the fear, it was too late.

"I want you to do one for thing for me," she said.

"Okay." Daniel's voice was barely audible.

"Make your world as big and endless as it can be. Don't hold back, don't come back, don't miss a thing. Can you promise me that?"

"I'll do my best." He lifted his chin and put on a brave face.

"And don't think about me."

He took her by the hands. "I will never, ever not think about you. You'll have to accept that."

Natalie's breath came out in ragged burst. "I'll accept that. But you have to leave me behind. Don't contact me. I—I don't think I could stand it. We both need to be able to move on." Her chest trembled.

They gazed at each other in the dark quiet, as if willing the moment never to end. But, of course, it had to.

"I get it," he said, so hurt he sounded almost angry. "You've given me no option."

"I'm sorrier than you could know." If she didn't get away from him soon, the tears would come.

"I think I do know." Daniel stood and took a step, then turned back. "Will you give me something to remember you by?"

"If I can, I will."

He pulled his phone from his pocket and scrolled. The strains of "My Eyes Adored You" broke the silence, blending with the soft sounds of crickets, rusting leaves, and the distant call of an owl. He held his arms open. "One last dance?"

Natalie rose and moved toward his embrace, her heart cracking into a million pieces.

CHAPTER 49

*N*atalie held Rebecca while she sobbed in her arms.

"Rebecca, please stop crying," Natalie said. "You're hysterical."

"B-b-b-but that was the m-m-most beautiful, heartbreaking, romantic end to a relationship I've ever h-h-heard." Another round of wails filled the shelter. Dogs barked, cats meowed, and even the chickens outside in the coop clucked extra loudly. "How are you not in bed buried under the covers? I would be!"

Natalie kissed the top of her friend's head and untangled herself. "To be honest, I'm numb. And I have no time to wallow in a broken heart. I should never have given you all the details." As it was she'd hardly told Rebecca any details, except for their last dance. Natalie would never be able to hear that song again.

Three nights ago, after Daniel left, Natalie allowed herself to crumble. She spent the night and the whole next day with Cece, crying, apologizing, and swearing on her life that going forward she'd devote her entire self to rescuing and reviving the Lurensky Dance Academy. No more distractions or left turns or forays into misguided endeavors.

To her credit, and as expected, Cece forgave all of Natalie's neglect and inattention. Making amends with her best friend at least cured some of her angst.

Natalie adopted tunnel vision. She'd be a horse with blinders, unable to see anything other than what was directly in front of her. Right now, that was one red-headed, runny-nosed, sweet girl named Rebecca.

"Dry your tears. I'll be fine, but I do need to be at the studio in fifteen minutes, so please give me the paperwork for that town council thing. And whatever it is we need to submit to the historical society. Oh, and did you tell me you know a guy who repairs old plaster? I've got to get someone to look at—"

"Natalie, hold on." Rebecca sniffled and blew her nose. "Tessa and I are taking care of everything having to do with the historical society and town council. I'll find a plasterer, so don't worry about that. You and Cece have to put all your energy into figuring how to keep the school running for the next few months."

"Okay, you're right," Natalie said, impressed by Rebecca's ability to switch gears and become the decisive one. "Thank you."

"I'll bring the paperwork to you as soon as I finish up here." Rebecca's eyes welled up again. "It's time for you to say goodbye to the puppies. They're going to their forever homes in a few days."

"Oh, yeah, I knew that." Natalie could only keep so much emotion at bay. A tear escaped. "How's the mother doing?"

"Poor thing, her babies are leaving her, except for the one. She'll get over it though. Dogs are very resilient."

Natalie took an extra minute to check on the playful puppies who had at least tripled in size since the night they were born. They were jumping and playing and chewing on each other, while climbing over their mother.

"Good luck, you cutie-pies. And you, too, little mama."

Natalie didn't dare stroke the mother. One touch of her silky fur would set her back even more.

NATALIE STAYED true to her promise. Nothing unrelated to the studio received one minute of her attention. Kaylee, thank God, was staying on track. After Elaine learned of Natalie's crisis, she promised to watch over Kaylee to make sure Natalie wouldn't get sucked in again. The puppies, six weeks after their birth, and their mother were sent off to their forever homes. And, painful as it was, Daniel left her alone. He, too, kept his promise.

Within days of the flood, renovations were underway. Half the town participated. Every handyman, electrician, plumber, and painter stepped up and pitched in, most of them working at discounted rates.

Natalie stood beside Cece in the middle of the studio, watching the transformation.

"I can't believe how many people are helping me," she said. "I feel like the guy in 'It's a Wonderful Life.' What's his name?"

"George Baily. I love that movie. And you are a modern day version of him. Everybody here is talking about what you've done for them or for someone in their family over the years."

"What my mother did, too. She was tough as nails but had a huge, generous heart."

Grinding noise filled the room as a man with goggles and gloves pushed the blade of a power saw through damaged plaster. Somebody else was on hands and knees prying up floor boards and dragging them out to the dumpster.

Natalie watched, momentarily falling into a trance, until Cece tapped her arm.

"Come on, let's get some coffee."

"Okay." Natalie followed Cece outside.

When they crossed the street into the park, Natalie turned

and looked back. "You know, even with all these people working, it's going to take months for the studio to be usable again.
The insurance and grant from the town council won't be nearly
enough money. I'm probably going to have to take out a loan."
She'd already borrowed against her house to pay for her mother's care. There was still some equity, but that house was her
nest egg. "Or reconsider Maura's offer."

"To sell your business? Are you kidding?"

"Maybe just part of it." Natalie pictured a magnificent sculp-
ture breaking into pieces.

"Hold on, just, Jesus, hold on. If you really want to sell a
portion of your business, why not ask me?"

"You?"

"Yes, me!" Cece practically yelled at her, but nicely. "I believe
in this dance school. I would love to invest in it. Then we'd truly
be partners."

Natalie considered the unexpected offer. Cece knew everything about the studio and its history. She even understood the
finances better than anyone.

"Are you really interested?"

"I wouldn't haven't brought it up if I weren't. The Lurensky
Academy was, and is, a major part of my life. Investing in it
would be much more than a financial transaction. I loved your
mother so much. And I love this school as much as you do."

At least as much, Natalie thought. *Probably more.*

CHAPTER 50

*M*aura, Cece, and Natalie met at an empty space halfway between their two studios. It was over a thousand square feet. The wood flooring was worn in spots, but at least it was wood.

"This used to be a restaurant?" Natalie asked.

"It did," Maura said. "A failed family business, but my brothers and I still own the property. And since I'm the only one who's local, I'm in charge of it. I never thought about using it as a studio, but it really is a great space for it."

"It could work," Natalie said. Her feelings for Maura had warmed. She had called immediately after the flood to express concern and sympathy. At first Natalie thought it was an act, but after several conversations, her belief in Maura's sincerity grew.

"I like it," Cece said. "Needs mirrors and barres, obviously. But the bathrooms are in good shape, there are shelves to use as cubbies, and with two rooms we can do group lessons in one area and private in another."

"It'll be perfect for Ashley, too," Maura said. "She can work with Cece here."

The more Natalie thought about it, the more she liked it.

"It's a good solution," Cece said.

"I'm glad you think so." Maura exhaled, as if relieved her idea appealed to them. "And I'm sure most of your students will stick with you since it's not that far of a drive."

Natalie and Cece exchanged glances. Maura was offering them the space at a ridiculously low rent. There was nothing in it for her, except keeping Ashley's training going.

"Maura," Natalie said. "Remember when you came to see me three months ago and asked me to reach out if anything changed?"

Maura froze, mouth open and eyes wide. "Are you serious?"

"I am. Obviously I was wrong. Predicting the future has never been my strong suit, and now that everything has changed, I have a proposal for you."

AFTER ALL THE numbers were crunched and every angle considered, Natalie sold off over half her business. She maintained thirty-six percent, while Cece and Maura each took thirty-two. They merged and became known as Lurensky Ballet and Dance with three locations.

The infusion of cash paid for the quick build-out of the new location. The insurance settlement wasn't enough to repair the damage to the studio, but the town council and the historical society stepped up. Thanks to the money from her new partners, Natalie was able to invest in the business—she gave all of her instructors small raises, paid herself for the months she'd worked without compensation, and even put a small chunk into her savings account.

Her partners' contributions gave her breathing room, and their devotion to maintaining the Lurensky name and reputation gave her comfort. For the first time since her mother's illness began eight years ago, Natalie was not in it alone.

Maura could hardly contain her excitement over having her name associated with Natalie Lurensky's. And Cece was the pillar of strength and commitment she'd always been.

They lost only a handful of students, but gained some new ones. Progress was getting back on track. A different track, to be sure, but a solid one that Natalie knew she could stay on for the long run and head in the direction she needed to go. Her business would not fail. Her mother's legacy would not fade.

TESSA AND NATALIE stood in the park across from the old Mayfair Hotel on a warm Sunday morning at the end of May.

"Construction's coming along," Tessa said. "There's already talk about a grand reopening."

"Yep, grand reopening." Natalie entwined her fingers and put her hands on top of her head. "I can't believe I'm going to have to plan another event. Just one more thing to worry about."

"Let me do it," Tessa offered.

"I couldn't do that," Natalie said, although she wished she could.

"Why not? I can plan a party in my sleep. Plus, I have caterers and vendors knocking down my door to work my events. I've lost count of the favors they owe me. We can get donations, sell tickets, make it a fundraiser."

"You're already taking charge. And brilliantly so." Natalie checked herself. For the first time ever, she had to run every decision by others. "I need to talk to Cece and Maura, but I'm sure they'll be on board. It's a tremendous gift, Tess. Thank you."

Tessa squeezed Natalie around her waist. "Happy to help. Now, if you'll excuse me, I must go. Finally, I have a night with no obligations and a husband who is not on call. We're going to drive out to that place you recommended where you went with —oh, sorry, never mind."

"It's okay, you can say his name. Where I went with Daniel." Natalie felt a pang of regret, or perhaps it was loneliness. She couldn't tell the difference.

Natalie spent the next few hours in her office, cleaning out the desk and taking down all the photographs. The carpet would be ripped up, the wood floor underneath refinished, the walls painted. It was a much needed refresh, and long overdue.

At noon, Natalie took a break. She strolled through the park toward Nutmegs. At the pond, a few children stood on the bridge tossing bread to the ducks. Natalie allowed herself a momentary lapse into a sweet memory, the day Daniel brought Lola to Clearwater. It felt like a lifetime ago.

At the edge of the park, a crowd had gathered next to the *Furry Friends Pet Rescue* van. In the midst of the crowd, Natalie spotted Kaylee wearing a bright blue *Furry Friends Volunteer* t-shirt.

"Natalie, hi!" Kaylee waved. Her hair, back to its original color, was wound into a messy bun on top of her head. She looked like the sweet teenager she used to be.

"I'm so glad to see you." Natalie hugged her tightly. "You look great. And I hear from Elaine that everything is going well."

"Super well," Kaylee said. "I'm following all the rules, and in September I'm going back to school. I'm thinking I want to be a veterinarian someday."

"That's phenomenal," Natalie said, delighted by Kaylee's motivation and turn-around.

"It's going to take a while, because I have to work while I go to school. But even if it takes a few extra years, who cares? Right?"

"Exactly right."

"Oh, and, um, I'm really sorry about the studio," Kaylee said. "I saw what a mess it was."

"Thanks, but it's working out, slowly but surely."

"Just like me, huh?"

"Just like you." Natalie cupped her chin. "I'm very proud of you, honey."

Kaylee did a little twirl—her dance skills still remained—and went back to work.

At the curb, the van door slid open, and Rebecca stepped out onto the sidewalk with a crate full of mewing kittens.

"Hi, Rebecca." Natalie's voice was chipper after seeing Kaylee doing so well. "Adoption day, huh?"

"Every other Sunday." She held up her crate. "Just got a bunch of kittens if you know anyone who wants one, hint-hint."

"I've got more than enough on my plate, but thanks."

"Excuse me, Rebecca," a volunteer said. "What should I do with this one?" He held a small cage covered with a pink towel.

"Oh, just give it to me. And you take the kittens out to play in the center pen."

They traded crates, and the volunteer carried off the kittens.

"What's in there?" Natalie pointed at the pink towel.

"Nothing." Rebecca put the crate in the van.

"Come on." Natalie grew curious. "Is it something weird like a snake or a monkey?"

"That's so totally funny!" Rebecca's laughter was forced. "Hey, if you're getting coffee at Nutmegs would you—"

"Rebecca, you are so transparent." Natalie reached in and lifted the towel. "What's this?"

Rebecca groaned. "I didn't want you to see her. It'll only make you sad again."

The mama dog had been groomed, her coat clipped short and stylish with little pink bows on each ear. On the door to the crate was a card that read: *foster only.*

She looked up at Rebecca. "I thought she was adopted."

Rebecca shook her head. "It didn't work out. The family that took her said she was too needy and decided to just keep the puppy. So, we got her back."

"Then why isn't she up for adoption?"

"Because I'm concerned about her. We have to figure out the right kind of household. She's having a hard adjustment—trembles all the time and only calms down when somebody holds her."

"Can I hold her for a little bit?" Natalie reached for the hook on the cage.

"It's not a good idea, Nat. I mean, you're in a very vulnerable state, and if you get all attached to her again it'll—"

"Oh, please," Natalie said, opening the little door and coaxing the dog into her arms. "She's not a child, just a dog."

The moment the silky coat touched the side of Natalie's neck, she knew Rebecca was right. Attachment closed in on her like a clamp.

CHAPTER 51

"*I* want her," Natalie said.

"You what?" Rebecca's eyes popped. "You've never had a dog. You have no idea how much attention they require. If you need a pet, a cat is way more independent. Besides, you can't replace a boyfriend with an animal. It never works."

Natalie stroked the sweet dog and received gentle kisses in return. Was she trying to fill the hole in her heart with a pet? And if so, would that be such a bad idea? The dog needed a home, and Natalie needed—she needed something. "Let me try, Rebecca. I'll take good care of her. And God knows you could use one less animal in the shelter."

Rebecca twisted her lips side to side before a reluctant smile emerged. "Wow, I can't believe this. You and a dog?"

"It's crazy, I know, but I can do it." Natalie didn't question her decision for even a second. "I'm excited. I'm going to be that nutty dog-mom who carries her little pup in a pack or a purse or a stroller everywhere. She'll be our dance school mascot, and the children will love her. I love her." Natalie's eyes filled with tears as she buried her face in the dog's fur.

SHE NAMED HER ODETTE—THE virtuous heroine in Swan Lake, Natalie's favorite ballet. Within two days, Odette's whimpering subsided, her appetite grew, and she even learned how to play fetch. Finally, the poor, overworked breeding machine had the joyful and spoiled life she deserved.

And Natalie's heart healed a little bit more.

TWO WEEKS AFTER ADOPTING ODETTE, Natalie was driving back to Clearwater from the new studio. Maura's old restaurant space had been transformed into the perfect venue for large beginner classes as well as advanced and private lessons. Maura and Cece had established a new schedule, hired three new instructors, and launched night-time classes at the new location. They even rented out the space four mornings a week to a yoga instructor, which added a nice boost to their bottom line.

As for Natalie, she took a step back, finally free to not micro-manage every detail. Merging her studio with Maura's and making Cece a true partner was one of the best decisions she'd ever made. Only second to her decision to adopt Odette.

She reached into the fleece lined car seat and stroked her dog's warm fur. It was mid-afternoon on Saturday, and Natalie couldn't wait to get home, change her clothes, and take Odette on a walk in the park.

Natalie opened her front door, dropped her bag on the sofa, and set Odette on the floor. The happy dog scampered into the kitchen to her water bowl. After a refreshing drink, she sat and wagged her tail, anticipating the treat Natalie gave her every time they got home.

"You are just the smartest little girl, aren't you?" She held up the cookie. "Speak!"

Odette let out a fast yelp, received her snack, and trotted off to her spot on the couch.

"I'm going to change," Natalie said, kissing the top of her head. "And then we'll go out."

Yep, she had definitely become that crazy dog-mom.

She'd just pushed her feet into sneakers and clipped Odette's pink leash to her pink collar when her cell buzzed. Natalie retrieved her phone from the bottom of her bag and read the text.

> I'm sorry to bother you, but I can't find my Giants cap anywhere. Did I leave it at your house?

She froze. The three little dots bounced as his texting continued.

> I think I put it on the coffee table... have you seen it?

Natalie hesitated, her hands shook. It had been over a month since their break-up. She started to type a reply, but then deleted it. This was ridiculous. They were adults. She was fine. Their relationship had been brief—it wasn't that hard to move on.

She tapped his number. It rang two times before he answered.

"Hello?" He sounded like he had no idea it was Natalie calling, but of course he knew.

"Hi," Natalie said. "It's me."

"Right, um, I know I promised I wouldn't—"

"It's okay," she said, steadying her voice. "I haven't seen your hat."

"Could you look around a little? I've torn my place apart trying to find it."

"It's just a hat, Daniel. You can buy a new one."

He didn't respond right away, and Natalie immediately knew she'd said the wrong thing.

"It's, um, not just a hat. My dad bought it for me right before he died. We'd gone to a Giants game, and he surprised me with it at the seventh inning stretch."

Natalie swallowed and blinked on watery eyes. He'd never told her the hat story.

"Let me look around, hold on a sec—" she shook out the blanket, scooted the coffee table over, then bent down and checked under the sofa. There it was—the black and orange cap he had on the first time they'd met. She stretched her arm out to reach it. "Good news. It was under the couch."

"Really? Oh my God, thank you. I'll, um, I'll come get it, if that's okay."

"Sure, why don't I—"

"You can leave it somewhere if you don't want to see me," Daniel said.

So much had happened since they parted ways Natalie didn't know what she wanted. But it sounded juvenile to be unwilling to see him for a minute to hand him his baseball cap. Or maybe he didn't want to see her. "I'm okay with it if you are."

"Oh, well, then—" he sounded surprised. "I'm about forty minutes away. Where should we meet?"

"How about Nutmegs? I know you know where that is."

Daniel chuckled. "I do. Maybe I'll pick up a sticky bun for Lola while I'm in town."

"Sounds good. See you there." Natalie tossed her phone to the side and turned to Odette. "I can do this, I'm a big girl, no reason to be nervous."

As soon as Natalie got out of her car and saw him standing on the patio under a yellow umbrella, she second guessed herself. She took a breath, picked up Odette, and walked toward him.

They wavered around each other for a moment before moving in for an awkward hug.

"Here's your cap."

"Thank you." Daniel clutched it then put it on his head. His wavy brown hair had grown longer, his beard thicker. It made him look a little older and more rugged. Daniel reached out and scratched Odette behind the ears.

"What have we here?" he asked, accepting her licks on his hand.

"I adopted a dog."

"Wow, that—that's great. I mean, really great."

"She is great." Natalie repeated the overused word.

"What's her name?"

"Odette. I named her after the princess in Swan Lake."

"Princess Odette." Daniel continued petting her. "It suits her."

Emotion pulled Natalie in opposite directions. One side of her brain told her to say goodbye and get away from him as fast as possible. The other told her to linger in his presence and allow the flutters to flutter a little longer.

Daniel held up a pink bakery box. "I hope you weren't planning to get a sticky bun, because I took the last four."

"They make them every day, so there's always tomorrow." Natalie stood in place, waiting for him to make a move toward his truck or say he had to get going. But he didn't.

"Well, Odette and I are going for a walk," she said it as if it were just information and not a way of departing.

"Can I join you?"

No, no, no, no...

"Oh, sure, yeah. Why not?"

Why not? Really? Are you out of your mind? The voice in her head would not shut up.

Daniel put the bakery box in his truck, and they crossed into the park, Odette prancing between them.

"When do you leave on your trip?" Natalie asked. "I thought you'd be gone by now."

"Turns out moving takes a lot longer than you'd think. I'm still packing my apartment and putting stuff in storage. So, maybe another week or two." He slowed his steps as they passed the duck pond. "What about you? I drove by the studio. Looks like you're making progress."

"Oh, a lot has happened since the flood." Natalie gave him the long-story-short version. They walked and talked. "What's happening with your sister and Lola and the new boyfriend?"

He smiled and grimaced at the same time. "Aah, the boyfriend, Gordon, everyone loves him. Even I love him. He's a good guy, and it looks like he's in it for the long run. I won't be as central to their lives anymore, but that's okay. It's the way it should be."

They sat on the steps of the gazebo. *The way it should be,* such a simple explanation, a cliché maybe, but a basic truth. Seeing Daniel again, saying a final goodbye, would bring closure. And making sure he didn't give up his dream had absolutely been the right decision—*the way it should be.*

"So tell me," she said, trying to sound light-hearted. "Where are you headed? What's your itinerary?"

"Well, first I'm gonna head north, go into Canada. Then I'll come back south and hit the national parks. From there, I'm not sure. Probably travel Route 66 for a while. I told Lola I was going to find all the best ice cream shops in the country, and I intend to do just that." He pressed his lips into a wistful, regretful smile.

"It's going to be amazing," Natalie said. "I think it's a good thing that you don't have it all planned out, that you're just going to see where the wind blows and the road takes you."

Daniel turned his attention to Odette, and the little dog hopped into his lap. She stood on hind legs with her front paws on his shoulder and licked his cheek. He laughed and scratched her sides. "She's a sweetie. Too bad I don't have a dog to travel with me."

"Easily solved. Rebecca has a shelter full of them."

"Yeah, well, it seems you got the pick of the litter with this one," he said. "Can she go with me?"

Natalie pulled Odette into her lap and kissed her. "This dog never leaves my side, so if she goes, I go, too."

$\mathcal{N}$atalie gulped, and the flutters turned to heart pounding panic.

"That's not what I meant, I mean, I was kidding. Not about Odette leaving my side—she doesn't. But about, you know, the other part."

"I know what you meant," Daniel said. A light sheen of perspiration shimmered on his skin. "It was just an expression."

"Yeah, right, exactly." Natalie set Odette on the grass. "One of those silly things that falls out of the mouth."

"Exactly."

"Exactly. Unless you want…" the words stuck in her throat.

"Unless I want what?" Daniel's head tilted.

"Unless you want us to go with you." Natalie couldn't believe what she'd just said. "Wait. I'm sorry, that's ridiculous. Nobody invites themselves to go on someone else's trip. It's presumptuous and—and impulsive."

"Right. And you don't do impulsive."

Natalie covered her mouth and shook her head. "I don't know what's come over me, but I—I think I want to go with you."

Daniel swallowed hard, his Adam's apple moving up and down his neck. "Slow down. I've spent the last month in agony —missing you and dreaming about you and beating myself up for falling in love with you. So don't mess with me, Natalie. I don't think I could stand it. Do you really, really want to go?"

"Maybe. Yes. I don't know." The what-if worries began. "What if we fight?"

Daniel stood and pulled her to her feet. "We'll make up," he said.

"What if there's an emergency?"

"We'll fly back."

"What if you get tired of me?"

"That will never happen." He picked her up and spun her around. "There's no what if question you could ask that I don't have an answer to. I swear, I've never loved anyone the way I love you. And I will win your heart or die trying."

Natalie stroked his bearded cheek. "You already have, detective." She picked up Odette and snuggled her between their bodies. "Hear that, girl? We're going on a road trip!"

NATALIE OPENED her closet and pushed everything to the side.

There it was—a brand new, never used suitcase. She lay it on her bed, opened it, and filled it with clothes and shoes and dog toys.

Natalie had turned her world over. Her business would be left in capable and dedicated hands for as long as she was away, a yet undetermined amount of time. There wasn't anything that couldn't be handled by somebody else, at least for a while.

Rebecca would check on Natalie's house. And she'd keep the Mustang running by driving it around town on weekends, but only if she wasn't transporting animals.

Patty would inspect the renovation at the studio daily,

confirm that work stayed on schedule, and reprimand contractors as needed.

Tessa would handle everything having to do with the insurance, grants from the historical society, and various town council issues.

And Cece, well, she'd manage everything else.

The freedom Natalie had dreamed of had arrived.

IT WAS near the end of June. The night before Natalie's adventure began, she met her four best friends in front of the studio to say goodbye, all promising frequent calls, video chats, and texts.

Rebecca refused to let go of Natalie. She clung to her like a needy monkey until Patty pulled her off and launched herself into Natalie's arms.

One by one, they bid goodbye.

"This is really hard." Tessa dabbed her eyes with a tissue "I'm going to miss you. But I'm so happy for you."

Natalie released Patty and embraced Tessa. "Thank you for being the big sister I never had."

Tessa wriggled. "Don't get all mushy, please. I can't handle it. Besides, I have something for you." Tessa opened the trunk of her car and removed an enormous basket.

Natalie took it from her and set it on the steps. "It weighs a ton. What did you put in there?"

"Every one of your most favorite snacks, a few bottles of wine, and a load of ridiculously overpriced dog treats."

"Thank you, Tessa." Natalie wanted to hug her again, but they'd both fall apart if she did. "For everything."

"You bet." Tessa backed up with a wink and a smile. "Come on girls. Those two need some time alone."

Natalie and Cece stood side by side as their three friends crossed into the park and disappeared into the darkness.

Natalie let a sob escape.

"Oh, no," Cece said. "If you start crying, I'll start crying, and we'll never get through this."

Natalie blew her nose. "You're right. I'm not gonna cry. Honestly, it's not like I'm leaving forever."

"I hope not," Cece said. "But this is what you always wanted, to leave our suffocating small town behind."

The two childhood best friends sat on the steps in front of the studio where they'd sat a million times before, the very spot where they'd shared their dreams decades earlier.

"I'm not sure what to say." Natalie had no idea when she'd return. "But I'll be back eventually, at least for a visit."

"Of course you will," Cece said. "And we'll all be here waiting for you, no matter how long you're gone."

Natalie leaned against Cece. "If it weren't for you, I couldn't do this. I would never go with Daniel if I didn't have you to watch over everything. You've given me my freedom, Cece. You are my roots and my wings."

"We've come full circle." Cece sniffled. "You gave me my dream-come-true seven years ago. And now I'm here so you can have yours. Destiny, don't you think?"

Natalie glanced upward. "Yes. We were meant to find each other on these steps waiting to begin our very first ballet class."

"Hard to believe that was what? Thirty-five years ago?" Cece broke down. She buried her face in Natalie's shoulder and cried like a child. "We'll sit on these steps again someday, just like this. Won't we?"

Natalie wiped away Cece's tears and wrapped her in her arms. "Yes, we will, my friend. I promise."

CHAPTER 53

*W*ith her boyfriend and dog, Natalie visited places she never thought she'd see—the Grand Canyon and Mount Rushmore, big cities like Chicago and out of the way spots she'd never heard of.

They stayed in motels and hotels and campsites along the way. They devoured bags of pistachios and Tessa's gourmet treats.

Almost every day was an adventure. On quieter days, Natalie and Daniel would sit and hold hands and watch the wind blow.

They discovered more things they had in common—love of country music, mocha chip ice cream, old train stations, dry martinis—and a few things they didn't.

Their compatibility exceeded Natalie's expectation. Never before had she known such contentment or felt such profound love. Daniel fulfilled her in body and soul. She let go of almost every worry and reveled in a state of unencumbered bliss. Her cell phone rarely rang. She hardly ever checked email. She'd even blocked all social media. It was like turning back time.

As for Odette, she became the princess her name inspired.

Spoiled and doted upon and loved. She usually preferred Daniel over Natalie, which endeared her to both of them even more.

Three months after their trip began, as summer melted toward fall, they returned to California at the request of Lola, who missed her uncle desperately. Natalie rented a car and slipped into Clearwater surreptitiously. The only one who knew she was coming was Cece.

It was late at night when they went to the dance studio. Natalie viewed the main ballroom with discernment. She could tell immediately what was done to her and Cece's high standards and what needed further attention.

"It's coming along," she said, trying to sound optimistic.

"It is." Cece ran a hand over a smooth ballet barre. "I know it's not perfect yet. And I was hoping we'd be farther along by now."

Natalie sensed concern in her voice. "I feel terrible not being here to manage this. Maybe I should stay a few weeks and help get—"

"Absolutely not. You're living a dream with Daniel. And we're all enjoying it vicariously." Cece smirked at her. "Don't you dare mess it up."

Natalie wavered, but she appreciated Cece's firm instruction. Since she'd been away, fleeting twinges of guilt poked at her regularly. But they always passed quickly, like a fly buzzing by.

"Okay, well, I'll be checking in more often going forward. Can't believe Nutcracker is only three months out. How are rehearsals going?"

"Just fine, that's all you need to know," Cece said. "And you'd better be here for opening night."

"Of course I will." Natalie had no idea where she and Daniel would be by the time the holidays rolled around. But no matter what, she'd make the trip, even if only for a few days.

One of the best parts of her adventure with Daniel was the

freedom—no plans, commitments, or obligations. But an occasional flight home was expected and easily arranged.

Natalie spent the night at Cece's house, not wanting to attract any attention. The next day, she drove to Oakland to meet Daniel at his sister's house.

Although anxious about seeing Jennifer—it would be their first interaction since the disastrous day when Natalie hit rock bottom—she was looking forward to seeing Lola again.

They were in Jennifer's house barely five minutes when Lola yanked on her Uncle Danny's hand and dragged him to her room to see her new soccer shoes. Gordon, delightful and cheerful, said he had to run to the store, leaving the two women alone.

Natalie offered Jennifer a tight smile.

Jennifer mirrored the expression. "Let's go to the kitchen."

"Can I help prepare something?" Natalie followed Daniel's sister, playing it cool. "I'm not exactly a whiz in the kitchen, but I'm happy to chop vegetables or something."

"That's okay," Jennifer said, "have a seat. I make a mean dry martini."

Natalie propped herself on a stool. "Daniel must have mentioned my drink of choice."

"He did." Jennifer shook the cocktail shaker with expertise. "I spent a year tending bar at some dive restaurant before Lola was born. I can make any cocktail you can think of, as well as a few I invented."

She poured the icy liquid into two martini glasses. "Cheers."

"Cheers," Natalie said.

"To the future," Jennifer added.

"That, too." Natalie sipped. "Excellent martini, thank you."

Jennifer took a long drink and set her glass down. "I owe you an apology."

Natalie choked. "You do get right to the point, don't you?"

"I try. Although I wasn't so good at it last time we were together."

"Well," Natalie said. "I didn't make it easy for you."

Jennifer sat next to her. "I shouldn't have interfered. And I'm sorry I did. My brother is more than able to figure out his life."

"Listen, I understand what you were trying to do for Daniel. And I accept your apology. I've learned a lot about your relationship and how protective you are of him. Truthfully, I admire it. I'm even a little envious. Having a sibling you adore is quite a gift."

To Natalie's amazement, Jennifer swiped at her eyes and sniffled. "Thank you for making my apology so easy. Saying 'I'm sorry' is not my strong suit."

"I'm glad we cleared the air."

"Me, too, which leads me to a request, a small favor. It's no big deal. Take maybe an hour or two."

"Sure." Natalie assumed it was something easy like looking after Lola.

"It's tomorrow at noon, are you busy?"

"I don't think so."

"Oh, good. Could you be like a maid of honor?"

"What?"

"I know it's sudden, and you and I hardly know each other, but Lola's too young, and I have no idea how—"

"Wait a second," Natalie said, trying to get a grip on this insane conversation. "You're getting married?"

"Gordon's the best thing that could've happened to me. And neither one of us is getting any younger. Do you have a dress you could wear?"

"I'm sure I can find something." Natalie raised her martini. "To the bride."

ON A SUNNY, warm afternoon with only family and a few friends present, Daniel gave his sister's hand in marriage to the man she'd met at a paint store only five months ago. Gordon was loving and funny. And most importantly, he adored Lola, and she adored him.

Two days after that, the newlyweds took off to Hawaii, and Lola flew with Natalie and Daniel back to the East Coast.

Natalie fell in love with her 'niece', the cheeky little girl in the tutu and Giants t-shirt who had charmed her the first time they met.

In Washington DC, they visited the Smithsonian. Their favorite was the Natural History Museum, where Lola was captivated by elephants and fossils and the mega-toothed shark. She declared then and there that she would one day be an archeologist.

After putting Lola on a flight home, they meandered up the East Coast, stopping in random places and lingering in locations they especially enjoyed.

Weeks went by. No plans, no obligations, no rush.

THEY WERE on a beach off the coast of Maine. It was a cool and breezy afternoon, and they snuggled next to each other wrapped in blankets with Odette snoozing between them.

"Do you know the date?" Natalie asked.

"No. Do you?" Daniel brushed her hair out of her eyes.

"I think it might be November. It feels like November, crisp air and crunchy leaves."

"I like November," Daniel said.

"I do, too. In Clearwater, the holidays start right after Halloween. The whole town explodes into Thanksgiving. Nutmegs brings out the best pumpkin bread you've ever tasted.

Betsey's Blooms turns into a garden of gorgeous autumn flowers, Mariano's hosts a fall festival in the gazebo that's—"

"Are you homesick?" Daniel asked.

Natalie considered his question. "Not exactly. Just nostalgic. What about you?"

"I miss Jennifer and Lola, sure, but I never had a home like yours. You have a magical world in Clearwater." He kissed her palm. "Whenever you're ready to go back, it's fine with me."

"Go back?"

"Go home," he said. "We can't live on the road forever."

Natalie's eyes teared up. Crying came more easily now. She'd cried at Jennifer and Gordon's surprise wedding; she cried when Lola flew home; she even cried the other night when they watched an old movie. "But I don't want this to end."

"What do you mean by *this*? Because we—you and me and this pup—there's no end there. I'm all in with you. And I'll move to Clearwater in a heartbeat. I want it all. The crazy small town gossip, sticky buns every Sunday, dinners with your fabulous friends, walks in the park, dance recitals. I want to be there. And I want to be with you."

Natalie sniffled. "But what about your bigger life?"

Daniel cupped her face and drew her toward him, their lips melting into each other. He held onto her with an intense strength, a determination to never let go. Without releasing her, Daniel drew back, his lips beside her ear. "You are my bigger life. And I will do everything in my power to be yours."

EPILOGUE

*T*hey headed back toward California at the end of November, taking it slow, seeing a few places they'd missed along the way, and savoring the last days of their adventure.

Natalie and Odette arrived home in early December. Daniel didn't exactly move into Natalie's house, but she made him bring enough stuff for a long-term stay.

On a Sunday afternoon, a week after their return, they went to take a look at a cozy cottage on a hill above the lake, a place where they could build their love nest.

"I think it's great," Natalie said, peering out a big picture window with a view of the water. "What do you think?"

Daniel gathered her in his arms. "The most romantic thing I could say is that if you love it, I love it."

"But do you?" Natalie dialed back her enthusiasm. "Because if it's not what you—"

"It's perfect." Daniel took Odette from Natalie and ruffled her fur. "And I do love it. It's got a fenced yard for this one, a garage for the Mustang, a patio in back for a barbecue, and a loft for when Lola spends the night. She'll love that." He jiggled the ladder as if testing its stability.

"We'll make it into a little hideaway for her." Natalie kissed him on the cheek. "Look at us. Our first big decision together, and no disagreement. We really are the perfect match."

"I agree with that, too." Daniel opened the front door of their future home. "I'll call the realtor tomorrow. Now, let's go eat. I'm starving."

"See? I am too. We agree on everything."

~

"This town sure loves Christmas," Daniel said as they strolled Main Street one evening. Fresh wreaths adorned with red holly, tiny pinecones, gold ribbon, and twinkling white lights hung on every lamppost along Main Street. Festive displays filled every shop window. And the scent of fresh pine filled the air.

Natalie slipped her hand into his pocket, nestling her fingers into his warm palm. "You think it's over the top?"

"Absolutely. And just the way I like it."

Natalie still marveled at the fact that less than a year ago she'd been a different person living a different life and existing in a different world, resigned to a future without inspiration or dreams. Now she viewed everything with a fresh mindset. Her childhood home was not a trap anymore. It was her touchstone.

And the love of her life had joined her.

~

The week before Christmas, Natalie, in formal attire, arrived at the community theater for opening night of The Nutcracker.

The entire town had gathered in front to greet her, the honoree. She wore her long red dress with sparkly silver sandals and a black cashmere cape. Daniel, dashing in a dark suit and red tie, offered her his arm. Together they climbed the steps, like royalty entering the ball.

The tribute to Ilana Lurensky opened with a video production highlighting the entire history of the Lurensky family dance school interspersed with live ballet in front of the screen. Tears moistened Natalie's cheeks as she viewed clips of her mother dancing and photos of her from when she was a prima ballerina in Europe.

The final image was one Natalie did not expect—a picture of her standing between her parents at high school graduation. She gasped and turned toward Cece as the music faded and applause crescendoed.

Cece's eyes glistened. "Did you love it?"

"So much." Natalie swiped her tears away. "It was perfect."

The performance of The Nutcracker was magnificent. For the first time ever, Natalie watched from a seat in the audience instead of from backstage.

Ashley was the most exquisite Sugar Plum Fairy Natalie had seen in over a decade. No doubt, the young ballerina would make her professional debut in a few years. And Natalie would be there to witness it.

The reception was held at the studio—in the newly and beautifully renovated grand ballroom of the Old Mayfair Hotel. An enormous Nutcracker-inspired Christmas Tree took center-stage. A trio of carolers in costume sang holiday songs. Guests filled plates from a lavish buffet. Servers wound their way through the crowd carrying silver trays of sparkling wine, eggnog, and hot cider.

Tessa's magic touch was everywhere.

Natalie spotted Maura standing alone beside the Christmas tree.

"Congratulations," Natalie said, a light touch on Maura's back.

"For what?" Maura asked.

"We have an up and coming prima ballerina, don't we?"

Maura smiled up at her. "It wouldn't have happened without you."

"I suppose that's true."

Maura's gaze was sincere. "I could never have done it on my own. Thank you for believing in me."

Natalie drew in a breath at Maura's vulnerability. Perhaps it was the champagne or the storybook atmosphere or the glorious night. Whatever it was, Natalie appreciated her candor.

"I'm glad I did," Natalie said. "And I thank you, too. Not only for trusting me, but also for helping me realize how much I needed support. Since we came together, I've learned that relying on others is not a weakness. And that revelation has changed my life."

Maura inclined her head. "Even when we think nothing will ever change, change happens."

"It does." Natalie sighed. "Hard to believe we're standing together like this. Friends and now partners. My mother would approve."

It felt good to be honest—liberating, comforting, empowering.

They were interrupted by the entrance of the entire cast from the show. The guests burst into applause, especially when Ashley made her way in, the last to enter.

To Natalie's surprise, Kaylee, wearing a leotard and ballet skirt, was in the midst of the youngest dancers, rounding them up and keeping them in order.

She spotted Natalie and ran over. "I'm so happy to see you."

"What's this?" Natalie's laughter twinkled with delight. "Do you work for us now, too?"

"Just volunteering for tonight. But I love being back at the studio with the little kids. They're super cute."

"I'm so happy to see you, Kaylee. Things are going well, aren't they?"

"They really are, thanks to you." She gave Natalie a hug before returning to her charges.

At every turn, Natalie was in awe. The people, the décor, the food, the drinks, the music. And the tribute to her mother, all of it beyond expectation.

"Hey you," Cece said, grasping Natalie's hand. "Come with me." She guided her outside to where Tessa, Rebecca, and Patty were waiting on the veranda.

Tessa handed her a glass of champagne. "We just wanted a quick moment to toast your homecoming and to tell you how much we missed you."

"I totally missed you," Rebecca said. "I was afraid you weren't ever coming back."

"Well, I'm back and here to stay."

Patty stepped forward. "And the detective is coming with you, too. Don't ever forget, I was the one who told you that a hot fling was exactly what you needed."

"And then your fling turned into the most romantic love story," Rebecca said.

"It really did," Cece said, embracing Natalie around the waist. "Now, snuggle up my friends, I have a toast to make."

They tightened their circle.

"To our dear Natalie," Cece started, her voice hitched. "Tonight you're the star of the show, but you are and always have been *our* shining star. These last few months without you, well, it was like we were incomplete. A piece of us was missing."

Natalie regarded each of them—Tessa, the great sommelier and the fantasy big sister who had been by her side for as long as she could remember; Rebecca, the wild, red-headed everywhere girl with a love-filled heart and a contagious enthusiasm nobody could resist; Patty, the little one with the biggest mouth who showed up in Clearwater for a quick stay and never left; and Cece—the great Cecilia Rose, the magnificent ballerina who seven Christmases ago reentered Natalie's life and became her best friend once again.

With all the challenges and heartaches Natalie had faced over the years, she'd never had to face them alone. Few were blessed with such depth of friendship. And she'd been blessed four times over.

"I'm so lucky to have you all."

Tall and strong and sturdier than ever, Natalie embraced her precious friends.

The stars were finally aligned, and for the first time in over twenty years, Natalie knew she was exactly where she was meant to be.

I'VE DONE IT, Mamma. I've lived my dream and spread my wings. And the roots you planted have brought me home.

∾

AFTERWORD

Dear reader,
Thank you for spending your reading time in Clearwater! There are so many books to choose from these days, and I'm truly delighted you selected one of mine.

If you enjoyed One Last Dance, please tell your friends and post reviews on Amazon and Goodreads. Reviews and personal recommendations are critical to a book's success. Thank you!

Review on Amazon:
Review Link for One Last Dance
Review on Goodreads:
Link to Goodreads

You've reached the end of the Clearwater series—at least for now. If you read One Last Dance out of order, no problem! Each novel stands alone with its own main character and complete wrap up, no cliffhangers. All the books in the series are listed in order on the "Also By" page.

If you'd like to send me a note, please do ~ my email is: juliemayersonbrown@gmail.com.

I love book clubs and chatting with readers! If your book group reads one of my novels, let me know.

Finally, keep up to date with me and stay in touch by subscribing to my newsletter and joining my reader group on Facebook.

Links for E-readers:

Julie's Newsletter

Julie's Reader Group on FB

Julie's Website

ABOUT THE AUTHOR

Julie M. Brown is an author, playwright, and essayist. A California girl all her life, she now lives in Palos Verdes, a Los Angeles suburb, surrounded by trails, horses, and wild peacocks. Wife, mom, and dog-lover, Julie enjoys mentoring young writers and interacting with readers and bookclubs. She's an active member of Women's Fiction Writers Association.

When not writing, rescuing dogs, or baking banana bread, Julie can be found in a quiet corner somewhere with coffee and a laptop.

View my website
juliemayersonbrown.com
While you're there, be sure to subscribe to my newsletter ~ it's a great way to get in touch and find out about my new books and projects.

Let's connect on social media, too!

ALSO BY JULIE MAYERSON BROWN

THE CLEARWATER SERIES

Long Dance Home

Road to Somewhere

The Lonely Sommelier

The Everywhere Girl

One Last Dance

A Clearwater Christmas ~ a YA holiday novella

Welcome to Clearwater
A Box Set of the first three novels in the series

~

The Accidental Life of MF Ascher
Under the collaborative pen name, Ivy H. Booker

www.ingramcontent.com/pod-product-compliance
Lightning Source LLC
Chambersburg PA
CBHW051953240626
47153CB00005B/1745